Within the Gray

Within the Gray

Jenna Ashlyn

atmosphere press

Copyright © 2020 Jenna Ashlyn

Published by Atmosphere Press

Cover design by Ronaldo Alves

No part of this book may be reproduced except in brief quotations and in reviews without permission from the publisher.

Within the Gray
2020, Jenna Ashlyn

atmospherepress.com

In Loving memory of Denver Wilson Ash III (1969-2010)

With a special dedication to the man that made me feel safe enough to truly love again, Shawn M. Sexton.

1

Like a barren tree limb, Terra collapsed in the ashes. She was stuck in a loop of hallucinations that made her mind scream. At first, she thought she was dreaming, but knew it was something more. As smoke filled her lungs, Terra remembered that moment. That moment when everything changed. A life full of love, of hope... turned desolate and everything went black. The bustle of life was muted in an instant, replaced with deafening silence. Her thoughts, her breathing, and even her heart seemed to stop. Yet those words still echoed in her mind.

"I'm sorry, your husband has expired."

In that moment she fell into a chamber within her mind, collapsing within a place of echoing despair. Lost, within the Gray of her mind. People that once surrounded her were now merely ashes that clung to her skin. Alive, in her death she arose. Smoke-filled memories surrounded her, hiding the engulfing flames of passion, expired. Searching across the Gray, the light of hope was absent from her horizon. Whispered words of the past swept through her hair like the calloused touch of his hands. A reminder of hope, now torn from the destruction of him. Her body wasted from that moment, she looked down at the emptiness that her diamond ring now represented and knew her young family would never be the same. Her skin cracked, dry as the bark on a tree from the memories that raked across her skin. There was no sound, no color, and no breath. It appeared there was nothing, but smoking embers. Gasping, Terra stood up. Reaching down she felt her gauze dress and saw the once snow-white fabric, turned gray, flakes of ash covering her naked feet. Her gaze wandered, searching, as the heated wind raked through her fiery hair. She was alone. Around her, she could see the sharp edges of mountainous rocks. They were broken in black shards like a shattered mirror reflecting the darkness of day. The smoke swam around her, pushing her forward towards the shoreline. The water oozed like black oil against the horizon and licked the shore like thick bubbles of misery.

Driven, her feet drug against the rocks. Terra reached down, trying to stop moving, but she only fell forward. She felt the heat of blood between her toes, but instead of a rich red, it was as black as a raven's feather. Against the shards, her body seemed to echo like an eternal loop in tiny mirrors.

Forward, her body moved without her. Terra's heart raced, only able to see the black ocean cresting gray against the shore. She opened her mouth to cry out, to scream, but was only met with silence. The dark ocean was only a few feet away. Her body tensed trying to produce sound. Every muscle clenched, every ounce of breath within her escaped. Still, there was silence. Pulling against the smoke, she dug her feet into the ashy sand until finally, she collapsed. Terra could feel movement behind her. Turning, she saw them. Hundreds of gray figures walking blindly. Each haunted individual headed towards the black depths. Crouching against the black sands, she watched as one by one their feet touched the ocean. Continuously, they walked into the depths until their heads vanished into the oily darkness. She felt tears streaming down her face, but they evaporated in a moment. Her eyes shot across the horizon, searching for a glimpse of hope. She kept looking for color, or a whisper of sunlight in the suffocating heat. Finally, she saw a square of light against the Gray.

Quickly she began crawling. Her knees scraped against the tiny shards tearing at her skin. Pain shot through her body like a thousand needles as she gasped for air. The pressure of the smoke pushed against her with suffocation. But Terra only forced herself harder along the shoreline to the window of light. After an eternity, she finally reached it. A tiny square of color stood above her. Timidly, her hand tried to reach forward to touch the window within the Gray only to discover that it was part of a door; she collapsed from exhaustion. It was untouchable. Tears ran down her face like oil as she continued to search. Her screams echoed through her mind as she pounded against the Gray.

***

Then, just as quickly, she felt the cold. Opening her eyes, she was blinded by bitter lights and muffled voices as strange figures rushed towards her. The light grew brighter, as she felt them place her in bed. The crisp sheets brushed against her skin like an unwelcome cocoon.

"Terra? Terra? Can you hear me?" he exclaimed. "What's wrong? I'm here. You're at the crisis center, you've had a hard couple of weeks, you were having a nightmare."

"What do you mean?" she asked looking into his eyes. "I wasn't asleep, I was in this place..." she screamed. "There's no way that was a NIGHTMARE! I can still feel the ashes against my skin! The heat! The smoke! Look! You can see the cuts on my legs! You're lying! What is this?!"

"No, Terra... you've been here the whole time."

"That can't be true. I am bleeding. My knees are scraped up from crawling through the rocks." She exclaimed pulling up her dress so she could see her legs. "Look at these cuts. How do you explain that?"

Looking down he ran his hand across the cuts. "You must have hurt yourself on the floor. Right now, you just need to calm down and rest."

"But I am calm! This did NOT come from the floor?!"

"No, you're not calm. Wow, that nightmare must have really did a number on you. I'm going to call the doctor. Maybe they have something that will help calm you down." He whispered. Gently, he pushed her matted hair back from her face and stood. "I will be right back."

"NO! Don't go! I don't want to go back to that place. You can't leave me." She pleaded as she pulled away from his touch.

"I'm only a volunteer, there's nothing else I can really do. You will be ok. I will be right back."

She watched him rush out of the room, the door closing hard behind him. Grabbing her thin white blanket, she clutched it to her body. The air felt like ice against her skin, and the rough blanket barely shielded her from the bitterness. Everything around her felt sterile. A drastic contrast to the smoke from the Gray.

"Rough couple of weeks?" The man's words echoed through her head.

Taking a deep breath, she looked around. *Why am I here?* Laying her head against the pillow, her eyes searched the ceiling counting the tiles, as her mind reeled. Then like a gentle fog replacing the smoke in her mind, she saw him, his blonde hair gleaming in the sun. She remembered how he used to smile, and the way his body felt against hers as they slept. Darren was, but now... he was gone.

Like a rushing cloud she remembered everything. The day they met, the way his lips tasted like cherry cigars, and their wedding day. *Why am I still suffering? Wasn't it supposed to get easier?* She knew that her mother, Sheila, had just put her in the crisis center for a little rest.

"You're young," her mother had said. "It's hard to become a widow at thirty. You just need some quiet time to get through this."

Terra knew she wasn't crazy. *I just need time to get my act together.* Closing her eyes, she tried to slow down the avalanche of emotions. Calmly, she made herself take slow, deep breaths, imagining herself on a swing looking up through the leaves of an old maple tree, the warm kiss of sunlight on her skin. She could almost smell the freshly cut grass.

Hearing the door again, Terra sat up. "You're back. I'm sorry if I scared you..." she whispered, the sight of the stranger overwhelming her with guilt.

"It's ok. I've never had that happen before. I just walk

around and bring in movies and books for everyone. I heard you screaming...you sounded terrified...but you seem better now. Or is that just an act?"

"I think I just needed a minute to wake up. Did you find someone?" she asked, putting her feet over the side of her bed.

"Yes, they said that you should be ok, but they were going to give you something to help with anxiety. They said that it would be good if I kept an eye on you. You haven't had any visitors." Slowly, he walked towards her. "My name is Paul; I don't think I ever told you that. Your name is on the door, or I wouldn't have known yours. They talk about you a lot. That is, the other patients talk about you... nothing bad, I promise." He smiled. "Do you mind if I sit down?"

"It's nice to meet you, Paul." She answered shaking his hand. "I'd love for you to stay with me for a while. My family is just trying to give me time. I promise, I'm not crazy." She giggled uneasily.

"I know, don't worry. This isn't where they keep the crazy people." He winked as his finger brushed across her hand as he released his grasp.

For a moment, her eyes found his, and her breath stopped. Quickly, she looked down at the floor as guilt swept over her. She didn't know this man. How could she possibly feel something like this? So soon after her husband's death? What would he think of her? She was in a "quiet" place because of what had happened. Now, she had seen something in the eyes of a man she had just met. *This isn't right; it's not possible.* Looking up, Terra caught Paul's warm brown eyes staring into hers. There was something about his eyes, something different, tender, and forgiving. *Maybe I'm just lonely. He's right, nobody ever comes to see me.*

They were giving her a little too much space. She felt her heart racing. Looking down, she noticed her hands shaking as she placed them under her legs, hoping he wouldn't notice. She felt the edges of her diamond ring digging into her skin as she tried to keep her body from betraying her.

"Are you cold?" Paul whispered. "I can see if I can find you an extra blanket...."

"That would be nice," she stated, staring at the floor, knowing the cold wasn't the only thing making her shiver. *Of course, he would try to be considerate.*

Paul knew she was frightened, but when he looked into her eyes, he felt something hiding behind her fragile strength. He just couldn't understand why she was alone. Her hands were interesting. They were soft, but in contrast, her nails were bitten down almost to where they bled. There was a raw beauty about her. Her hair was a mess of fiery waves that fell down her back, not smooth but rough and tangled against the ivory dress that was wrinkled from sleep. Paul imagined her walking in the sun, the light dancing in her eyes, the breeze caressing her skin.

Standing up, he walked just outside the door to a small oak cabinet. As he opened it, he lifted a stack of blankets and put them aside. Then he found it, hidden in the back under all the rough and worn blankets. It was a dark crimson and still as soft as the day he left it. It was his favorite from when he had stayed there, and he knew that's what she needed. He only hoped Terra didn't see the look in his eyes. She needed a friend, not an admirer.

Walking to her, he opened the blanket and wrapped it around her. "Hang on to this. I believe it's one of the nicest blankets in here." He smiled down at her.

Looking up, she noticed that look in his eyes again. What was he thinking? He seemed so caring. Did he pity her? In that moment she was thankful for the blanket to hide her messy appearance. Terra didn't want to be a charity case. She really needed to pull it together. How long had it been since she brushed her hair? She couldn't even remember how long she had been there crying in her bed. How could anyone have been talking about her? She wasn't sure she had left her room more than a couple of times. Then again, it didn't take much to get people talking. She couldn't imagine what he had heard about her.

"How did you say you knew my name?" She asked, diverting her eyes. They fell to his lips; they were normal lips. They weren't big; they weren't small. There were a couple of hairs hanging down a little longer than the rest of his mustache, just barely curling down his lip to his mouth. His goatee was rough. She imagined him roughing it up with his hands when he got nervous.

"The other patients say you haven't come out much. That you lost your husband," he answered, glancing at the small patch of freckles under her eyes. "Does it bother you that I knew your name?"

"No... not really... I just didn't know how you knew me." Glancing down she noticed his hands. He had strong hands, clean and a little rough. But, not too rough. The sleeves of his crisp button-up shirt were rolled and pushed to his elbows, the blue warming his pale skin.

A couple strands of hair fell onto his temples, framing

his eyes. "I guess I really don't know what to say."

"You don't have to say anything, but maybe you could get out of the room and watch a movie or something. There's some of those new adult coloring books, too. For me, it really helps to find something to express myself with. Do you have any hobbies or anything that you like to do?" He asked sitting down across from her.

"I don't know. Darren and I did everything together. We used to take pictures of things we found interesting. He loved to cook, and he loved to dance with me while we cooked. He stole a lot of kisses." She smiled, looking down at her rings. "That seems like an eternity ago." She stuttered glancing into his eyes. "Sometimes it feels like it would be selfish to want to love again."

"It's not selfish to want to be happy, Terra."

"I've had my happiness..." she stated bluntly. "How many other people can say that?" Standing up, she walked to the edge of the room. "There should really be a window in here." Reaching up, she touched the block wall. "I miss being able to see outside."

"You can see outside from the TV room." He said walking to her. "Do you want me to walk you down there?"

"No," she laughed. "I'd probably scare everyone. I'm a mess."

"You may be a mess," he laughed. "But you're still stunning," he caught himself whisper under his breath. "Do you have a bag or anything that I could get for you?" He recovered, hoping she hadn't heard him.

"Somewhere... I guess maybe under the bed?" Terra questioned. Did she really hear him call her "stunning"?

He looked nervous as he got down on his knees to

retrieve her small black bag. "Here you go. I should probably give you some space. After all, you don't really know me. You don't need some stranger staring at you," he stated, turning away.

"Paul..." she muttered watching his embarrassment. He had stopped walking, but he didn't say a word as she walked towards him. Reaching down, she softly placed her hand on his arm. "Come back sometime soon... please."

"I'm so sorry if I made you uncomfortable," he stated. " I didn't mean to say anything," he mumbled, placing his hand on hers.

"I wish you would say more, but I don't deserve it. I'm not ready to hear anything like that. But I would still like for you to come back, though. You are the first person I've talked to in days."

Squeezing her gently, he stepped away. "I will be back...probably tomorrow. But you must make it out of your room by then? I hate to see anyone lock themselves away like this."

"I will try if it means you will come back. It gets lonely in here." Grabbing her hand again, he looked into her deep-sea-blue eyes.

"Tomorrow," he stated firmly and walked away, leaving her standing in the middle of the stark room.

The door sounded like a thousand hammers as it shut behind him and his dark hair disappeared from her view. Looking down, she felt every hair on her legs standing on end. Her hair felt flat against her head, the tangles rough against her cheek. Stunning? He must have been crazy, she thought to herself. Grabbing her bag, she started to look through it, unable to remember what she had packed. If he was going to come back, if she was going to leave the room and go to therapy and face what had happened, she had to at least brush her hair. There was barely anything in her bag. All she saw was a little blue sundress, her makeup bag, and a hairbrush. There wasn't much she could do with that, unfortunately. Grabbing the hairbrush, she made her way to the restroom and looked in the mirror. She barely recognized her reflection because instead of a well-polished woman, she only saw swollen eyes and oily skin, a shadow of her former self.

Turning on the water she splashed her face and gasped at the cold. It was August, and she was freezing. Grabbing a towel, she scrubbed the water from her face and headed back to the blanket that was laying half off her little bed. Wrapping herself up, she couldn't help but shake. Her hands quivered as she touched the brush to her hair. It hadn't been brushed in days. Blankly she sat and stared at the wall, imagining the sunlight that must have been on the other side. Her breath came quickly, as her body began to shake. What if something bad happened to her? What would happen to her daughter? How could he die and just leave her alone like this? Closing her eyes, she felt her chest tighten. Pain coursed through her body as tried to catch her breath. She felt her little dress moving against her chest. Falling back against the bed, she held the blanket tighter against her body.

"Count, just count..." she told herself. "It's just an anxiety attack, you can get through this." Slowly she started counting to herself. "1... 2... 3...nothing bad is going to happen." She whispered. "4... 5... 6... it's going to be ok. 7...8...9... I can get through this."

Still clutching the blanket, she sat up and grabbed the brush again. Trying to control her breathing, she focused on a small crack in the wall, running the brush through her hair. It was painful, but it was good to focus on, she told herself. "Focus on the feeling of the brush going through your hair."

Soon, her heart rate started to slow down, and her breathing eased up. It was only a little better, but it was something. Since Darren passed, this happened a lot. Anxiety attacks came out of nowhere. She couldn't imagine him being gone.

"How could he leave her? How could he die so young? How was she supposed to raise their daughter alone? Where was the rest of her family? How was she supposed to do this alone? Why hadn't they visited her? This couldn't be real. It wasn't possible," she told herself. But as she looked down to her dirty, wrinkled white dress, she knew it was.

Getting up, she began to walk around the room, the panic still gripping her. She knew she needed to find a better way to manage her feelings. Terra felt the heat around her body. She felt it as though someone was holding a torch to her face. Walking in a small circle, she started trying to relax again.

"Count, just count..." she told herself. "It's just an anxiety attack, you can get through this." Slowly she started counting to herself. "1... 2... 3... nothing bad is going to happen." She whispered. "4... 5... 6... it's going to be ok. 7... 8... 9... I can get through this."

She kept wishing that Darren was there to hold her, to tell her everything was going to be ok, but he was gone. Reaching down, she pinched herself.

"This can't be real. It must just be a bad dream. If it's a dream, it won't hurt when I pinch myself, and then I'll wake up, and he'll be lying beside me in our bed... at home." She hoped. "Ouch," she cried.

Laying down on the bed, she felt the salty water cover eyes with the warm moisture of tears. Her body shook as she grabbed the blanket and buried her face in the pillow. She couldn't believe this was happening to her. She was only thirty years old. She had found the love of her life, her soulmate. She didn't know how she could expect to love like that again. How could anything replace the passion that they had experienced together. It was impossible. Laying there, she still felt his body against hers. She smelt the musky scent of his after shave and felt the roughness of his hands wrapped around her. The tears kept coming until she heard a knock on the door and one of the counselors came in.

"You need to come to group therapy now," the woman stated dryly. "It starts in about five minutes, Terra."

"I CAN'T GO ANYWHERE LIKE THIS!" Terra screamed. "I need a shower, I need to stop crying!"

"Well, right now you need to take one step at a time. I'm glad you want a shower, but you need to be going to these therapy sessions. They will really help," she stated as she walked out of the room.

Moments later, an older man appeared. His gray hair blended into the white walls, but his large blue eyes looked like they could see through anything. He just stood in the doorway leaning against it with his arms crossed.

"Do you really want to get a shower, Terra?" He asked bluntly. "I'd love to see you get out of this room, see you being more like yourself. Then maybe we can talk. Will you do that?"

"Yes, but I don't want to talk in group, I'd rather just

talk to someone. I don't want everyone to know my business. They don't need to know what I'm thinking, how I'm feeling. This is happening to me, not them." She sobbed walking towards him.

"Come with me, then. I will watch for you. We will talk then."

Grabbing her bag, Terra followed him down the hall, still holding onto her blanket. She hoped the warm water would help soothe her anxiety. The last thing she wanted to do was tell anyone what she really felt. What did they expect her to say? It was too much for her to handle at one time. She knew that maybe if she tried to live, tried to do normal things, maybe she could find a little piece of herself again. Maybe she didn't have to think about Darren all the time. After all, she didn't want to be one of those women who couldn't find the will to live after their husband passed. She'd heard of it happening to older couples that had been together for years. People who were supposed to be soulmates dying within weeks of each other, sometimes only days apart, and other times it would be within a year. Terra knew she didn't want to be like those couples. Even if he was the one true love of her life, she knew there was more to think about than him. What would happen to their daughter, Autumn? She was so full of life, affection, and laughter. She could always make Terra smile. Maybe she just needed to let herself forget enough to pull it together. She knew she couldn't do it for herself, but maybe she could do it for her.

The water felt like heaven against her skin. Closing her eyes, she felt the bubbles from the soap erase the stress from her body. Keeping her eyes closed, she leaned her head against the wall and waited to run out of hot water.

Letting herself sob, she allowed her tears to escape down the drain. At least in here her cries couldn't be heard. So, she let herself cry, trying to get it out. Keeping it bottled in had only led to nightmares. She was at a breaking point. How much more could she really take? How long would she mourn him? She felt her life calling for her, but she couldn't seem to reach it. Terra knew she had to take it one step at a time and had to do what was necessary to move forward.

2

There was a crispness to the humid August air. The leaves were richly green, but he knew fall was coming. Paul couldn't wait to watch the leaves turn to crimson and gold. He strolled slowly down the bike path. He needed a little time. He'd been alone for a little over a year, but it felt like an eternity. Even when he was still with Patricia, he had felt alone. After a while, it had become normal. But now, he liked being able to do whatever he liked without being questioned constantly by a nagging wife. There was a sense of freedom that came with solitude. It had never bothered him, until the previous day. Volunteering at the center had always been rewarding, but meeting Terra had changed him. The world around him seemed somehow more beautiful, the leaves on the trees sounded musical as they blew in the morning breeze. He had always loved his morning walks on the local trail. It winded through the town just far enough from the road to muffle the sound of traffic. The path was covered with trees and wildflowers. When the leaves changed, he knew it would be like walking into a painting.

Every day he parked his truck at the end of the trail and walked his way to the center. It was his way of doing something good for himself. When he got there, he would visit with the patients and he loved to bring them new movies to watch. The stigma surrounding the place was awful. Some people looked down on those who spent time there, but nearly everyone eventually did. Whether or not they chose to admit it was another thing entirely.

For him it had been a long and complicated journey of obsession, anger, and depression. At first Paul had attached himself to everyone around him. He had tried to make everyone happy and had forgotten the things that he loved. During his marriage, he had abandoned his own passions for hers. It had been like going through any addiction, but this was an addiction to pleasing others. Even a year later, he had to watch himself carefully. While he loved helping others, he had to be careful not to make their problems his own. He had intentionally avoided relationships to foster and develop a relationship with himself. Now, he saw the world in a new light and had stopped relying on other opinions to give himself worth.

Maybe today would be a good day to take in some of the flowers that surrounded him. A few wildflowers would help warm the place a little. He remembered how the sterility of the place got to you. There were times when it felt like he was in a cave. He would have loved to have seen just one of the black-eyed Susan's that covered the sides of the trail. They were his favorite. He loved how warm the color of their petals made him feel. Paul loved warm colors; they kept him grounded. He appreciated the natural beauty of things. Grabbing the small journal in one hand, he began gathering flowers. Some of the flowers were golden, others were a crisp white, but he kept looking for something red. Even if he found one, it would be enough to slip into the pages of the journal. It was for Terra; he couldn't stop thinking about her. He wished he knew more about her, the real her. There was a delicate strength about her. She was the kind of woman that made a man want to nurture and protect her even though she didn't need it. He had always pictured himself being the kind of man that would hold a woman, a lady, when her strength failed, and she needed an anchor. He had always wanted that for himself, too, a place where he could be vulnerable.

Paul had always wanted to feel the tender arms of a woman when times were hard. Everyone was vulnerable sometimes. His ex-wife had never allowed him that luxury. Every time he tried to get close to Patricia, she had pushed him away. The things he bought for her were never enough. She would have hated the wildflowers on the trail. The only flowers she liked were roses, white roses. He really didn't like white anymore. Between white roses and the white walls of the center, he had learned to hate the color. It reminded him of loneliness, something he had conquered. He had friends, he had family, and most of all he knew he was making a difference with his daily visits. Sometimes the kindness of a stranger changed everything.

Helping others was one of the few things that helped him cope with his depression. After all, you never really conquer it. It sticks with you like a pair of concrete shoes, holding you down to the ground when you want to fly. Paul tried to do his best during the hard days, when he didn't want to get out of bed and even the paint on the walls seemed to taunt him. Those were the days when he really needed the center. It helped to remind him that there was always someone going through something worse than what he was on that day. Yesterday had been one of those days. He had skipped his walk and just came in between meetings. It had been a quiet day. It was all he could do to pick his feet up and really say hello to anyone. He had forced himself to go in and see the others. He had hoped that someone would need him, make him feel a little less worthless. There were a lot of times that he felt that way. He knew it wasn't true, that he had value, but his mind loved to play tricks on him.

Paul remembered all the conversations he had with Patricia. Endless talks about working on the garden, planning, and another vacation she had to go on. Things she didn't really care about. They were her distractions, to keep him busy. It didn't matter how many houses he showed to people, how many offers he wrote, or how many homes he sold. It never seemed to be enough for her. His depression had been a lot worse until he learned that her opinion wasn't the only one that mattered. Still, at times, he heard her words, and it was like pouring salt into an old wound. She had destroyed a part of him that he feared he would never get back. Why was it so hard for a man to feel needed? If a man could be strong and still need to feel safe, then it doesn't make a woman weak to want to feel loved or needed.

Why did women seem to run in extremes? Either they wanted a man to do everything or nothing for them at all. Because of that, Paul had embraced his loneliness. He found ways to occupy himself. At first it was just with his music but while it had helped him to express himself, he was still lonely. He had played guitar for most of his life and while he had always loved the idea of being a rock star, he found symphonic pieces suited him. Paul would spend days lost in the art of layering sounds. At first, he would start with a melody line, a bass, and slowly he would hear the different instruments in his mind. It had always been one of his favorite things to do, but Patricia had hated every moment of it. Most of his equipment he had lost because of one more thing that she needed. But then, as he finally had the chance to play again, it allowed him to look beyond himself and see the world for what it really was. That part had come easily, like a fog lifting from his eyes. It was the most obvious when he was showing houses. Young couples would make an appointment to see a few of the listings. They rarely agreed. A lot of people didn't seem to care what their spouse felt about a home. You couldn't tell until you started to show them different homes who the dominant person was. Oftentimes, it was never who you would have expected.

    Almost to the center, Paul glanced down at the flowers he had gathered. To him, they were beautiful, naturally beautiful. They were not trying to be a rose; they were wild, and there was freedom in that. He loved their raw beauty. Reaching in his pocket he pulled out a pocketknife and cut them to the same length. He would have to take one of the glasses from the cabinet for them, but he knew the counselors wouldn't mind. In his other hand, he held a little journal. It was an earthy green with a white butterfly etched in gold. He used to hate butterflies, because of Patricia, but this one reminded him of Terra, even if it was white. He hoped it would help her find a way to express herself. She obviously hadn't been going to group therapy; maybe this would help her get started. It was hard to talk to strangers about what you were thinking and feeling, and that was a feeling he knew well. The little journal wasn't much, but maybe it would be what she needed.

***

Terra laid quietly on her bed as she counted the ceiling tiles again. Morning therapy... the thought of it frightened her. But she knew she had to try. Her daughter needed her. Sitting up, she grabbed the hairbrush. Her hair felt smooth and silky again. It only took a moment to brush through it, and then she was up, heading down the hall to the common room. That's where everything happened. Finding a seat closest to the window, she sat quietly while the others sat around her, and she tried not to notice how happy they appeared. Her attention was drawn outside to the trees. The wind seemed to make them dance. Their leaves waved back and forth while the smaller limbs made them rise and fall. It was simple, yet complicated. The bark on the tree was cracked and reminded her of how her skin felt when she was in the Gray. It wasn't smooth like some and she soon found herself tracing the lines as she looked for unusual patterns. She loved trees.

"Terra, welcome to therapy," the counselor stated. "Are you with us, Terra?"

"Yes, I'm here... I'm sorry, I was just a little distracted. I haven't looked out of a window for a while." Startled, she tried to look at everyone around her.

"I understand, try to stay with us. Everyone has a story, and it helps to really hear each other," he stated dryly. "What is said in here is confidential. You cannot tell anyone what you see or hear." Leaning back in his chair, he motioned to everyone, "Who would like to share first?"

"I guess, I will," a little voice whispered from the far end. "I usually seem to start these." Standing up she turned to face everyone. "I'm here because my parents drive me crazy. I'm eighteen years old, so I'm an adult now. I shouldn't have to babysit my little brother, so they can go have dinner once a week. So, when they left, I left. I went to my boyfriend's house because I don't have to do what I don't want to do," she stated almost proudly.

"How old is your younger brother?" Terra questioned, puzzled at why she would seem so proud of acting so rudely.

"He's five, and that's plenty old enough to be at home alone." The girl nodded her head and sat down. Crossing her arms in front of her, she sat at the edge of her seat. "He doesn't NEED a babysitter, and they don't need to go out for dinner ALONE," she mocked.

"Five, seriously!" Terra fumed at her. "You have got to be kidding! You left a five-year-old alone! Were you at all concerned? Did you at least call and tell your parents you were leaving?"

"It's okay, we don't pass judgement here. You need to calm down, Terra. I'm sure Kim did what she thought was right." The counselor looked narrowly at Terra. "Why don't you share with us now."

She looked at him, folding her arms in front of her. "I'm here because something bad happened to me and I need time to recover," she stated with a glare.

"Is that all you want to say, young lady?"

"Yes, that's all I want to say. But maybe you should say

something to her. She's eighteen years old. She should show some responsibility and realize that her parents need to go out just as much as she needs to, if not more. You don't dry up when you get married. Love takes patience. Love takes time," Terra answered, standing in front of her chair.

"Well, what happened to you? Did your man cheat on you or something? He probably did..." Kim mocked, as she leaned back in her chair. "He probably hated you!"

"No, you're wrong, little girl. You're completely wrong! HE DIED, and not in an accident; he was extremely sick. But you wouldn't know anything about real life. You're just a child doing childish things!" Turning, Terra moved her chair out of the way, making a hole to escape from. "If this is what group therapy is about, don't count on me coming back, not around her."

"Terra, it's ok. You need to stay for just a little while longer. While we may not agree with Kim, she can express herself. This is a safe place. Just like you can express yourself. She's not the only one here. I'm sure if you give it a few more minutes you will find that hearing someone else's story may help," the counselor calmly remarked, gesturing for her to sit. "Kevin, why don't you share with us now?" he stated looking over to an older man in the corner.

Slowly, the other man stood and rubbed his hands down his jeans as though he were dusting crumbs from his lap. "My wife of thirty-eight years left me for a younger man after I had heart surgery," He mumbled quietly as she sat down again hanging his head. She saw a small tear in the corner of his eye.

She heard the pain in his voice. Maybe death wasn't

the worst thing that happened to someone you loved. She heard his breath coming slowly, evenly. With one finger she saw him wipe away the tear as he tried to sit up a little straighter. Looking around, he caught her staring at him. He smiled softly and then looked back down to the hand in his lap. Even from a few feet away, she saw the pale while line where his wedding band used to be.

"I'm so sorry that happened to you," Terra replied, trying to be as private as was possible.

Everyone grew silent for a moment, and then one by one, the other three people in the group shared their stories. Looking out the window, she watched a small red squirrel run up the side of the tree. It had no idea the pain that was within these walls. It didn't know that the people within found hope watching it scurry up and down the tree.

"Terra... Terra?" Kim asked quietly. "That's your name, right?"

"Yes, sorry. I must have drifted off for a second," she answered, noticing how the others seemed to stare at her.

"I do that, too!" The older man laughed from beside them. "All. The. Time."

"I just wanted to let you know that... I do care about my little brother. It's hard to be the one responsible so my mom can go do whatever she wants," Kim answered, reaching for Terra's hands.

Looking in the young girl's eyes, Terra softened, remembering what it was like to be a young mother. And she thought about how she felt when Sheila was constantly disappearing without explanation.

"You know... I kind of know how you feel. My mom was gone a lot when I was growing up. I'm not sure what she was doing, but one day she went from going out at night to working all the time. It was like something in her snapped," Terra explained, taking Kim's hand. "I think that, and well, I have a little girl that is stuck with my mother, and it scares me for her. I don't know what's happening to her. I don't know how she feels... It's hard," Terra sniffled. "I didn't mean to take it out on you. I overreacted."

"You may have overreacted, but I... Maybe I need to think about what's going on with my mom? I don't know, but the way I have been doing things has only put me back in here. Over. AND. Over. AGAIN. I don't want to do things the same way anymore."

"Well, I love little kids; they're innocent. What they are going through isn't their fault."

"No... you're right, it's not their fault, but it's not mine either."

"The way you look at it IS your fault."

"You might be right," Kim answered with a sigh. "I don't want you to be right, but maybe you are. You are the first person that has ever made me think."

"Thinking is dangerous sometimes," Terra replied coyly.

Soon enough, therapy was over, and still she found herself drifting off, watching the tree. Her hands were folded neatly in her lap, as everyone around her continued the conversation. There were only brief moments when they would get her attention that she participated. Terra couldn't think. The only thing she could do was remember. She remembered standing in the kitchen waiting for Darren to come home. She always tried to keep dinner warm, if possible, waiting for him to come home. That night was no different. He had asked her to pick up a bottle of Long Island iced tea; he wanted to celebrate. He had just received a promotion at work. He wouldn't just be fixing the cars in the back anymore. He had finally made it to the sales floor. It made sense. Nobody knew those cars like he did. Terra couldn't be prouder of him. All the long hours had finally paid off. A few of their friends were waiting in the dining room for him to come home, and she had sent Autumn, to stay with her grandmother. It seemed like it would be a nice night to celebrate when he finally got home. She always worried about him getting in an accident. She worried about him working all the time to try to take care of their family. She hadn't known what kind of a night it would be.

Terra never was much of a drinker; she preferred to sip a glass of wine and be the sober one. She loved watching the hilarity. Darren was funny and affectionate when he drank. She had loved watching him relax, but she was a worrier. He had a few blockages around his heart a year or so previously, so she watched him closely. Every night she held her hand over his heart as he slept and would awaken each time it fluttered or skipped a beat. She didn't always sleep well, but she rested easy knowing that the blood pressure cuff and nitroglycerin were close. Trips to the hospital had become commonplace. Darren had been in at least once every six months for a heart catherization, and each time they patched him up and he had been fine. He had become so much healthier in that last year, was eating better, and had even gone through cardiac rehabilitation. He'd never needed open heart surgery, and for that she was thankful. He was a big man and would have been hard to take care of. She hated all the long hours he worked, but he insisted that he was fine. Darren had tried to get social security disability, but they had turned him down twice, so he felt he had no choice but to work hard to support his family. After work, he would come home, eat dinner, and try to watch a little TV with Terra and Autumn, but it never lasted long. Almost every night was an early night as he fell asleep on the couch with his head on Terra's shoulder, his arm draped around her shoulders. She had grown to love those moments, even though she had to be aware of him all the time. She was always close by. She didn't go out much, but she loved every moment with her family. The love she had with Darren was like nothing she had ever experienced.

She remembered the first night they had met clearly. It was as though only a moment had passed in six years. A mutual friend had set them up on a blind date. She was nervous to be meeting a stranger in the middle of a parking lot, especially for a date. Terra waited looking for him to arrive in his old Chevy S-10 truck. She watched each truck as it drove by, wondering if it was him and secretly hoping that he wouldn't show up. The idea of going out with someone she had never met made the hair on the back of her head standing up. But when he pulled in next to her, it was like a moment from a dream. It was as though she had seen his eyes before and was immediately drawn to his smile. Getting out of the truck, he walked over to her.

"Excuse me, miss, I'm Darren," he spoke gently, leaning down to the window. "Are you Terra?"

"Yes, I'm Terra..." she mumbled as she tried to grab the handle of the door.

Swiftly he opened the door and gestured for her. "It's

nice to meet you. Are you nervous?" He asked as he held out his hand for her. His eyes sparkled under the lights as he touched her hand gently. "Have you thought about what you would like to do tonight?"

"I really don't know; I hadn't really got past the idea of a blind date..." She laughed as she looked into his deep blue eyes.

"Well, ma'am, if you like, we can just stay here for a few minutes and talk. Then if you feel comfortable, we can decide then," he calmly reasoned.

As they leaned up against the side of their vehicles, she couldn't help but stare. His eyes had a kindness to them, his light brown hair was cut short to his head, and you could see just a few wrinkles starting in his brow. Standing next to his truck, she felt his ruggedness. He must have been more of an outdoorsy type of guy because his hands were large and rough. They weren't the hands of a man who sat at a desk. Darren had said he lived close by, but listening to his rich southern accent, she knew he hadn't always. She loved listening to him talk. Meeting him had felt like déjà vu. Instantly, she had known that they were meant to at least meet one another.

"So what kind of things do you like to do?" he asked, leaning up against the door of his truck.

"I don't know. I guess the same kinds of things everyone else does," she answered, smiling back at him. "I'm not too complicated."

"Well, give me an example," he laughed.

"I like to try new things, but I really love taking pictures."

"A photographer, that's interesting. My friends didn't really tell me that much about you. I know they just set up the Christmas lights down at the park. Have you been to see them yet?" Darren asked as he got his bottle of soda from inside the truck.

"I haven't, actually. I feel a bit guilty about that," she laughed as she stepped towards him. Terra couldn't explain how warm she felt around him.

"Come with me.... I want to take you," Darren suggested as he stepped closer to her. He held out his hand to her.

"Okay," she whispered, taking his hand.

Walking to the other side of the truck, she felt his rough hands against her soft skin. His hands were so big that she could wrap her hand around his thumb. Swiftly, he opened the door for her and waited for her to get in. As he closed it, he ran to the other side and jumped into the truck. Looking over at her, he stopped for a moment with his hand on the steering wheel.

"I'm glad I had the chance to meet you," he stated, reaching his hand down to hers. Gently, she put her hand next to his as he brushed his thumb across the top of her hand. Taking a deep breath, he looked deeply into her eyes for a moment. "Are you comfortable?"

"I'm okay. I'm not hard to please," she answered, watching his hand leave hers and start the truck. "Have you seen the lights yet?"

"No, I haven't, but I hear they're beautiful," he smiled. "I think it will be nice to see it together, something different."

As they drove away, she watched her car disappear. She didn't feel hesitant anymore. Her heartbeat like a hummingbird's wings every time their eyes met. It had been an amazing feeling. It was comfortable. Terra had never felt anything like it before. Reaching down, she adjusted her skirt, her hands gripping the sides of the fabric, she looked out over their little town. That night felt different. Glancing over at him, she saw his eyes watching her and she couldn't help but smile. Looking down, she watched his hand touch hers. She loved the way he touched her. Darren was gentle, his eyes were warm. Looking over at him, she imagined her hands on his face, the way his lips would feel against hers.

3

Terra's eyes fluttered open. She didn't have a good night's sleep. Her mind was filled with memories and questions. Looking across her room, she flinched against the emptiness. There was nothing there that reminded her of home. She couldn't decide if that was a good thing or a bad thing. Regardless, it didn't seem to stop the memories or the tears. There was nothing to distract her.

Rolling towards the wall, she found the extra blanket Paul had given her and pulled it close. She wasn't used to being alone. A blanket was a poor substitute for the warmth of someone's touch, but it was something to hold onto.

Closing her eyes, her thoughts drifted to the past. She remembered the Christmas lights from their first date. They had been the most beautiful she had ever seen. He had been such a gentleman. While that wasn't a rare thing in their little Ohio town, it was for her. Terra remembered him opening the door for her and immediately holding his arm out for her. Putting her arm in his, she had nestled close to him to shield herself from the cold. Although she found herself staying quite warm that night, she had loved being close to him.

The night was full of warmth and color. The lights shone in rich gold, reds, and greens. They hung from balls in the trees and were strung across the sidewalks like a canopy. There were Christmas trees lining the sidewalks that different groups had decorated. Each of them had a different theme. Each year they had expanded the lights in the park, and this year they were especially memorable. Soft music floated through the air around as people walked casually through the canopy of lights. It was like something from a story book.

"It's beautiful tonight," Darren whispered as he leaned down to her. "I didn't imagine them being like this."

"It's amazing, I don't think I've ever taken the time to do anything like this," she replied, looking across the park. "I really should have."

"We're getting near the center; will you dance with me?" He smiled, holding his hand out to her.

"I'd love that," she grinned.

Taking her hand, he pulled her close to him. She felt his hands caress the small of her back. His eyes looked down into hers, as she slid her hands to his broad shoulders. She saw the gold reflecting in his eyes as they swayed. Diverting her eyes, she looked over to the fountain next to them. The granite pillars were wrapped in gold, she had always loved that fountain. But it only distracted her for a moment as she felt his hot breath next to her hair. His thumbs gently caressed her lower back as he slid her a little closer to him.

"It's been a long time since I held a lady. Is this bothering you?" Darren whispered, leaning into her ear.

"It's okay if you don't want to be this close."

"I... don't... know... is this really appropriate for a first date?"

"I think what's appropriate is up to us, really. We are experienced adults. We're not little kids, so it should be based on what we are comfortable with. For me, I feel close to you. I want to touch you, so badly. I know that sounds bad, but I really don't mean it in a bad way. You feel so soft. I've been waiting a long time to feel something real, something sincere. I feel like I've known you, for a long time." he uttered as he pulled away just enough to look deep within her eyes. "I promise, I mean you no harm."

Terra felt his shoulders tense beneath her hands, his eyes widened as he held her. Looking up at him, she couldn't pull away, her body seemed to melt under his touch as they swayed to the gentle rhythm. She wanted to say it was okay, but she couldn't seem to find the words. She had only known him for a few short hours. Could she possibly let herself lose control, even a little? She was normally rational. But here he was, a warm stranger with his hands on her back pulling her closer to him. How could this be happening to her? It couldn't be real. The thought of love at first sight, soul mates, and being swept away seemed silly to her. But here he was, leaning down looking into her eyes as though he were peering into her soul. Closing her eyes, she took a deep breath, and found herself leaning against him. Darren's arms were around her now. He was so warm and so gentle. She felt his breath in her hair, as he held her close.

"Thank you," he sniffled. "I've never had anyone fit so perfectly against me."

Opening her eyes, she saw a single tear escape his eyes and slide slowly down his face. Reaching up, she took her finger and gently swept it away and rested her hand against his cheek. She felt one of his hands travel up her back to her hair. He stayed there for a moment gently running his fingers through her hair, gently arranging it away from her face until he could rest his hand gently against her cheek. Cradling her face in his hand, he leaned down to her and like a whisper his lips brushed across hers. She felt warmth flood her body like a wave as she pushed herself against him just a little harder. Pulling his face closer, she let her lips caress his again.

Wiping away a tear, Terra sat up in bed. She still felt his lips pressed against hers. Their first date hadn't lasted much longer than that. He had been a gentleman, after all. It was the first of many dates, many memories, and many unforgettable moments. The reality of him being gone sent a shiver up her spine. She would never feel a touch like his again. He had been one of a kind. Their love was like a fairy tale with a tragic ending.

Swinging her legs over the side of her bed, she glanced over to the single white daisy resting in the glass beside her. What would she do now? Could she manage to raise their daughter alone? Could she manage to be without him? He had become a part of her. It was like losing a part of her soul. The only thing that held her now was emptiness.

Terra felt her chest get heavy as the questions taunted her mind. Gripping the side of the bed, she saw her knuckles turn white. Her heart started to pound as her eyes closed tightly, her mind growing dizzy.

"1... 2...3... It's going to be okay," she stated aloud to

herself. "4...5...6... I can get through this." Rhythmically, she let her breath go in and out as she slowly counted.

"1...2..3... it's going to be okay. 4...5...6... I can get through this." Again, she counted, as she tried to regain control. Still, her breath didn't slow; her heart kept racing. Her head spun.

"1...2...3... It's going to be okay, she stated aloud to herself. "4...5...6... I can get through this." Rhythmically, she let her breath go in and out as she slowly counted again.

Reaching to the table, she grabbed the daisy from the glass. She focused on the green of the stem and the smell of its petals. Leaning back against her pillow, she pulled the blanket to her. Pressing it against her chest, she focused on the pressure and the smoothness of the fabric against her arms as she held it. Looking up at the smooth white ceiling, she began to count again and after a while, she began to feel a little better.

Swinging her legs over the side of the bed, she felt the cold floor against her bare feet. She hated cold. It just increased her loneliness. Looking towards the bathroom, she pulled herself from the bed and headed towards the restroom. Her legs felt heavy as she dragged them along, but she knew the water would be refreshing. Terra was overwhelmed with thirst. She needed to feel the warmth of the water against her face and the feel of the brush going through her hair.

Anxiety was taking its toll on her senses. She had never had an attack until Darren had passed. The thought of going through life without him seemed impossible. But the fear of living like she had been for the past few days was paralyzing. Staring at her reflection she saw the redness in her cheeks, her swollen eyes, and the dryness of her hair. Frozen, she thought about those warm moments in the sun with Darren. But they drifted away like dust as she reminded herself that he was gone.

"He's gone," she mumbled, trying to convince her reflection. "Darren can't come back. He died, Terra. He had to move on, and now so do you." She whimpered.

How could telling herself this possibly help, she wondered. Feeling her legs give out she felt her knees collide with the rough tile. With her hands on the floor, she felt the tears rush from her eyes. Moans escaped her lips as the cries continued. He was gone; she knew she had to accept it, but it seemed impossible. How could this be real? Everything she had ever dreamed of had been ripped away from her in an instant. She refused to think about that night. She wanted to forget everything and pretend that she had never met him. Why had she let herself fall so hard for him when she knew he had health problems? Had she really believed that she could make him better? Why hadn't he listened to her and taken better care of himself. Had Darren expected her to do everything for him?

She felt her body change. Her eyes tightened as she gripped the side of the sink, pulling herself back to her feet. Taking a deep breath, she felt the heat rise in her. She was angry. She had given everything to him; she had given six years of her life to a man who didn't listen to her. He didn't try to keep himself healthy. Darren had refused to take his blood pressure medicine. He had refused the healthier foods that the doctor had recommended and drank caffeine even though it effected his heart. Now, she was alone with a daughter to raise. With the economy the way it was, how was she supposed to do that? It had been years since she worked full-time. Her little part-time job and selling photography sessions were not going to be enough to provide for their daughter. Why hadn't they invested in life insurance? Stomping back to the bed, Terra sat down. Grabbing the brush, she ripped it through the tangles, as the door to her room slowly opened.

"Terra, I've missed you!! How are you!" Sheila proclaimed; her sugary sweet voice echoed as she entered the room.

"Hi, mom," Terra stated, rolling her eyes.

"That's not much of a greeting, dear, now let me look at you! Oh, you don't look like you've eaten a bite! Here, I brought some things from home."

Wheeling in a red leopard suitcase, Sheila rushed over to her daughter and pulled her up from the bed in a hug. Her short blonde hair was rough against her skin as it rubbed against Terra's cheek. The stench of cheap hairspray invaded her nostrils as she continued to hold onto her. Her full figure pushed up against Terra as she shook her from side to side.

"How is the food here?" Sheila asked finally pulling away from the embrace.

"It's fine, Mom; it's not bad. It's just food," she mumbled, plopping back onto her bed.

"Are you eating?"

"Yes, of course, I'm eating. I'm not going to starve myself."

"Well, here's your stuff!" She smiled. "I hope I remembered everything."

"Thank you."

Grabbing the suitcase, Sheila threw it on the bed. Within moments, it was open, and the contents organized into neat little piles on the bed. Terra saw a couple of satin gown and robe sets, another hairbrush, a little makeup bag, and a couple of outfits. Beside those were books, bottled water, shampoo, conditioner, lotion and what seemed to be half of the local body works store. Standing up, Terra grabbed at the clothes, hoping Sheila remembered her favorite dress. It was a long maxi dress that was covered in monarch butterflies. It was bright, vibrant, and reminded her of happy days, but it wasn't there.

"Where's my butterfly dress?" Terra asked as she stared at all the neat little piles. "You bought all of this didn't you?"

"Well, yes, of course I did. I didn't want anything to bring back any memories. You don't need to dwell on the past," she reassured.

"But I love my butterfly dress. I didn't mean for you to go out and buy me a bunch of stuff. I can't afford all of this."

"You don't have to; this is my treat. How often do I get to spoil my little girl?" Sheila squealed.

"I don't really need to be spoiled by you, Mom." Grabbing the makeup bag, she quickly thumbed through the contents. Most of it was expensive brands she had never tried. "I like the makeup I already have. You don't need to do this."

"I know I don't need to, but I wanted you to have something nice. Do you like the nightgowns I got you?" she inquired gesturing towards them.

Reaching over to them, Terra pulled out a beautiful emerald green robe. As she held it up, she noticed the beautiful lace that trimmed it. Her fingers reached down and felt the smooth fabric and the delicate lace that trimmed the sleeves and hem. Grabbing the delicate chemise, Sheila handed it to Terra. The thin straps were delicate, and it, too, was trimmed in lace. It wasn't a revealing set but was elegant. Looking over on the bed, she noticed that the second gown was the same but was ivory and covered in elegant pink roses. Catching her breath, Terra dropped the green one on the bed and reached for it. Grabbing the robe, she tried it on and went to the mirror. It was soft and brought out the natural tones to her skin. It reminded her of the roses in the courtyard. Her favorite roses. For once, Sheila had given her something she really loved. Wearing them in a crisis center seemed to be a bit overdone, but maybe her Mom was right. Maybe a little luxury wouldn't hurt right now.

"You know, Terra, you have always loved nice things. It won't hurt to focus on yourself a little right now," Sheila whispered as she rested her hand on her daughter's shoulder.

"They're beautiful," she sobbed as she wiped away a tear. "These might actually make me feel a little better." Glancing over to the table, she noticed her white daisy and smiled.

"Where did these come from?" Sheila asked walking to her little table. "I don't remember these being here."

"The journal is just something they had," Terra replied, snatching the journal from the bedside table. "And they had flowers out on the table yesterday, and I asked for one to keep in my room."

"Well, that's good, for a second there I thought you might have an admirer," she laughed. "I'm sure many men would want to prey on you now thinking you have insurance money to burn." Giggling she sat down on the bed.

"I don't have any admirers, where would I find one in a place like this?" She tried to laugh. "I haven't thought about anything like that."

"And you shouldn't! What would people think of you flirting with some strange man. That would be horrible!"

"I've never been flirtatious, so I don't think we need to worry about that," Terra smirked walking back over to the bed. "What did you bring me to wear? I can't wear these to therapy, after all." She remarked sliding the robe from her shoulder.

"Well, I wasn't sure what you would want, so I got you a nice pair of pants, a couple tops, and a nice new pair of boots, of course. I know it's not much, but Autumn is hoping you will only be gone a couple more days. We don't want to disappoint her."

"Where is Autumn?"

"Oh, don't worry about your little girl. She's safely tucked away at the neighbor's house. " Sheila waved as though she were trying to push away her question. "You know what I noticed as I came in today? I saw a man around your age in a button up shirt just sitting in a chair looking outside. I wonder what he is in here for? I bet he beat his wife or something like that. You never can tell with people!"

"I wouldn't assume that!"

"Well, tell me about him. He has dark hair, a medium build. It looks like he lifts weights or something. He's fit, but not in a steroid way," she laughed.

"Oh, I don't know. That doesn't sound familiar, maybe he's just visiting someone," she lied. "Why didn't you bring

Autumn?"

"I told you. Don't worry about Autumn. She doesn't need to see you in a place like this, around all of these crazy people." Walking towards Terra, she grabbed her hands. "You don't want her thinking something is wrong with you. That's not what she needs right now, honey."

"THIS PLACE? This place isn't for crazy people. It's for people who are just needing a little help. Everyone needs a little help sometimes. My daughter needs her mother right now, and I need her. How dare you keep her from me! She just lost her dad; she doesn't need to be afraid of losing me too!" She stated as she grabbed her hands away. Terra began throwing her clothes back into the suitcase and slid it under her bed. "YOU shouldn't be so judgmental. Is that what all of this is - a bunch of stuff to help your CRAZY daughter come to her senses?"

"Of course not! But, honey, these other people...you need to be careful around them," Sheila cooed as she reached for Terra's hands again.

"These people? There's nothing bad about these people," she yelled, pulling away from her mother. "They are just like me. They are not crazy."

"Well, you can tell yourself anything you want if that is what helps get you home," she laughed, patting her shoulder.

"Tell me about Autumn, how is she doing?" Crossing her arms across her chest, Terra plopped down on her bed. "What do you mean by safely tucked away?"

"I just had Michael watch her, so I didn't have to bring her here. This is no place for children," she answered as she sat next to her.

"Maybe not, but she's only five years old. You can't just

leave her with anyone. There are people that don't understand little kids. They might leave her alone." She stated walking towards the door. Looking out of her little window, she looked around for a friendly face but didn't see anyone.

"Michael would never do a thing like that. You're being silly! Besides, we've been together for a long time; little Autumn knows him well. She sees him all the time. It's not his fault you don't pay enough attention to know how important he is in my life. He wants nothing more than to be a part of our family. He basically saved my life." Walking over to Terra she grabbed her hand. "Why don't you come over here and tell me how it's going. What are you talking about in therapy?"

"I don't get to tell you that. I'm not going to give you more to gossip about. And what do you mean by close friends?" Terra uttered turning towards her. "Are you screwing him, Mom?"

"I don't see where that's any of your business, young lady..." Sheila giggled walking towards the door. "Oh, enough about me, young lady. You need to shake this off so you can get back to town. Everyone misses you."

"Who, exactly, is everyone?" she asked.

"Well, me for one, but there are others. You know what I keep hearing? People are saying that Darren was doing drugs and sleeping around with some woman at that car lot. That's how he got that promotion," she whispered, stepping away from Terra.

"MOM, NO! You can't be serious. Darren would never do something like that. He loved us. He would never sleep around, and he would never do drugs. There wasn't anything like that going on at the car lot," she growled as she hit her mattress. Standing up she walked over to her mother. "Where did you hear this crap?"

"Well, how else do you think he got that promotion? Through hard work? Think about it, Terra. Don't be so naïve. Is it so farfetched that he was doing a little bit of crack because he was stressed out from working so much? Don't you think he wanted to get ahead for you guys, so he started sleeping around, hoping that it would help him get the promotion. Come on, think about it!" Sheila scoffed.

"I'm telling you, there's no way he would do anything like that. He was a good faithful man. Nobody has any business talking about him like that."

"But honey, don't you remember all of those late nights? All of those times when you worried about how late he was going to be home?"

Unfortunately, Terra remembered. There were times when he worked nearly eighteen hours without even a phone call to tell her he was going to be late. She hated those nights. She hated not knowing when he would be home. Every night she was afraid that he wouldn't come home at all. She even remembered stopping in for a visit at the car lot one time and finding that he wasn't there. She had waited four hours that day. But he never came, and she had never mentioned it. Why accuse him of something when he came home every night and loved them, held them, and worked so hard to provide for them. Darren supported her artwork and her photography. He had been the first that ever really had. How could she question him? He was the one to stand by her side when she had won her first photography award. And he had been there when she had the honor of being featured in her first solo gallery exhibit.

"Mom, none of that is true and you know it. Maybe you should go. You need to get back to Autumn," she sighed pointing towards the door. "You know how I feel about gossip."

"Are you sure, dear? I can stay as long as you like."

"I'm sure. I would like to get a shower and get some rest. And the shower isn't in my bathroom. It's down the hall, so you should probably go ahead and go," Terra quickly answered.

"Okay, okay. I'll go. You just need to focus on taking care of yourself," Sheila whispered as she hugged her daughter again. "You know what might make you feel a little better? A close friend of Darren's. You know Greg calls and asks about you every day. You should talk to him! He's so cute and you guys have a lot in common. He even gave me a note to give you. They wouldn't let him see you OR talk to you. How crazy is that? Okay...I'm going. I will see you in a couple of days. Be sure to read that letter!"

Watching her mother walk away, Terra looked down at the letter. Her hands shook as she reached to grab it off the table. Her eyes stared through the paper as it rested in her hands. She wanted to believe he had good intentions or maybe he had apologized. Either way, this wasn't a letter she was prepared to read. She wanted to forget that night and everything that had happened, a luxury he wasn't allowing. With a sigh she slowly opened it, knowing she couldn't escape him.

Terra,

I miss our time together. It seems like forever since I saw you. We are both in this together and I wish I could be there to help you through this. I miss Darren just as much as you do but most of all, I just miss you. I miss your beautiful smile and the way you hide your face when you laugh. Your eyes would always sparkle when you saw me, or I always thought it was because of me. I'm glad I could be there with you that night, in that moment, when everything changed. Maybe now we can be together. You know how much I have always wanted to be around you. You always meant more to me than Darren ever did. All I want is for you to let me take care of you. Please be okay. Get better, so I can see you. I know that this is what he would have wanted. Nobody can help you through this like I can.

    Love,
    Greg

Glancing over the words, Terra shook her head as she stared at the floor. Crumpling the scribbled words, she shoved the page violently in the trash and headed for the door. From his words, Sheila probably thought they were lovers. *That's all I need.*

"Mom," she called out. "Don't bring me anymore letters from Greg. That's not who I want to hear from right now. I prefer to get through this on my own. Tell him THAT next time he calls."

"But you need him, darling."

"No, Mother...I don't need anyone. Depending on a man never got you through anything, why would I try it?"

"Fine, be that way, but they really do come in handy," Sheila winked.

Watching her mom leave, she let out a sign. She loved

Sheila, but she was exhausting. She was the kind of mother that believed nothing was ever good enough. It didn't matter how hard she tried or how well she did at anything, it was never enough. She had hoped to make her proud when she grew up, but that wasn't going to happen sitting in a crisis center. Even as a child, the honor roll was never good enough. She was always pushing her to do better, be more involved, and be more popular. Terra, on the other hand, just wanted to be herself. She had always been artistic. She loved writing, painting, singing, and even dancing. If it were possible, she would have believed that Sheila hadn't been her real mother. She had always been a bit of a daddy's girl, so when news came of their divorce, Terra hadn't been sure how to feel. Thankfully, they both seemed to be happier apart. Unfortunately, he had vanished right after the divorce, and she wasn't sure why. He was like a vapor. Her mom had simply stated that he had to go away for a while. No matter how hard she had pleaded for answers, they never came. Terra knew there was more to the story, to Sheila's story. That's the way she was, though; you only found out what you had to know or discovered on your own. Her mother was too aware of town gossip to let any negativity reach the ears of the community. After the divorce, everything changed for both, and Sheila had begun her sales career, something she was very good at. Sometimes visits with her mom could be fun. They would talk about her latest shopping adventures and the newest hairstyles. On other visits, she was overwhelmed with the gossip of the town. It had often made her wonder what her friends knew about her.

The news of the gossip around Darren's death didn't help Terra feel any better. What she hated the most about the town gossips was that most of the time there was some truth to their stories. They were just exaggerated. How much truth was behind the story about him? Was that why that night he had seemed a little different? Had he been taking drugs. She had never really done anything like that. She had no idea what the warning signs were. It was something she had never really considered. If he had been, it would have worn down his heart. There were so many questions, and she knew that they would never be answered. The only thing she had now was what she hated the most, town gossip.

The night her life changed, that led to THAT MOMENT was still more of a nightmare than a memory. It all started simple enough, a hug and kiss at the door, the I miss you's, and the I'm-so-glad-you're-home greeting that happened every night before. He wanted to start the celebrating right away, so the music played, the pizza was eaten, and drinks were poured. It was a hard-won promotion that he had worked years for. Darren usually only had a drink or two occasionally. It was always just enough to calm his nerves and to make him feel normal. This night, however, was different.

Their friends had gathered and while it wasn't a party, exactly, they were all ready to celebrate and enjoy a child-free evening. They had all gathered around the back patio. The fire glowed in the moonlight; it was a warm spring evening, and the moon shone like a diamond in the black sky. The stars twinkled above them as their laughter floated like music in the air. The glasses swirled with alcohol, and the ice melted quickly.

Sitting back, Terra watched Darren and their friends drink glass after glass of Long Island iced tea. It was hard to keep up. She couldn't help but smile as she watched him laugh in the middle of the group. He'd lost his shirt some time ago and hadn't seemed to notice. His southern accent grew thicker as the alcohol levels increased in his blood. Leaning his head back, she saw him notice every light in the night sky.

"Hey, Greg, come over here..." Darren waved his friend over. "I'm so glad we met. You have been with me through everything. You were there when I didn't have anything, when I was alone, and nobody loved me. Thank you so much for everything you've done for me," he mumbled as his arms wrapped around Greg. "I don't know what I would have ever done without you."

"Hey, man, it's okay, I wouldn't have it any other way," he laughed nervously. "I'm always happy to be around you. You are one in a million, Darren." Leaning away from him, Greg gave him a quick fist bump and walked towards Terra. "I think he might be a little drunk."

Laughing, Darren refilled his glass and staggered to the middle of the group. The reflection of the small fire made his skin look redder than usual. His eyes glistened as he looked at everyone. "All of you mean so much to me, you have no idea...how much, really."

Stuttering, he found his way back to his chair. "You all should just stay here tonight. We have plenty of room."

"Well, I was hoping that would work. Where else would we go?" Greg laughed as he nudged Terra. "I would not want to drive like this, and I'm sure you don't want to drive us all home."

"Terra, come here, baby," Darren motioned for her, as he patted his lap. As she sat down on his lap, she gently took his glass and put it on the table beside her. Looking into his eyes, she saw them water. There were tears in the corners of his eyes. He had never been much of a crier. He had always been tough. He didn't like to express his feelings often, but when he did, he really did. Most of the time, he showed her in a lot of other ways. She hated to admit it, but he hadn't been around much lately. He was constantly at the car lot, working long hours. Darren came home late every night. He had been for months. She knew that he had been really pushing himself. He was always tired and while she adored him, she was tired of feeling alone, never knowing when he would be home. She missed their evenings cooking together in the kitchen.

He had loved to grab her as the music played. Pulling her into a slow dance, he would serenade her with the words to her favorite song. He had shown his love for her in every way. But in recent months, he had grown distant, almost absent from their lives. They barely talked anymore. Every night she watched him slowly fade into the night. He would sleep on their couch until Terra had cleared the dishes and made sure Autumn was in bed. That's when she would wake him to join her upstairs in their bedroom. Cuddling close to her, he would always hold her tight against him, so tight she could barely breathe. Then, eventually he would roll over and she would rest her hand against his chest. Every day was the same. It was a lonely existence, but she had always adored him. For better or worse, in sickness and in health, that is what she had vowed to him. She honored him and put him above all other things in her life. He had quickly become her life, and she spent most of her time making sure he took his medicine, ate well, and rested enough to keep going. He had gotten so much stronger lately, but she hated that she barely saw him. Sometimes she would try to surprise him at work, but oftentimes, he would be out on a service call. Sometimes he was just not there. On many occasions, she had left the lot with her head down, leaving behind the little lunch basket she had prepared for them. There were many times that she had felt isolated from his world, but it was on those days that he came home and reminded her of their love and their time together. He would bring home not just any flowers, but they would always be her favorites. Darren knew that stargazer lilies and pink and cream roses always made her smile. It was on those nights that he whisked her away to the bedroom, holding her close to him. They were only able to be intimate occasionally. It was difficult for him now. His body had changed him, and nothing really seemed to help. It was difficult, and she had felt their connection dwindling.

On many occasions she had caught his friends watching her. She worried about what intimate secrets he might have shared with them. Lately their gazes had grown longer and more frequent. They didn't bother to look away when she would catch them anymore. They just kept staring. Terra had learned to keep her distance from them, especially when they would come over during the day while Darren was working. She hated to be rude, so she had grown accustomed to sitting on the patio, as their daughter would swing on her playset. The phone was always close by. She was tired of feeling alone. Her heart ached for him when he was gone. Every moment was like torture.

"You know I love you, don't you?" Darren asked as a tear slowly trailed down his cheek. "I would do anything for you." Pulling her closer to him, his lips brushed against hers. "I love you so much, baby."

"I know you love me, Darren. But you never seem to be around anymore. It really hurts being alone. I don't feel like you love me like you used to." Leaning away she looked deeply into his eyes and kissed him gently on the forehead. "Will you be around more now that you got this promotion?"

"I don't know. It's a lot of responsibility. I can't guarantee anything but that I love you. I will always love and adore you and Autumn. You are everything to me."

"But we miss you, we really miss you."

"I'm so sorry baby, just know that I love you, no matter what you might hear about me, always know how much I love you."

Leaning up against his chest, Terra felt his heart beating. The alcohol didn't seem to have had much of an impact on more than his emotions. Closing her eyes, she let herself melt into his embrace. His arms were so warm around her. She felt his kisses on her forehead, as he pulled her even closer to him, so close she could barely breathe. His breath was hot against her skin, as it came in rapid gasps. But soon, it slowed as he quickly fell asleep. Gently, she moved his arms away and stood up next to him. Like every other night, he had drifted away. Reaching over, she grabbed his glass and started gathering the trash from the evening.

"Here, let me grab that for you, Terra," Greg commanded from behind her.

"No, it's okay. I'm used to it."

"You shouldn't be. Let me help you."

Brushing up against her. he grabbed the glass from her

hand. She felt his eyes staring into hers. He was close, too close. Quickly he gathered the trash and headed inside. Their other friends had left a while ago. It was just the three of them now. Glancing back at Darren sleeping soundly on his chair, she headed inside. She knew she needed to make up the couch and clean up for the night. Grabbing the extra sheets and blankets from the closet, she started putting the couch together for Greg. He had been staying over a lot lately. His wife had left him recently and while they had been trying to work through things in therapy, it didn't seem to be helping. As she stretched the blanket over the couch, she felt him behind her, watching her.

"You know, you're a beautiful woman, Terra. You shouldn't have to feel alone," he whispered in her ear. "Darren told me he hasn't been able to-"

"I'm not alone. I'm with Darren," she quickly answered.

She felt her body freeze as he touched her. She felt his hand gently drift up her arm. Tugging at her shoulders, he turned her around to face him. His eyes were piercing, like he saw every insecurity and every moment she ever felt alone. She felt his strong hands resting on her shoulders.

"You don't have to feel that way, he would understand if you had your needs met... elsewhere. He told me... he can't.... well, you know, he has a hard time. He worries about you. He said you were amazing. He said everything about you is amazing. I have always wanted you, Terra, always."

"Like I said, I'm fine. I'm not alone, Greg. What do you want from me? What do you want, exactly?"

"I want you, all of you. You're alone in this house every

day when Autumn is in preschool and yet you never leave. He barely touches you; he barely kisses you. I know, I've been watching. A woman like you should never be neglected."

"I'm not neglected, really. I'm okay."

"No, Terra, I know you're not."

Terra felt her eyes moisten as he looked at her. She watched his eyes leave hers as he took all of her in, his grip only grew stronger as he pushed himself up against her. Losing her balance, she felt her legs give out as she landed on the couch behind her.

Sitting beside her, his arms reached around her and pulled her against him. His arms were strong as he turned her to face him.

"Darren won't mind if I kiss you, if I touch you. Like I said, he's all but asked me if I would help him take care of you," Greg whispered.

Terra couldn't move as she felt his lips press against her. At first, he was gentle. Then the kiss grew harder as he pulled her even closer to him.

"Please, let me have you," Greg commanded.

She felt her body collapsing against the couch as his body pushed her down. Her hands tried to push him away, but he was stronger and harder than she was. He just kept pushing until she was laying there beneath him. She felt his hands drift up her legs, pushing her skirt up to her waist. His hands were hard as they pushed her panties to the side. Reaching down she felt him kiss her belly. His gaze on her body felt like hot coals against her skin as he explored her.

"Greg, please stop. This isn't right. What if Darren catches you..." Terra cried as she fought against her own body. Caught between passion and loyalty, she tried again to push him away. "Please stop."

"I know you don't really want me to stop. Darren isn't going to catch me touching you, kissing you. If he didn't want me to, he wouldn't have told me how you feel, how your kisses taste, or how much he loves being with you. He wouldn't have told me how lonely you have been or how he can't seem to fulfill you anymore. He practically asked me to take you."

Her hands pushed against his shoulders, as she tried to sit up. Grabbing her legs, he spread them open and kneeled over her. She saw his chest moving rapidly with his breaths as he looked down on her. Closing her eyes, she felt his hands open the buttons on her blouse and push it to the side. Tenderly she felt him lift her bra and quickly take her breast in his mouth. Gasping, she tried to sit up again, but his body was too heavy.

"Did you hear that?" Greg panicked standing to his feet. "Get up, I heard a crash." Grabbing her hand, he pulled Terra to her feet just as Darren ran inside to the restroom. Quickly, Terra closed her blouse and ran to him. He was grasping the sides of his toilet gagging, vomiting. Automatically, she grabbed a washcloth and held it against his forehead and filled a glass of water.

"Are you okay? Is your chest hurting?" she asked rubbing his back.

"Yes, it's really bad this time, please... help... me," Darren cried through the vomit.

"I'll be right back; I'm going to go get everything."

Running to the kitchen she reached into the cabinet for the blood pressure cuff and his medicine. They were up higher than usual, and Terra cringed as it came crashing down on her. Pressing the button, she waited for it to turn on as she ran back for the bathroom, but it didn't. The batteries had been removed. Opening the drawers, she dug for the batteries of their faithful blood pressure cuff.

"Greg, find the keys, we have to get him to the hospital."

Rushing back to the restroom, Terra opened the aspirin and handed it to Darren. His skin was pale and covered in sweat. His eyes were swollen from tears. His hand was clenched against his chest as he leaned over their toilet. Grabbing the water, she handed the aspirin to him. His eyes seemed to stare through her as he quickly swallowed it.

"Come on, we have to go," she commanded as she tried to pull him up.

"I can't move, it hurts!" Darren whimpered.

"Move, Terra, I will get him," Greg shouted from behind her.

Grabbing onto Darren, Greg pulled him up from the side of the bathtub. Pulling him gently, they headed towards the car as Terra quickly got in the driver's seat and started the car. She was thankful that the hospital was close. When they arrived, she watched him calm down. aybe it wasn't that bad, she thought to herself. Just like usual, she watched them take an EKG, draw blood, and wheel in the x-ray machine. This is normally when she took a moment to catch her breath. He was stable, so she headed to the hallway with Greg tagging along behind her. Leaning up against the wall, she focused on the cold against her cheek. She knew it was going to be a long night.

"I'm sorry, Terra," Greg whispered from behind her.

"I hope I didn't hurt you."

"No, I'm fine, but I told you no..... what if something happens to him? What am I supposed to do?"

"He will be fine. He's done this a lot; he's always going to be fine. He's at the hospital; he's safe now."

"I could never betray him, Greg.... never. I hope you understand that."

"I do, I'm sorry...."

"We don't have long; we need to get back in there. They are done with the x-ray." She stated walking back inside of his room.

Walking to her husband, she grabbed his hand and felt his grip tighten against her hand. His skin was colder than normal, and his eyes were glassy as she looked at him.

"I'm scared, Terra. I don't want to leave you and Autumn. I'm so sorry. They asked me if I had been drinking and now, they are going to treat me just like a regular drunk."

Darren's tears flowed quickly down his cheeks as he held onto her hand. As he tried to look away, she watched him try to wipe away the tears. They hadn't hooked the monitors back up after taking the x-ray. She knew they would be back in soon, so Terra watched him closely. His breathing was slow, a little slower than normal. Looking towards the wall, she watched his eyes slowly close and his head droop to the side. She felt his grip loosen as his breathing stopped.

"NURSE! NURSE! Somebody help!" she screamed, holding onto him. "Come back to me, Darren!"

Rushing in, they pulled her out of the room and quickly closed the curtains. She saw them moving quickly, as Greg pulled her away, back into the hallway. There they were met by another young nurse who took them into a quiet room. The room was inviting with a nice sofa and peaceful pictures on the walls. There were flowers in the corner and magazines on a table. Sitting down, Terra tried to calm down.

"This is different. This is NOT okay..." she cried looking up at Greg.

"No, he's going to be ok, just be strong for him. They are going to pull him out of this," Greg answered as he grabbed her hand.

Pulling her hand back from Greg, she shuffled to the room window. She saw them wheeling his bed out now. They were moving him, and she saw him look down the hallway towards her. But she knew there was no way he saw her through the little window. Pulling the door open Terra ran towards him. Hoping to see him alive, just to see that look in his eyes. The one that reminded her of how much he loved her.

"We're taking him up to the Cath Lab. His doctor is already there waiting on him. You need to head to the second floor, and they will be out as soon as we can to update you, ma'am," the nurse called out to her as they rushed him away.

"Darren, I love you!" she called as he disappeared around the corner. At least she had that. No matter what happened, she knew that her last words to him were that she loved him. It was a habit of theirs. Every time they spoke, when they went to sleep, and when either of them left, the other they always expressed their love. They knew that anything could happen, at any time. You never know when you will speak to someone for the last time. They had lived by that and built their relationship around it.

Now it was a painful reminder of how true it could be. What if?

Grabbing her hand Greg headed down the hallway to the elevator. He didn't say a word. He didn't need to. He saw the way she had looked down the hallway where he had disappeared. He knew that she probably wouldn't hear him anyway. She was lost. Her eyes were blank, her mouth was half open, and she walked slowly as though she were stuck in a dream. Putting his hand on her back, she led her to the second floor waiting area where they ushered her immediately into a quiet room. They had been in this room before. Both sat there staring blankly at the dry erase board in front of them. It was the same one they had used to describe how they had placed stints around his heart after his first heart attack. He had survived a ninety percent blockage in the widow-maker. They had showed Terra and a couple of their close friends who waited how they had entered the vessels around his heart and placed several stints, not just in one area, but in several. It had just served as a reminder. Darren was strong; he could survive anything it had seemed.

"It's going to be ok, right?" Terra asked, as she stared blankly at the wall.

"Yeah...they have him where they need him. If nothing else, they can open him up and do whatever they need to do. He's in good hands," Greg answered.

"I hope we got him here fast enough. I can't believe the batteries were gone from the blood pressure cuff. I told him I needed a manual one just in case, but he insisted that I didn't need it. If I would have had one, maybe I could have done more."

"Don't do that, don't blame yourself for anything. Do

you understand me?" Sitting back, she heard people rushing up and down the hallway passed their door. She saw dozens of people in blue scrubs cross by them. Each one moved faster than the next. Taking a deep breath, she leaned up against the back of the sofa. Watching the second hand on the clock tick away, she counted the minutes and compared it to his previous visits. It hadn't been long, but it felt longer, a lot longer. Terra couldn't stop watching the clock. It was as though it was drawing her in. It was all she saw. Outside, the nurses stopped rushing and she felt herself start to relax. They would be in soon to tell her he was okay, just like every other time. It was going to be okay. It had to be. It was always okay. He was young and strong. It was just a rough night. Maybe he would need open heart surgery. She didn't really know what the future would hold, but she believed everything would be ok. Finally, she watched two people approach and slowly open the door. She couldn't help but smile a little. She felt relieved. He was out of the lab and now it was time to find out what the plan would be to help him.

"Are you Darren's wife?" the doctor asked plainly.

"Yes, I am."

"Ma'am, we did everything we could."

"So, what's the plan, does he need another surgery?"

"Ma'am, I'm sorry, but your husband has expired."

"What?" Terra whispered. "What does that even mean?"

"He's gone, I'm sorry."

In that moment Terra felt her heart beating inside of her chest. She felt every breath she took as her eyes looked down at the empty table in front of her. Her voice felt frozen, and she couldn't seem to move. Their voices faded away; all that was left was silence.

4

Heat from neighboring flames melted her dress to her body. The stench of old smoke smothered her as her eyes were baked by the floating embers of a distant fire. Above her, the silent horizon of an abandoned time screamed its smoky gasp as she watched the horizon move in heated ripples of air.

As she arose, the ocean nipped at her feet while the door teased her with an imagined breeze. This time she couldn't feel the pressure pushing her from before. Bolting to her feet, she stepped away from the black waters and looked within the window that taunted her. Beyond the glass, she could see dancing trees and a path created by grass and petals from cherry blossoms. She saw water glowing, dancing like a ribbon amidst the green, creating a path through a plush carpet of blooms. Squirrels scurried up branches of weeping willows, and birds guarded their nests. The faint scent of honeysuckle drifted through the cracks as she searched for an opening, a knob... anything. Still it silently stood, as invisible as her husband. Like him, the door was dead, an idea that couldn't be touched.

Reaching down, she continued to search for a way in. The door felt strong and still, but was nothing more than the view on the other side. She never wanted to look away from the paradise beyond. Then she felt it, a hole lying against the door, a glistening glow against the darkness, a tiny escape.

Where in all of this, would a key be hidden? Still... the waves continued to crash against the shore, oblivious to her. Reaching down, she touched the glass and dug her fingers, still bleeding, into the splinters it had created. Searching. Blood oozed from her fingers as pain shot through her as each piece cut deeper and her back collapsed. *There had to be something.*

The tree beckoned like an oasis among the embers, as Terra crept to the center of the broken shore, her haven within the Gray. She longed for its perspective as it overlooked her. In this way, the tree was a king. *Why am I here?* Stepping forward, she watched the water crash a few feet away, each time coming a little farther as the shattered mirrors nipped at her toes. Each one cutting deeper.

In the glass, she could see herself but not her reflection. Each piece was a memory. Crouching down, she watched her face change, the moment she was told of Darren's death. She saw her body stiffen and eyes glaze over. A shiver ran down her spine as she relived those painful words, words she hoped to never hear. Everything was silent, but she still heard them echo in her mind. Tears raged within as she watched the scene play through broken glass.

In the next glass, she saw her daughter's birth play out like a movie. She saw tears as she held swaddled Autumn in safety, her fresh baby skin covered in kisses as their hearts beat together. Her tender eyes barely open as she slept peacefully against Terra's breast, the scent of baby powder flooded her senses with the warmth of the moment captured. Her mind reeled as she watched her memories play out. Her happiest moment and her greatest sorrow played side by side on the shards beneath her. To the left, she watched moaning desperation and to the right, tears of joy sprung from her eyes like laughter.

Looking down the glassy shores, she could see movement in each shard, tiny memories in an endless loop. There were happy memories, sad memories, and memories forgotten. Taking a few steps forward saw her first day of Kindergarten. Her hair tied in pig tails as she rushed to find her name at the table. She felt hope; she felt the joys of new crayons and fresh wooden pencils. Reaching to a shard for a closer look, the mirror turned black, and her memory disappeared and dropped it to the ground as she felt movement in the distance, something was coming. Looking against the smoky landscape, she saw the heads of people. They were coming again, thousands of them. She knew they were headed to the black waters. Running against the broken glass of her memories she raced towards the tree. *What if the smoke pushes me again? How can I stop this?* Reaching the tree, she grabbed a lower branch and held on to the petrified branches as black as the oily ocean waves that crashed.

They were coming.

Why were they going blindly ahead? Like robots they drug themselves forward. Each step looked painful as shattered sand was drug along. Desperately, her hand reached for them, but there was no sound, no recognition.

Their gaze was steady, skin as cold as death, and their arms hung limply at their sides. Unreachable. Unstoppable. She tried to scream, pushing her voice to be heard, but she was met with silence as they pushed ever forward. Again, she pulled from within and pushed her breath into a scream, her mouth opened wide to let the sound escape, but it was met with invisible silence. Again and again she tried to stop them, but one by one they walked towards the oily waves.

Rushing to the tree, she grabbed the lowest branch and climbed away from them. She could feel the sharp steeled bark pressing against her legs as she climbed up. The leaves were like razor blades as the smoky haze ripped them against her. Yet still she climbed, looking over the black ocean. She could see its oily presence touching the gray horizon beyond. Helpless, she watched people begin to disappear within the waves. Each one shuffled within the depths as their heads disappeared one by one into the deep. She could see nothing beyond the black surface that was so devoid of life. No ripples greeted their presence as they marched forward and she watched helplessly as each of them was swallowed by the midnight sea.

Turning, she faced away from the waters to the wasteland. She could see nothing but the pebble sands and broken rock. Squinting her eyes to the smoke, she could see something far in the distance. Like a skeleton broken against the rocks, she could see pieces of steel. They rose and fell against the gray sky, like a lost city. Looking at it reminded her of dread. Terra could feel the air being sucked out of her lungs, like a vacuum. Her body grew weak against the bark as she clung to it. She could feel herself falling. Twisting, she tried to grab onto something, anything as she fell. Her hand reached for another branch, but as she did, the smoke blew it out of her grasp. She could feel her hands reaching, tugging they tried to find something to keep her from the sharp rock below her. She could feel the razor leaves cutting her as she grabbed for them.

Twisting her body, she wrapped her legs around the lowest branch, just in time to stop her fall to the rocks below. Her arms burned as she pulled herself onto the limb. Her breath was coming rapidly now as she tried to refill her lungs. Looking into the distance, she could see a cloud of smoke rushing towards her. Like a sandstorm, a wave of smoke and ash funneled towards her from the darkness. Climbing down, she huddled between the rocks. Closing her eyes, she braced herself against the storm. She could feel the heat coming for her. Her breath came in shallow gasps as she tried to guard herself against the smoke. But it still came for her, she could feel her lungs burning as she searched for oxygen. Pushing herself further between the black rocks, she covered her mouth with the edge of her dress. She knew it would be over soon; the sudden burst of ash felt like fire on her back, and all the air that she had fought to recover escaped with a silent scream.

***

Looking inside of Terra's window, Paul saw her thrashing. The pillows had been tossed from her small white bed. One lay crumpled in the corner of the room, while the other lay silently on the floor beside her. He heard her coughing, gagging as her arms grabbed at the air. Flying through the door, he knelt beside the bed.

"Terra... Terra, wake up!" Grabbing her hands from her throat, he pulled them down to her sides. "You have to wake up, now!"

"OOOOOOOooooo..." Terra moaned as her face grimaced.

"Wake up... sweetheart... you have to wake up..." he pleaded as he held her firmly.

"Owww...aaahhh...NOOOO..." she continued groggily.

"SNAP out of it," he pleaded with tears welling up in his eyes. "You can do this..."

"I'm awake...." she gasped, as she coughed for air. "Let.... go.... of.... my WRISTS!" Sitting up, she grabbed at the blanket, holding it close to her chest. What had just happened, where had she been? Looking over at Paul, she felt her wrists burning from where he had held her down. "Why were you holding me down?" she yelled, glaring into his eyes.

"I'm sorry, I'm so sorry, you were hitting yourself. I didn't want you to get hurt. What were you dreaming?"

"I'm not sure it was a dream. It's this place.... I can't describe it. It was like being stuck in a different place without light, color, or sound. It's hot and full of smoke. That's what happened when I first met you..."

His eyes were warm as Paul listened to her. She felt the concern in his voice. Her memories rushed through her mind as she tried to gather herself. She didn't want anyone to see her like this. Clutching the blanket tighter around her, she looked over at Paul. There was no way he could ever understand how alone she felt. Nobody understood her. They had never been to a place that taunted you with your worst nightmares. Darren had left her behind. How could she possibly be loved by another man? Looking into his eyes again she wanted to scream. How could Paul try to be compassionate towards her? He was just another man. Would he be like Greg and just try to take advantage of her?

"I used to have dreams like that, but for me... I felt like I was drowning. Maybe it was because I was drowning in my own emotions. It still doesn't make sense to me," he answered, watching her eyes dart around the room. "Here let me help you." Gently pulling the blanket from her, he spread it out evenly over her. The sheets were a mess underneath her as he tried to drape the blanket around her. "Would you mind if I held you for a little while?" he asked, trying not to stare at the cream and rose satin gown she wore beneath it. He saw her legs folded in front of her as she sat up, the edges of her gown inched up her legs as he tried to cover her.

"Why would you want to hold me?"

"Because I know what it's like to feel alone. I know what it's like to hold onto this blanket, searching for comfort. Maybe I can help."

"You just want to take advantage of the situation..."

"No, I wouldn't do that, Terra. I'm not that type of guy."

"Aren't all guys that type of guy? Can you really say that you don't want to touch me?"

"No, they're not. And yes, I would love to touch you! I can't deny that. But I would never want to hurt you or make you uncomfortable. If you ever give me the chance to touch you, I would want to touch your heart, your mind, and your soul, before I would ever REALLY touch your body. And I'm not here just because of that, so please don't think that way. I know something of what you are going through, maybe not exactly, but I'm trying. You just need to let me in. You need to let someone in."

Staring into his eyes, Terra loosened her grip on the blanket. She knew he was right about the blanket. It really didn't help, but it was all she had in this place. She saw the tears filling the sides of his eyes. His lips had quivered as he spoke to her. What was she supposed to do, how was she supposed to feel? Nothing seemed normal anymore. What were the rules? Were there any rules? Her mind was racing. Yet still, she felt herself inch over in the bed. Lifting the side of the blanket she tapped the mattress beside her for him to join her.

"In a lot of ways.... you've already touched my heart, just by being here. I just don't know what to think anymore. There's so much I haven't told anyone. Something else happened that night, after Darren died. I just...."

"It's okay, you will talk about it when you're ready. Have I really touched you? I want to help you and be here for you, I just don't know how. The last thing I would ever want to do is scare you."

"Well, I can let you try... what harm is there in that?"

Sliding off his shoes he sat down beside her. Paul felt her body stiffen as he put his arm around her. He felt her breath quicken as he felt her skin against his. Lifting the blanket, he saw her pale skin peeking out from beneath her satin gown. She looked so delicate, so vulnerable. He could see so much of her beneath the blanket. As he leaned back, he felt her cuddle up against him. Her fire-red hair tickled the side of his face.

"What happened to you, Terra? What happened that makes you afraid to be close to me?" he whispered softly in her ear. Taking his hand, he brushed the hair away from her forehead. "You can tell me anything, I won't tell a soul." Leaning down he allowed his lips to brush against her forehead. He could feel the warmth of her skin against his. It had been a long time since he had been this close to a woman. He felt her jerk beneath him. "Was that okay, Terra?" He asked hopefully.

"It's okay," she sobbed. "That's not why I jerked. It felt beautiful. The last man that touched me wasn't so gentle, and that's all I can really remember. I can't feel anything else anymore. All I can feel is him...." she sobbed into his shoulder.

"Do you want to talk about it?"

"I don't know if I can. I'm afraid that is all I will ever feel. I don't want to be afraid."

"You don't need to be afraid of me."

"Can I ask you something?"

"Yes, you can ask me anything, Terra."

"Is it hard for you to sit here with me?"

"I love being able to hold you, letting you cry. I want to be here for you."

"No, that's not really what I meant."

Looking down into her eyes, he saw something different. He couldn't be sure what she was really asking, but he knew what he was feeling. It was hard to lay beside her underneath the blanket. His entire body felt like it was on fire as she cuddled up against him. There was so much more to her that he needed to know.

"Terra, I don't think you need to hear anything else right now."

"Maybe not, but maybe I want to hear what you are thinking."

"My thoughts are not what's important right now. Yours are."

"This isn't just about me, Paul. There's something to this. I don't really understand it, but there is."

"I'm glad you feel that way, but I can't ignore what you're going through."

"Why can't we? I would love to ignore what I'm going through," she scoffed.

"Because, this isn't the place to build a relationship. I can't do that to you. Right now, you're confused and... "

"Show me, Paul, show me what you want? If you can't say it, just show me," she whispered looking up into his eyes. "It' been years since anyone really touched me. The last man that tried, hurt me; he was forceful. He didn't listen when I told him not to. He kept pushing, trying to convince me that was what I wanted. He held me down, Paul. He... wouldn't take no for an answer."

"What did he do, Terra? How far did he make it? Did he...."

"No, but it was close, really close. He tried twice that night, the night Darren died. I just want to remember that I won't always be touched like that. I don't want to have nightmares. I want something good to remember."

"Calm down... you're going to have an anxiety attack," Paul answered, wiping the tears from her cheek. "I saw you with your mom. You're stronger than that... Be... brave..."

"WHAT?! You're not going to tell me to suck it up are you! The whole boys-will-be-boys thing? That's what Sheila always told me. I don't believe that. I believe that men are responsible for their own actions. I have a right..."

"Yes, yes you do!" he interrupted her. "You have a

right to feel the way you feel. There's nothing wrong with that. You have every right to be angry, but use that anger, channel it to make you stronger," he answered grabbing her hands. "You don't need me. You don't need anyone. You just need to take this one moment at a time. Control what you can control right now, and that's your reaction. I am not rejecting you, Terra. But you know you don't need me."

Gasping, Terra pushed his hands away. Doing it Sheila's way was a bad idea, and she knew it. *At least he doesn't disagree with me. It's about time that someone didn't.* She thought to herself. Turning away from him, Terra collapsed on the bed and closed her eyes, shutting out the world, shutting out the man that was trying to help her. He was right; she didn't need him.

"One thing at a time?"

"Yes, one thing at a time. Break it down to the ridiculous. Every. Single. Day. Then you will see your progress."

Turning back to him, she let herself rest against the pillow. Keeping her eyes closed, she thought of warm places and sunshine. The sand on the beach, the sound of ocean waves, and she let them overwhelm her senses. Taking deep breaths, she counted each second in rhythm with her heartbeat. She could feel the scratches on her legs from her dream and she thought about that place. The idea of going back there was terrifying. Still she pushed it away from her mind and thought of the way the sugary sands would feel against her toes.

He loved watching her. She was peaceful as she slept. Today she had a small smile come across her face. He only hoped that her smile was for him. Terra was experiencing so much right now; he remembered what it felt like when his world suddenly changed. Paul would have given anything for someone to reach out to him. It would have stopped him from doing a lot of things. Reaching over to her, he gently combed her hair out of her face. He knew the door would open soon, and it would be time for morning therapy. He had always hated when they came in to drag him to sessions.

"Wake up..." he whispered, caressing her hand. "You need to wake up."

Slowly, her eyes fluttered open and as she looked at him, a smile spread across her face. She laid there for a moment then gently pulled back the covers. Paul watched silently as her legs were revealed. Her gown was pushed up around her waist as she sat up. Swiftly he turned to reach for her robe. Grabbing her hands, he pulled Terra to her feet and wrapped the robe around her. Looking down into her eyes he wrapped his arms around her, pulling her close for just a moment. Taking his hand, he brushed the hair away from her eyes and ran his fingers through her hair.

"You need to get dressed..." he whispered in her ear, trying to catch his breath. Grabbing the robe, he pulled it closed. "You know I don't want to leave, but if you don't get out there soon, they will come in here."

"I know, but I don't want to pull away. You feel so nice," she mumbled as she looked longingly into his eyes. Taking a step back she started to rummage through her dresser trying to ignore how she felt. Hadn't she just yelled at him?

"You should probably hurry. You never know when that door will open. Besides, I don't want to push you... or me... I just don't think it's a good idea. I just might kiss you if you're not careful."

"Well, I guess we don't want that do we?" she sighed, trying to feel more like herself as she headed towards the restroom.

As the door closed behind her, Paul fell to the bed. What was he going to do now? Taking a deep breath, he tried to push it out of his mind. After all, he still had to go to work. How was he supposed to focus when the only thing he thought about was her? As he walked to the mirror, he checked himself. He heard the water running in her little sink as he ran his fingers through his hair. Straightening his polo shirt, he caught the reflection of one of the counselors behind him.

"You're in here awful early, Paul. Is there something we need to talk about?" she smiled coyly at him. "I'd give you a lecture, but I've never seen you smile like that. How is Terra? Is she getting ready?"

"Yes, she seems fine. I hope she's fine," he stuttered. "She's getting... dressed."

"Okay, well, she's going to be out of here soon, maybe you should keep your distance to make sure she's okay. Neither of you need another disappointment."

"I don't think I can do that. There's no way I can stay away from her."

"Well, maybe try staying out of her room. You guys can visit in the common room," she smiled closing the door behind her.

Moments later, Terra reappeared. Her hair was neatly pulled back in a ponytail this time. He liked seeing her hair away from her face. It was something different. She was beautifully dressed in her white linen pants contrasting against her black georgette top. He couldn't help but smile. He couldn't wait to see her away from the crisis center. He wanted to see her in real life.

"I have to go; I have a meeting scheduled in about half an hour." He stated walking to her. "Can I have another hug before I go? You look beautiful."

"Will you come back today?"

"Probably not. One of the counselors came in. They said that you should be getting out soon. She also said that we need to be careful until you get out of here. I will be back in the morning, but if something happens and you leave before then... my number is in the back of your journal. I put it there when I bought it, just in case," Paul whispered as he headed for the door.

She hated watching him walk away without saying something. What was she supposed to say? She was so used to telling Darren that she loved him whenever they parted that she was at a total loss for words. She tried to shrug it off as she headed to the therapy room.

"WOW, Terra is smiling today, that's weird," Kim called to her.

"I do know how to smile."

"Yes, but what made you? That's what I want to know."

"Maybe I'm just starting to feel better."

"You do realize you don't get better all at once, don't you?" Kim questioned as she sat beside Terra. "I've seen a lot of people go through here. You would think I would get better, but I never really do."

"Maybe you need a positive influence in your life."

"Well, when I get out of here maybe I should come hang out with you. You just have to promise not to get too mad at me."

"You know I can't promise that," Terra laughed. "But maybe that's not such a bad thing."

"Ok everyone, are we ready to get started?" a voice rang from behind them. Walking to his seat, the older gentleman looked across the room. There were only a few of them left now. "Which of you will be starting us off today?" he asked, looking hopefully over their group. "Kevin, would you like to share something with us?"

"Well, I think I've come to realize that maybe it wasn't such a bad thing that my wife left me," Kevin remarked as he glanced over at the girls. "Now I don't have to worry about as much. I won't feel like I'm walking on eggshells around her. I'm free to reinvent myself if I want. I have a long life ahead of me. When she left, I thought that my life was over, but it's not. I've learned a lot from watching you girls."

"I feel like I should be more considerate of my parents and my little brother," Kim stated looking down at the floor. "Maybe they do need time alone. I never thought of adults being romantic, but I guess sometimes they are. I really miss my little brother. I loved the way he would run into my arms when I got home from school last year. Now it's time for him to start school, and I want to be there for him."

"I realized that just because my husband died doesn't mean I can't still have a little fun. I don't have to die; I can really live. I can appreciate life, knowing that nothing is promised to us. why live with regrets?" Terra mumbled looking towards Kevin.

Again, each of them shared a little of their thoughts and stories. By working together, they had learned a lot about each other. They inspired one another. Over a few days, they had learned to look a little beyond themselves. They all knew they had a long way to go. Life would be different outside of the crisis center. They would have to face the pressures of their own individual lives and the circumstances that had sent them there. Terra would face the death of her husband and all the memories they shared. Kim would face the frustrations of caring for her little brother, and Kevin would have to learn to live alone.

"Do any of you have any plans for when you leave? Do you have any ideas?"

"Well, Terra and I exchanged phone numbers. We're going to try to stay in touch. I don't really know how that will work, but at least I know I can talk to her and if I mess up, she will set me straight," Kim remarked smiling at Terra.

"I think I'm going to be moving in with my sister for a while, until I can get my own little place. Otherwise, I'm just going to take it one day at a time," Kevin stated looking out the window.

"I don't really have a plan," Terra mumbled. "I just want to try to get through this. Maybe I can find a job, somewhere. I need something to occupy my time, so I'm not sitting around."

"Well, I have already contacted your families, and told them that you all are ready to go home. Kim, Kevin, you two will be leaving us this evening. Terra, I'm sorry but your mother couldn't make it until in the morning," the doctor remarked. "So, you will have the place to yourself tonight."

As he walked away, Terra watched her new friends rush for their rooms. It was their time to pack. They were lucky that they had families ready for them. There was no doubt that they were happy to have them home. They would be greeted with hugs and happy smiles when their relatives arrived. It always happened that way for Kim and Kevin. Each time they had visitors, she heard the excitement echo through the halls. It was like watching a party she hadn't been invited to. Listening to them always made her feel even lonelier. This time would probably be worse. She only hoped that the walls of the courtyard would absorb some of the sound as they were able to leave. It would never be that way for her. Tomorrow her mother would come. Sheila always acted sweet to everyone, but her words cut like a knife.

Terra wasn't ready to hear the town gossip about Darren. It didn't really matter that she didn't want to know, her mother would make a point of telling her every lie, exaggeration, and hurtful thing that had been spread about them. She hated to think of what her daughter, Autumn had been exposed to. She had only been at the crisis center for a few days, but it felt like an eternity. A lot can happen in a few days. She had changed and was starting to feel a little different about her life. For years, she had kept herself stuck in their little apartment, waiting on Darren. She had spent the last few years taking care of him. She had tried to keep him healthy, but in the end, it felt as though all her work had been for nothing. Terra only hoped that maybe her efforts had given him a couple of extra years to see their daughter grow. She was only five years old now. Would she even remember her father as she grew up?

As the noise around her grew, Terra grabbed her journal and headed for the courtyard. She had always loved being outside, even in the August heat. It made her uncomfortable as the sweat would bead up on her forehead. It reminded her that she was still alive. She looked at things differently now. After all, you only experience pain when you're alive. Old age was a privilege that she hoped to experience. Darren had only been thirty-five years old when he had passed. It was her hope to live much longer than that. She just didn't know how she was going to live. She wanted to experience life again. There had been so many things she had missed in the past few years. Terra just didn't know where to start. How do you start living and appreciating life? As she sat beside her favorite maple tree, she thought back to her moments with Paul. Maybe giving him a chance and being with him was a start. For her, he was electrifying. He was gentle and caring. She hadn't felt that way in years, but she only imagined what the town gossips would say about them. Could she keep him hidden from her mother? The last thing that she wanted people to say was that she moved on too quickly or that she didn't love Darren enough. She knew she would never get them to understand how lonely she had been even before he had died. Yes, facing the real world was going to be tough.

    Closing her eyes, she leaned her against the bark of the tree. She smelled the sweet mixture of fresh cut grass and nearby roses. The breeze blew gently through her hair as she looked up through the maple leaves to the sky. It was a pale blue day without a single cloud passing by. She felt little pieces of the sunlight filtering through the leaves to rest on her face like a gentle caress of heat. How long had it been since she had been outside?

    Listening closely, she heard the little squirrel scurrying

up and down the tree next to her. Above her she heard the birds singing gently to her. She always loved the sounds of nature. She had missed them. Maybe getting away from town and her apartment would be a good idea. Maybe that would help her find herself.

As she looked down at her journal, she questioned what she really wanted now that her life was her own again. Did she want to go back to school? If she did, what would she do? Did she want to try something unusual? Move away to a different town? It was hard to imagine her life anywhere else, and even harder to imagine not having to take care of someone. She had loved caring for Darren, but now it almost seemed cruel. How was she supposed to live now, without him? In the past few years, life had passed her by. Her focus had only been on him and their daughter. She had spent each moment loving him. Terra cherished those moments with her family, but now it just made her feel lost and empty.

Grabbing her things, she began to stroll along her favorite path. She stopped to smell the wildflowers and noticed the texture in every petal. Terra loved their gentle beauty. She couldn't stop thinking about her dream. The Gray had seemed different this time. She remembered everything from both of her dreams. There seemed to be a reason for all of it. *Was it a place in her mind, was it her imagination?* She couldn't get those people out of her mind. Each of them so vacant in their expression. They seemed so empty. It was as though they were already dead, but not quite zombies. They seemed closer to just being soulless. The smoke had been so thick that she could barely breathe, and the heat made the August air seem crisp.

Sitting down on a bench in the corner she opened her journal. She had so much to say, so many things on her mind. Would she really be okay when she returned home? What if the dreams continued? She didn't have any medication for her anxiety attacks, and that terrified her. Terra hated those moments when she felt out of control. When her head swam, and it felt like she couldn't breathe. It reminded her of the night Darren had died. Would she be okay? She didn't know the answers, but she did know that she needed to keep pushing forward. Just like on other nights, Terra started jotting down her thoughts, hopes, and fears. Continuously, she wrote; page after page. Then something emerged from the chaos of her mind.

Spider Dreams

*Deep within a web
Created, I
full of traps
invisible to the naked eye
memories adept to hide
the heart of a spider
that strives.
A heart entrapped
in my own forlorn.
I step through
to avoid victims
that tried to find in which coffin I hide
my deepest desire
the passionate fire.
Within this web of callous,
retired
where to discover this heart of mine.
I am a spider,
that dreams to fly.*

5

It had been a while since he had felt such a contradiction in the air. As he walked away from the center, he smelled the crispness of the withered leaves on the ground. The sun was warm against his skin. He felt his face flush in the warmth of the August breeze. The air was heavy as was his heart. How could he become so attached to someone so quickly? He still felt her against him and the softness of her lips. Paul wanted to spend every moment he could with Terra. In only a few days, she had captured his imagination. His thoughts kept going back to her.

It hadn't been that long ago that his heart had shattered. It had been broken like a glass thrown against concrete. He had thought it would never heal. Paul remembered that moment as clearly as the day it happened. Everything had changed on that crisp summer morning. It had been a day much like this day, the sun was warm, and the air had been heavy. Paul had wanted to surprise his wife, Patricia with flowers. They had been through a lot lately. She had wanted a baby. It was all she seemed to think about. They had been trying for years, but lately she been more serious, more determined, almost obsessed with the idea. They had visited doctors, talked to adoption agencies and friends. He would have done anything for her, just to see her happy. This was just something he wouldn't be able to give her. The doctors couldn't seem to find anything wrong with either of them. For some reason, it just wouldn't happen. They had tried ovulation monitors, taking her temperature, and each little trick they found on the internet. Nothing seemed to work. They had given up on becoming parents. He had always wanted to be a father and wanted a child just as much if not more than Patricia did. When it didn't seem possible, he had started trying to do little things for her. He had bought her gifts, took her out to nice restaurants, and even took her on spontaneous trips. It didn't seem to matter how hard he tried; he couldn't make her happy. This was the only thing he couldn't give her. He just couldn't give her a child. There was nothing the doctors could do. They had tried everything. Today he just wanted to remind her of how much he loved her. They had their moments, but she was the reason why he kept going. He loved giving her the things she wanted. But lately, she seemed to want everything, but none of it made her smile. He missed her smile, her touch, and her kiss. She had a way of bringing a man to his knees. Paul remembered when they met. She always resisted him just enough to entice him to want her more. It was a game that they played. He changed his entire life for her. She was the center of his world. He had forgotten himself in her embrace. There hadn't been anything quite like her smile. The way her eyes would sparkle when she told him that she loved him was enough to make a magician cry.

Pulling in beside her little red car, he had hopped out of his truck and headed for the door. He had only been gone a few minutes. He pictured her surprise as she got out of the shower and found them sitting there on the bathroom counter. It would be easy to slip inside the bathroom and leave the flowers waiting for her. He couldn't wait to see the smile on her face. He had it all planned out. After she discovered the flowers, she would find him waiting just outside of the bathroom door where he would sweep her up into his arms and carry her to bed. He had a full day planned for them. It had been a while since he had taken her shopping, and Paul had been saving extra money each week to be able to take her on a shopping spree. He was prepared to take her wherever she wanted to go. She had never been much for surprises, but he was sure that she would love this one. But as he ran upstairs towards their bathroom, something seemed different. As he got closer to the heavy oak door, he heard her laughter chiming above the rush of the falling water. Smiling he reached for the knob. And then he heard it, a man's voice coming from behind the door.

"Well, Patricia, what is Paul going to do when he finds out you're pregnant?" he heard the man laugh.

"I don't know.... and I really don't care. He tries so hard, but he's clueless. How didn't he know about you?"

"Maybe he just loves you."

"Of course, he does. What's not to love?" she cooed. "I may be married to him, but I'm all yours, baby. And he will raise your baby, never knowing it's not his. We will have everything we ever wanted. We will have each other's passion, and I will always be here. He works too much to know the difference. And, we will have all of his money to spend."

"That's right, YOU are mine. You will never be his. That body of yours will always belong to me. Speaking of which, when are you going to stop sleeping with him. I don't want him touching you. I don't care if he is your husband."

Listening from outside the door, Paul felt his body shake with anger. The once tender flowers crumpled beneath his grip as he heard their words. Dropping his blazer to the ground, he grabbed the knob.

He felt the wall shake as he flung the door open. Surrounded by steam, Paul stepped into the bathroom and reached for the man's arm. Grabbing it, he threw him to the floor, crouching above him he felt his skull against his fists as the rage overcame him. Paul heard Patricia screaming behind them. But he was blinded by the sight of the man's naked body shining from the water that still clung to his body. He was slippery and hard, but was still no match for Paul as he drug him from the room and down the stairs. Opening the door, Paul threw the man outside into the sun. Slamming the door closed, he turned and looked to the stairs.

"Where are you, Patricia? How long have you been hiding this, PATRICIA? How long did you plan on using me? Did you really think I wouldn't notice that you were pregnant? Did you really think I would just accept that you got desperate enough to get pregnant by another man? AND you expected me to just turn a blind eye and raise the child with no questions asked? How stupid do you really think I am, PATRICIA?" he growled as he climbed up the stairs. Looking down at her naked body as she gathered the petals of the roses, he had brought her, for a moment, he felt sorry for her. Then he remembered each time she had pulled away from him, each time she had laughed at him, and had called him worthless. "So, tell me, who is useless now? Who is going to take care of you now? Will he spoil you and watch you cheat on him with another man because you got bored?"

"No... what do you mean, Paul? I don't want to lose you... I love you..." she whispered, glancing sweetly up at him. "I want you; I don't want anyone else. I just wanted a baby and I knew that you couldn't.... that you were infertile, so I just picked a guy to get me pregnant. It will save you a lot of money, baby. You know I love you. You know I did this for you!"

"That's not what it sounded like to me. I just heard everything you said. I'm not stupid. It sounds to me like he's been around for a long, long time. How long have you been with him? Is that why my underwear disappears sometimes? Is that why you never pick up the phone when I call home from work? Is that why you're never here when I want to surprise you at lunch? Maybe I should have listened to my sister. She said she had seen you out with some man. Hell, I just thought it was an old friend or someone like that. I never dreamed that you would be using my home, my money, and my life to keep another man happy. How long have you been doing this? How long?"

"I told you, it was just so I could get pregnant. I'm... I'm sorry... Paul, I'm sorry"

"How long? Or should I go downstairs and ask him. I'm sure he's still scrambling around in the bushes trying to stay covered so he can make it down the street to his car."

"Paul, how could you do something like that?"

"After what I heard, he's lucky to be alive.... how long Patricia?"

Looking down at her naked body, she took a deep breath. He saw her trembling as she tried to persuade him. Standing up, she reached for him, pressing her breasts against him.

"I guess.... I guess... it's been a while. A long while... but I only did it so you wouldn't have to worry about keeping me happy. You know it takes more than one man to keep me satisfied," she stated as she reached down for his pants.

"I think you need to go; you need to leave my house. Get dressed, grab his clothes, and leave. NOW! I've heard enough of your nonsense. Go find HIM. He can take care of you. Obviously, that's what you want. You've made it clear that you don't want me. Now, get OUT!" he yelled down at her. Dropping his grasp on her, he walked towards the bedroom. Taking her keys, he walked back to her. "Be out by this evening."

And with that, he had walked away. Away from his past, away from his life, and away from what he had planned for his future. He heard the tires squeal as he pulled away from their home. The smoke curled behind his truck like a tornado cloud as he raced away, heading towards the river front.

He sat by the river for hours that day. He had watched his entire life fade away in the bathroom fog. Paul couldn't remember the man's face, only the way it felt as his nose crumbled against his fist. He still felt the man attempt to struggle to his feet as he drug him down the stairs and into the bright August sun. In one moment, he had taken his wife's hidden guilt and thrown it into the light. He regretted his anger, but not his actions.

He had spent years cherishing her, overlooking her flaws, and spending every dime he had made to make her happy. What was he supposed to do now? He tried to figure out why. Why would she do this? Why would she betray him? There were some questions that he had known would never be answered. He had waited over a year for answers but nothing ever came.

Climbing into his truck, he felt his body relax. Terra, she was different. He had never been around anyone so intoxicating. Since the first moment he saw her, she had captivated his senses. She was wrapped in a gentle passion, and there was so much warmth in her eyes. He had only hoped that today wouldn't be the only time he would touch her. Again, he headed towards the river. This time it was for a different reason.

As he pulled into a spot facing the river, he felt the waters pull away the sadness and the hopelessness that had gripped him for so long. Stepping out into the light, he found himself leaning up against the truck. He had found his smile and for once he welcomed the heat of the hot summer sun as it burned away the memories of the past. He wanted to have hope for the future. He wanted the chance to fall in love again. Could love be possible for someone that had just recently been through so much? How could he expect that from her? She was going to be out soon and with that came a whole new set of challenges. Everyone reacted differently when they left the center. Some people attempted to hide their fears, and act like nothing bad had ever happened. Others tended to sink into their own misery until they ended up back at the center. He could only hope that she would be one of the few that would accept what had happened and try to find ways to cope with the pain. He knew he would have to be patient and wait for her.

Looking out over the water, he still saw Patricia's shocked expression when he had burst through the door of their bathroom. Her long blonde hair sticking to her back as her lover held her against him. The image of her sitting on the ground as she picked up the crushed rose petals had been burned into his mind. He remembered her tears, tears that poured from her eyes not for their love but for her love of another. He had spent a lot of time at the river in the months that had followed his revelation of how his wife had betrayed him. It had been the only place that had given him peace.

Maybe the waters could mean something different for him now. Paul knew that he had to make sure he had moved on. He had to face his life and find fulfillment without someone else standing in the way. He didn't need to depend on someone else's opinion to bring him happiness. He had known for a while that he needed to find his own joy. Every night he returned to their home. He was haunted by their memories together. He remembered everything about their lives together. He had loved to cook for her, but he hadn't used the kitchen in months. The bedroom had been quiet for a long time as well, as he often found himself falling asleep on their sofa, away from any real memories they had together. Paul had fought so hard to cope with his depression, but there were still so many memories that haunted him. It had never occurred to him to find a new place to live, a new home.

As he looked around their small town from the banks of the river, he finally imagined himself making a new life and getting ready to make new memories.

Stepping away from his truck, he strolled away and headed up the hill to their tiny small-town park. Everyone enjoyed walking down by the riverside, but today it was surprisingly calm. Walking down the sidewalk, he let his mind drift. He loved the historical part of town. It was quiet. Even when it was a busy day downtown, there were still a couple blocks of houses that stayed quiet. Then he slowly approached it, the house hidden on the corner overlooking the river. The large yard was hidden by shrubs and flowers as it the road curved around it. It was a big house that still felt like a country cottage, a hidden gem that most never even noticed. He stood there for a moment and wondered if he would be happier in a place like that.

"Hello, Paul?" a gray-haired man asked from behind the roses. "You're sure checking out my place awfully hard. What are you up to? Ready to see if someone could turn a profit by turning it into apartments?" he laughed.

"No, Russ," Paul laughed. "I was actually thinking of how beautiful your place is. I've been thinking about finding something for myself, a place where I could get a fresh start, maybe start a new life one of these days."

"Well, we have been thinking about selling out. I just hate the idea of it sitting empty waiting for some crazy investor to destroy it."

"I'd like to think you would know me better than that."

"Yeah, but if I just put it on the market, well, you never really know what could happen. Do you want to look inside? I don't think the Mrs. would mind. You could just give me your opinion on it."

"Are you sure? It doesn't really sound like you want to list it."

"Oh, I didn't say I was going to list it, just want your opinion," Russ giggled.

Following the old man inside, Paul couldn't help but admire the old oak floors, the beautiful crown molding, and the elegance of the stained glass in the door. The rooms were framed with beautiful archways and the stairs twisted up to the second floor. The house wasn't huge, but it was filled with an elegant charm. Heading upstairs he found himself admiring the bathroom with its ruby marble counter tops and large claw foot tub. Looking out the window, he saw an amazing view of the river as it twisted through the town. Outside he saw the brick patio overlooking the river. The lawn was surrounded by weeping willows and wildflowers. Russ took him all the way through the house, talking about how they had cared for each of the home's characteristics. It had always stayed in the family, but there was no one to pass it down to. They had all moved away to bigger towns and better opportunities. They had abandoned their small-town lives.

"Well, what do you think, young man?"

"Russ, I couldn't agree with you more. It would be a tragedy to let this place go to waste. It needs someone to take care of it, to cherish it."

"I'm glad you think so. I just don't know what to do, my old lady doesn't want me working in the yard anymore. It's just too much work for us. She wants to go into one of those little apartments on the other side of town. We're just not up to the work anymore."

"Are you serious about selling it?"

"Only to the right person, I don't want everyone walking through here; this is our home. I don't want people looking to see what they can steal."

"Would you consider selling it to me?" Paul asked, hopefully. It seemed a little crazy, but maybe a little crazy was what he needed. He had never been spontaneous, but he loved the idea of a new home and finding one close to the river was a bonus. "I could really appreciate a place like this."

"Did I hear him ask about buying the house?" a frail voice called from the other room. "Let him have it, Russ! We couldn't ask for anything better than that. We can be out in a month," she yelled excitedly.

"On one condition, young man. Well, maybe a few conditions. You can't resell it immediately. You love it like a beautiful woman, not one of those pretty girls, but one that drips with beauty. That's what this place is; it's not flashy, it's not perfect, but she has character... and you can never rent it out or turn it into apartments or some other crazy nonsense," Russ answered looking at Paul from over the top of his glasses.

"Sir, I assure you. I would cherish your home."

"Well, then, if you're sure.... consider it yours. But I want to see you find a young woman to help you turn it into a home. It doesn't need to be a crazy bachelor pad either."

"I'm not really the crazy bachelor type. I'm sure you know that. Can I draw up the papers when I get back to the office?"

"Yes, Paul, you can do that. I will be down there tomorrow. I want to make sure you get it right," he answered as he held out his hand. "Otherwise, consider it done."

"Yes, sir, thank you," Paul answered, shaking his hand. "What a surprise, I was just going for a walk thinking about how I needed to make some changes in my life."

"Well, the good Lord definitely led you here tonight. I look forward to working all of this out. Now get out of here, so I can tell my wife all about it."

"Alright, Russ, sounds good. I will see you in the office tomorrow."

And just like that, Paul had taken a giant leap of faith. No matter what the future held for him, he would be ready for it. Now all he had to do was iron out the details. As he walked back down the road towards town, he imagined a new life filled with new memories. Even if all he ever did was care for that home, he would be happy, but he couldn't help but imagine carrying Terra over the threshold. His smile broadened as he climbed back into his truck. It was time he headed for home. For once, he was excited to be there, as he imagined packing up and moving away from all the memories that haunted him.

Walking into his old house that night, Paul was overwhelmed by memories. He still heard Patricia's tears as she lay on the bathroom floor. He remembered the day he had grabbed a bottle of pain killers and had tried chasing them with a bottle of vodka. He hadn't wanted to feel pain anymore. That night he had sat in their bedroom, staring at their cherry sleigh bed. Visions of his wife with another man haunted him. Sitting in the chair he had sat there picturing his wife climbing on top of another man. He saw her screaming for him and laughing at Paul. Her words had echoed through his mind like a tormenting wind scraping across his face. As the bottle got emptier, his heart had grown heavier. It had only been a short trip to the restroom to find her old pills. In an instant he had held the entire bottle to his mouth and ate them like candy. Staring at the bed he had felt himself slowly drift away as the pills began to take hold of him. Still, all he saw was Patricia laying beneath another man, her nails clawing down his back, just because he hadn't been able to give her a baby. It was a miracle that his sister had stopped by. If it hadn't been for her, they would have found him days later, lying in a pool of his own vomit. He had always been thankful for that. That's how he had ended up in the crisis center. He had spent months there, trying to come to grips with what had happened. He had only started to be able to manage his pain when he had begun to help others. The last thing he had wanted was to face another day. In that moment he had wanted to die, he had wanted to fall asleep and never wake up. He had given everything to her, and she had only betrayed him.

Looking around he remembered his devastation. How much did he want to take with him? Their home was almost like a shrine of the past. He had bought everything that she had wanted. Everything from the couch to the drapes were her taste and not his. He couldn't even be sure what his tastes were. Walking through the different rooms, he looked at each little knick knack, each picture that still hung on the wall. Maybe he shouldn't take anything at all, he wondered to himself. Maybe he could just hold an auction and get rid of everything. It wouldn't be the first time someone held an auction as they sold out, but normally it was because they were moving to another state or retiring. Overall, the reason didn't matter to people. An auction was an auction. There wasn't much left anyway. She had taken most of it and had only left him the skeleton of their lives. For the first time, he was grateful. It was time to discover himself, to learn what he loved. She had taken away ten years of his life, and it was time for him to take his life back. He was done with living half a life and acting as though nothing bad had ever happened. Glancing around, Paul couldn't help but smile. Everything was going to change. Tomorrow he would start the purchase of his new home. It was a first step and an accidental beginning.

Sitting in the chair beside their old bed, he found himself laughing. Finally, he would get victory over her. Paul knew that his greatest revenge would be for him to find happiness without her. Looking around the room to the empty dresser and mirror, he saw the memory of her reflection, but this time it would really be over. There was nothing personal left of theirs. Most of the house was just a shell. He had moved his clothing to the downstairs hall months ago. It was rare for him to venture to the bedroom they had shared, but tonight he wanted closure. It was time to make sure it was all behind him. He had felt his mind move on long ago, but tonight he released his heart. After all, there was another woman who had begun to creep into his soul. What chance did she have, competing against the ghosts of the past? He was finished. Being with Terra had been a revelation. Paul's time with Patricia never compared to even the kiss that he and Terra had shared.

Grabbing a couple of suitcases, he headed downstairs and within moments he had packed away his personal items and headed out the door. It was time to walk away. Paul didn't want to wait, so he found himself driving quickly to the hotel next to his office. All he needed was clothes and a shower.

***

As she glanced over to the suitcases laying by the door, Terra felt her eyes getting heavy. It had been a long night. She had laid there for hours staring at the ceiling. She had a lot to think about, a lot to consider. How was she going to handle being home? Her thoughts kept going back to Autumn. She hadn't seen her since she had been at the crisis center. Terra had no idea how her little girl was handling the tragedy. She had lost her father. Sitting up, Terra looked around at the stark white walls. She was tired of the cold concrete, tired of laying in an uncomfortable bed. She had been staring at the ceiling for most of the night, worrying about her daughter and how she would handle walking into their apartment.

Leaving her room, she headed down the hallway to the courtyard. She felt the fresh dew of the grass between her toes as she stepped outside. She saw a touch of light filtering through the trees. It was like a tiny glimmer of warmth against the leaves as they rustled in the gentle breeze.

Wrapping her silk robe around her, she strayed away from the main path into the grass. She loved feeling the cool morning dew against her toes. Slowly she kneeled in the grass, feeling it against her legs she laid back and looked up to the sky. The stars were barely visible, but she still saw them glowing down on her. Closing her eyes, she breathed in the scent of the fresh grass around her. Terra was exhausted and she had a long day ahead of her. She couldn't imagine her mother getting there anytime soon. Sheila was the kind of woman that took half the morning to get ready.

"Terra? Are you in here?" they asked from the door of the courtyard.

"Yes, I'm here. Is it a problem me being out here?"

"No, but you should probably come inside. It's a bit early to be out here. You actually aren't supposed to be out here before nine a.m."

"I just wanted to get some fresh air. I didn't exactly sleep last night."

"That's really not unusual for your last night here. Paul is here, he stopped by to talk to one of our counselors. He's kind of waiting around and wanted to know where you were. I think you scared him," she laughed.

Sitting up, Terra watched Paul walk through the door of the courtyard. She saw his exhaustion. Obviously, he hadn't slept either. Pulling her robe tighter around her, she watched him approach.

"It's ok, I think you have the right idea. Do you mind if I join you down there?" he asked looking down at her pale skin in the moonlight.

"Sure, pull up some grass," she giggled.

Laying down beside her, he held his arm out to her as she cuddled up against him. Leaning her head against his chest, she felt his heart beating rapidly. His hand ran softly up her back as he squeezed her even closer to him.

"Did you have a rough night?" he whispered.

"Yeah, couldn't sleep. I'm worried about going home."

"It will be okay. You'll get through it. Mine was a bit crazy too, actually. Just a lot on my mind. "

"Good things or bad things?"

"A little of both I guess. I was hoping to catch one of the counselors, I need to run something by them, make sure I haven't lost it," he giggled lightly.

"I'm sure you haven't. You need to have a little faith in yourself, Paul."

"Can I ask you something and you be completely honest with me?"

"Of course, you can ask me anything. I'm an open book."

"Well, I guess I have a few questions. Are you going to forget about me when you leave here? And I guess I'm simply curious to know if in any way that lovely satin gown you're wearing was meant for me to see?"

"I'm not going to forget about you. I don't think I could. I'm not the type to forget about someone or just leave them hanging. And the gown, well, my mother brought me a couple and while I wouldn't necessarily wear them, I guess I had hoped that maybe you would see them. They make me feel beautiful, which really helps right now. I liked the way you looked at me. But I really wasn't trying to get you to do anything. I just wanted to feel nice. I wanted you to see me."

Rolling up on his arm, Paul looked deeply into her eyes. As he brushed the hair from her eyes, he ran his thumb across her forehead and let his lips brush against her forehead. Tracing her cheek with his finger he caressed her eyes with his lips as his face brushed against hers, he cradled her face in his hands. Looking into her eyes, he felt her cling to him. Bringing her knees up, she reached her hand out for him, pulling him down closer to her. As her eyes fluttered shut, she took a breath and looked into his eyes as he brought her face to his. Gently his lips caressed hers like a whisper. She could feel his heartbeat against her hands as she tugged on his bottom lip and his kiss deepened as a moan escaped his mouth. After a few moments she gently pulled away.

"We... should... stop..." she whispered between the caresses from his lips.

"Terra, you have cast a spell on me, one that I may never recover from. I've been like that since the moment I met you. All I could think about every time I saw you was what your lips would taste like against mine. Now...I know, and I just want to take you in my arms and hold you next to me."

"I love the way you kiss me. I love the way you look at me. I'm just afraid that it will be different when I leave here. I want to get to know you and make sure this is real and not just some kind of strange savior complex type of thing. And I'll be honest with you, right now I just want to feel you kiss me. I want to be in your arms and I feel like I should feel guilty about that. I want to completely surrender to your embrace. I want... you. But I want to know all of you. I can't let my emotions get away from me."

"I won't hurt you, Terra. There's just something about you. I know that sounds corny, but it's true. So, I really want to know that I have a real chance with you. Can I take you out some time? Maybe I could buy you dinner?"

"You have a chance, well, you have more than a chance, really. I would love to go to dinner with you. I'm just worried... Darren hasn't been gone long. Do you really think this is a good idea? I want to be with you, but should we be? Right now? "

"I don't know, I guess I never really thought about it.

Maybe I should have. If you're not sure… maybe, we should wait on dinner. Give you a little time to breathe? Is that what you really want?"

"NO, that's not what I want. I want you, but I also don't want to be an idiot and have everyone in town talking already. I hate gossip and I guess there's plenty of it surrounding Darren. Not to mention the fact that I don't know if I am even capable of love right now."

"You don't have to be with me right now, Terra. Maybe we can just hang out, be friends first. That's probably what we should have done before we kissed."

"I guess you're right. I hate the idea of just being friends. Besides, I can't stop kissing you… it's addictive," she replied hastily.

"Ummmm…. Maybe you can kiss me, just a little bit more," he answered sheepishly.

"Can I kiss you now?"

Reaching for Paul, Terra gently touched her lips against his at first; as he pulled her closer to him, he began to kiss her hard. His hand reached down her back to the bottom of her gown. Running his hand up her leg he held her tightly, gripping her against him. Terra felt him gasp for air as he kissed her and she saw his eyes fill with tears as his lips travelled down her neck.

Looking up, she saw the stars had disappeared in the morning sun. "Paul, you should stop, we shouldn't be doing this out in the courtyard."

"Unfortunately, you're right," he answered as he pulled himself away. "Hey, can I let you hear something? I wrote a song a while back that I want you to hear."

"I didn't know you were into music."

"Yeah, always have been," he answered pulling his

phone out of his pocket.

A few moments later, his music began to drift up from his phone. At first, Terra, tried to humor him assuming that it would just be some silly song like she had heard so many amateurs produce. Still, she wanted to be supportive. He had already done so much for her, and she wanted to show him that she cared about the things he loved. But then... as the music began, she felt her mind drift into the trees, her eyes closed, and suddenly she felt her breath fill her lungs with warmth. As the notes of the piano began to echo against the brass instruments, she began to imagine herself dancing to it. Her body longed to move in time to the rhythm he had created. She felt her eyes moisten as the music continued to echo through the courtyard and slowly a tear escaped to her cheek. She had never heard anything so breathtaking.

"I wrote that for my mom," he stated as the music faded away.

"I had no idea... how on earth did you do that?"

"It's a long process, one instrument at a time, every note is put in the computer one at a time and layered, tuned... I can hear them in my head. It's hard to sort it out sometimes."

"That was beautiful... I don't think I've ever heard anything so beautiful. Thank you for sharing that with me."

Pulling away he grabbed her hand and helped her to her feet. Closing her robe around her, Terra started walking towards the door. She felt the grass falling from her hair as she walked to her room with his music still echoing through her heart. Still, her body shook from the cold dew as though it had soaked through to her bones as she entered the air-conditioned building. Behind her, Terra felt Paul following her, watching her.

"Listening to your music made me realize that you haven't really told me much about that. I'd like to hear your story sometime. But right now, I really need to get dressed." Terra smiled as she took her robe off, revealing the tiny straps of her gown. "Can you step out for a few minutes? I really don't want my mother to come while you're in here helping me with that," she laughed.

"That's fine," he smiled. "Will you call me, soon?"

"Ok, I will, I really like being around you. It's crazy..."

"I will see you soon, Terra..." he whispered as he brushed his lips across her forehead.

She hated to watch him walk away, but at least the next time she saw him, she wouldn't be in the crisis center. She would be free from the sterile walls, free from the past and maybe she could truly embrace him with her heart. Terra knew that Sheila would be there soon but worried if she would really be ok leaving that place. Baby steps, making every little moment special, one at a time.

Glancing around the walls of her room, she felt her head spinning in the blur of white concrete blocks. They were closing around her like a chilly hand gripping her throat. Standing there it felt as though all the blood was leaving her body as the chill of the place enveloped her. The warmth of his kiss disappeared into the sterile air.

"I have to get out of here!" Terra told herself as she threw her gown to the little bed and grabbed her clothes.

Within moments she was dressed. With everything thrown quickly into her suitcase, she headed for the door. Without a glance back she headed down the hall to the little reception desk and to the door.

"Where do I sign out? I am just going to go. It's hard to tell how long it will take for my mother to get here. I'm just going to go out and enjoy the fresh air. It's really not that far from home," she quickly spoke to the paper on the desk, her eyes down. She instantly signed the papers that they handed her.

She didn't want to give them a moment to change their minds about letting her leave. Terra couldn't allow the walls of the crisis center to touch her again. She was done with nightmares and the bitterness that was trying to take over her body. Pushing through the cold metal door, she heard the door screech in protest. It was as though she heard the quiet screams of those who had come to stay before her. All of them had been tortured souls, some tortured more than others. But now, it was her turn to stand in the sunlight again. As she walked through the desperate shadows of the center, she felt the August air caress her long crimson hair. The sun kissed her skin as she stepped into the blinding white light of the sun. She felt the weight of the past leave her body as she continued to walk. She walked away from the cold. Terra tried to tell herself she was walking away from the past.

"Terra!? What do you think you're doing? Why are you out here walking BY YOURSELF?" Sheila screamed, stopping the car in the middle of the road. "Get in the car, young lady!"

"You know I'm a grown woman. I'm perfectly capable of walking home by myself!" Terra snapped, "I didn't want to be in there a moment longer."

"Just get in the car, Terra!"

Pulling over to the side of the road, Sheila parked her little blue convertible bug. Grabbing her suitcase, Terra threw it into the back of the car and climbed into the passenger seat, put her seat back a little and looked up at the sky. Reaching into the glovebox, she grabbed a little pair of sunglasses, sat back, and closed her eyes.

"Don't get too comfortable. We don't have far to drive. I need to stop by the BMV."

"Why couldn't you do that before you picked me up?"

"Because I need you there, and are you honestly in a big hurry to get home? You are going to have a lot to deal with when you get there."

"Might as well get it over with, I guess. Where's Autumn? I thought you were going to bring her to pick me up?"

"Well, I was supposed to pick you up at the center, and she REALLY doesn't need to see you there," Sheila replied, pulling into a parking space. "She can come to see you, just as soon as you get home and I know you are okay. The last thing that little girl needs to see is her momma losing her mind, crying, and screaming over some man!"

"I'm not going to lose my mind MOTHER, and that man... that man was my husband and her father, and he died. I have a right to cry and scream! But I'm not going to completely lose it as you keep putting it," Terra yelled, as she got out of the door and slammed the car door behind her. "What are we even doing here, anyways?"

"Well, as you said, he died, and you basically have next to nothing now. We had to sell the car to pay for the funeral, remember? He should have made sure he had life insurance so you girls would be taken care of, but that falls on me now. So, we are going to go in there, and this car will be yours, now. And you're not going to complain about it either. I'm going to make sure you are taken care of. AND you're not just going to be staying home all the time either; you need to get out and live a little. Now let's get in here and get this done so we can get you home."

"Why do I need to live a little? I know how to live my life; I don't need someone telling me how to do that.... and thanks for the car. BUT I still want to see my daughter. She is MY daughter, not yours, and you can't really keep her from me," Terra complained.

"Well, she is my grandchild, so my opinion does count, and I'm just looking out for the both of you. You can see her tomorrow, after you get through the first night at home, that should be plenty of time to cry," Sheila stated abruptly.

"So, you have already put me on a schedule as to how long I can cry and be upset? Is there anything else that you have scheduled for me?" Terra asked sarcastically.

"Maybe, I might have a few predictions," she laughed.

"You do realize that divorce and being widowed isn't the same thing, right?"

"Of course, darling, but it never hurts to reinvent yourself and go out and get a little action, remind yourself that you are still a woman. I think that you will have a little fun within the next week, and if not then I have completely lost my touch," Sheila stated turning towards her daughter.

"You seriously want me to go out and get laid? Is that really what I'm hearing?" Terra blushed.

"Why not?" she questioned, glancing over at Terra whose face had turned as red as her hair. "Unless... you already have? How on earth did you do that in there? Was there another patient or some poor helpless therapist?" she laughed. "Maybe you are my daughter, after all."

"MOM! Can we NOT talk about this? I seriously am not that type of lady."

"You don't have to be that TYPE of lady to have a little fun. Everyone deserves to have a little fun now and then, and right now, you need to remember that you are still alive. And there is nothing more alive than making love to a man. Everyone has needs, Terra. Even you, so embrace them. Just don't be crazy enough to bring a bunch of men around your daughter. And that's the end of the discussion. Let's go get this done."

***

Pulling into the little driveway Terra glanced up at the brick of the little apartment they had shared. Their home seemed lonely now; she felt the emptiness all the way to her parking space. How could she face it alone? Taking a deep breath, she grabbed her suitcase and headed for the door. Each step she took felt heavier as she got closer and closer. The morning sun had been replaced with the gloom of afternoon clouds and the threat of rain from the darkening clouds overhead.

As she walked inside, she felt the silence echoing through her mind as she locked the door behind her. The little house plants from the funeral were wilted and dry and the dishes were still in the sink from weeks before. She had only lasted a few days after the funeral. Just long enough for all the relatives to stop visiting. Her and Autumn had been fine until then. It had been easier with family around. But just as quickly as they had appeared, they disappeared.

The windows and curtains were closed and stood

quietly, waiting for life to begin again. It was as though their home had been frozen in time. She saw the light coat of dust on the tables and remote controls thrown haphazardly on the sofa. Walking to the windows, Terra threw open the curtains and windows, allowing their home to breathe again. Like her, it had withered from a boisterous center of activity to withdrawn solitude.

Looking around she saw the picture of her and Darren smiling at each other beneath a tree at the park. Instead of a traditional ceremony, they had picked a sunny day and a small field by the park to gather all of their friends together as they said "I do." There were pictures of them chasing each other around the stolen shelter house as he had smashed cake in her face. She had always loved his smile and his thick southern accent. They were what made him unique. His unpredictable antics were what had made her fall in love with him. He always surprised her. This last surprise hadn't been the best, however.

Walking around the living room, she saw the black guitar he had never learned to play still standing in the corner, and his favorite t-shirt was thrown on the recliner. Grabbing his shirt, she sat down and held it to her nose, hoping for a little hint of him. It was funny how a scent took Terra back to her last night with him. Closing her eyes, she saw the look in his eyes, as he confessed his love for her, the sincerity in his touch and the way his body felt as he had held her for the last time. Every curve of their bodies had fit perfectly together, like puzzle pieces. Together they had been a masterpiece. But now, they were nothing but a memory that would fade into the dark caverns of her mind. Like the small scent of his old shirt would fade into nothing, so would some of her memories. Looking around her little apartment, all she saw was him.

Taking her suitcase to the bedroom, Terra glanced down at their bed. The covers were still crumpled together in a corner, and their pillows were still pushed together as one. Like a fog she saw his hand reach out to her. *Come to bed, darling... I want you beside me.* Watching herself lay beside him in her memories, she felt his lips gently brush against hers and tasted the mint on his lips from his nightly routine. His breath escaped his lips and landed on her cheek as Terra closed her eyes allowing herself to feel his memory. *I love you. I don't know what I would ever do without you.* Then just as quickly the scene changed, and he was standing at the foot of the bed. *No, Autumn needs to go to bed. It's getting late. It's our time now. We focus on her all day long. I want to sleep with my wife!* The memory of his voice echoed through the emptiness as she smiled at the frustration of Autumn's toddler years. *I'm sorry I had to stay late at work again, baby...* he had whispered to her night after night. As she watched the memory of him crawling in beside her, Terra felt the warmth of his body against hers. All around her she saw shadows of him calling to her, loving her, and even the smallest of moments played out before her eyes. Each of them seeming more and more pointless as she remembered them. Every conversation tugged at her mind as tears filled her eyes. Collapsing onto the bed, Terra fought to catch her breath as sobs became muffled screams against their pillows. She saw him, felt him, and smelled him. She even tasted the sweetness of his lips after smoking a cherry cigar. Her vision was a fog of memories, and she was drowning in it. She felt herself gasping for air as she screamed out into the air.

"Why did you take him from me? Why do I have to be the one that is left alone, why? I don't understand!!! This wasn't supposed to happen!" she cried to the ceiling. "How am I supposed to go on like this? I'm too young to be a widow. Our lives together had barely begun. What about our beautiful daughter? What am I supposed to do without him? I never believed in soul mates until I found him, how can I ever expect to feel that again?"

Grabbing his pillow, she squeezed it to her chest as screaming tears escaped. Her body trembled as her breaths came in quick gasps and her eyes began to burn. Bringing her tattered fingernails to her lips, she struggled to find a raw edge to bite between her teeth but could only feel ragged nubs rubbing against her teeth. Her toes curled against her feet as she rocked back and forth in her bed, and she curled her legs up against her body. Then finally... it stopped. Everything stopped. Closing her eyes, her breath began to slow and eventually she sat up in the bed. As she closed the door behind her, she felt relief as the fog of memories began to fade back to the shadowed corners of her mind. She needed to close the bedroom door. Pictures were everywhere. Each of them smiled at her anguish, a gallery of memories that she wanted to forget.

Quickly she began turning them over, she couldn't bear to see his face, everywhere she looked. She felt her heart race as she took each one down. Even though she loved him, adored him, she knew she couldn't face him leaving her alone. *Why hadn't he taken better care of himself? Why hadn't he listened to her? Why didn't he take his medicine like he was supposed to?* He had developed so many health problems in the last few years because he wouldn't listen. No matter how she had pleaded with him, he had refused. *Why did he do this to her? It was his fault that he was gone, wasn't it?* Sheila was right, why didn't he at least make sure he had life insurance so that they would be ok?

Terra felt her skin getting warm, her face flushing as sorrow turned to anger. Grabbing a box, she started throwing everything of his into it. He wasn't here, and this wasn't going to be a place of mourning. It wasn't a place for the dead, but a place for the living. Grabbing a rag, she began dusting, cleaning, and changing their home into a place of vibrance. It wasn't her fault that he was gone. It was his. She was the one who had to move on and take care of their daughter; it was her who had to learn to live again.

He was dead, and he wasn't coming back. He didn't need his shirt, he didn't need the guitar he purchased and never took the time to learn how to play, he didn't need anything. All of it vanished in the closet under the stairs. How could she possibly live when her home was filled with memories of the dead. It was simple; she couldn't and she wouldn't. Her mind haunted her more than enough. Terra didn't need help remembering all the moments with him. Those memories were tattooed into her heart, and her mind had been ravaged by his haunted touch. She had to escape the shadows.

6

The stench of sulfur engulfed Terra as her eyes opened against the ash. The rocks pierced her skin as the smoke pressed her against them. Her white dress was painted with marbled veins of gray and black from the smoke. Her hair pressed against her neck like veins of tar attached to her skin from the black streaks of her tears.

In the distance, she could see the oily waters rape the glass shores. They crashed against the shards with fiery vengeance against the gray. Pushing to her feet, she felt the rock pierce her hand and her footprints left a trail as she drug herself to the tree. In the distance, Terra watched the others. Each of them hollow, mechanical as they walked. Her heart filled with dread as they headed for the shore. Clinging to the tree, she climbed to the branches above.

It was like steel, cold and sharp. The tree in the middle of the Gray wasn't rugged and earthy. It wasn't brown. It was something else entirely. It was more like a metal pole but still its branches spoke to her, called for her. It was her landmark. In its branches she felt safe. From the top,

Terra didn't feel the unnatural pull to the shore. From there, she watched empty souls disappear one by one. As she watched, the last person disappeared in the waves like a reverse water droplet. Around her the rocks stood like razors against the smoke saturated sky. Terra remembered everything, every moment, within the Gray. Searching through the horizon, she waited, watched, and tried to comprehend her surroundings.

Grabbing limbs, Terra slid down the side of the tree, her white gauze dress tearing against their roughness. Hitting the ground, the rocks pierced her feet. Falling to her knees, she gasped as the blood from her feet glittered against rocks. The land was empty, the smoke swirled her like a vapor. Turning away from the waters, she stepped away from the tree, searching. Now, ahead of her lay trees that were broken like daggers jutting sharply to the sky. Against the rocky horizon the sky swirled red through the smoke. Slowly she walked towards the fire.

What was causing the land around her to be devastated, full of smoke and fire? Why were these people so willing to walk into the sea? What was this place? Each step was a question as another rock dug into her and pain shot through her like daggers. Each step was an assault. Her breath came in gasps as her lungs filled with smoke. The heat made her sweat through every pore, but still she moved forward, needing to understand. Each shot of pain reminded her of her journey, her loss, and her emptiness. Each step a hopeful memory turned to heartbreak as tears carved through the ash on her cheeks, as with every step, the smoke became heavier and the air grew colder.

The steps came slowly as she pushed herself further. Closing her eyes, she remembered his face and his hand against her back, feeling loved, and the knowledge of him by her side. She longed to feel his arms around her again. She wished to see his face warmed by the fire as he held her close to him. She almost felt his lips kiss her gently. But now the warmth of those memories had vanished and were a reminder of what she would never have again. She felt her soul break with each step. Each memory brought her only emptiness.

That's when she saw the building, surrounded by broken trees like cat tails surrounding a pond. Like an abandoned factory, it stood, waiting almost moving in the air as she stared, trying to see the details. Squinting, she looked for doors, windows, anything to make sense of the structure. Red smoke poured through a small pipe on the roof. Continuously, the building expelled plumes into the thick air. Each of them looking more sinister than the last, like puddles of blood pooling into the sky. And there were people, but not like the ones that had walked into the sea. Their skin was gray, but not from the ash and smoke. It was a different kind of gray, reminiscent of death. The cold lifeless color of emptiness and soulless withdrawal. This was a different kind of cold. Her body shuttered as her sweat began to stiffen on her body from the changing temperatures. Stepping behind a rock she watched the deathly figures begin to pace in front of the structure. Wearing uniforms of black they stood, walking back and forth in front of the building.

Terra watched them scan the broken trees above them. Their lights darted across the rocks she crouched behind. Each beam was surprisingly bright as she peered through the cracks in her disguise. But no one strayed from their path. After a few moments she felt the lights stop. She could barely see them now, but still she waited. Staying hidden, she watched the structure breathe its bloody breath into the skies above her.

Slowly, she crept towards it, hiding behind each jagged rock, to the valley beneath her. With each step the air grew colder, bitter. The chill ripped across her face, freezing her hair to the sweat on her neck. Watching closely, she scanned the building for an entrance. *What were they guarding? Who were they searching for?*

Hiding between the rocks, she shrunk between their razor edges while the soot swallowed her toes as the ground began to quiver. The guards scattered against the wall as the gate lifted and another wave of the lost came towards her.

Quickly she stood and faced the direction of those headed towards the waves. Every few moments she would step back towards the building, vanishing against the crowd of darkness she hid within their emptiness. Terra kept her gaze forward, locked against the sky. With each step she felt the ground change beneath her. The soot became thinner, harder, and colder. It changed beneath her until it became as slick as glass. With a final step backwards, she darted behind the wall as the gate lowered, closing her in. Around her the light vanished and the shadows disappeared. *What had she done?* Deep within the tomb of lost souls she felt the emptiness engulf her. Her heart began to pound like a snare, enveloped in silent darkness she embraced the tomb around her. Placing her hands against the ground, she felt her skin sticking against the glass. Feeling the wall beside her, Terra slowly moved farther into the abyss, not knowing what she would find but needing to discover its sacred mysteries. Her body felt the struggles of many tears, many souls, many broken hearts that had been ripped away from the bodies of lovers grown cold too soon. The bitterness crept into her skin like the wailing of the lost.

Slowly she crept, keeping her body flat against the black glass floor. Silently she moved forward along the wall her body sticking from the frosty cold of the tomb. Reaching forward, she felt the walls change. Opening her eyes, she saw them. Ahead of her were cages, bars, covered in rust from tears of lost battles. She saw them clearly in the darkness. Figures naked, crying in the corners of cells. Her ears couldn't hear, but her heart felt every shout, whimper, and sob, from the prisoners. Forward she crept. Finding her feet beneath her, Terra ran her hands against the bars. Cell by cell she watched each stage of misery. The woman with her hair covering her face as she shook in the darkness. The man whose fists pounded against concrete in waves of percussion. The child, clinging to herself for comfort against the cold. Terra saw their anger, their despair, and their denial. In her mind, she felt their screams through the silence of the tomb. They cried out for help, they cried out for God, and they cried out for another moment. All of them mourning in their own way, all lost, and trapped within their minds. She felt their faith dying, their hopes diminishing, and their dreams.... they were already gone. Wall after wall, cell after cell, she saw them. She felt them and their emptiness. Terra felt in her heart that this is where the lost came to die.

Looking down the hall of cells, she saw her. A woman covered in ashes, pulling at her long red hair, streaked black. Her tears were the loudest. She felt her anguish more than any other as she ran to her but Terra's feet slipped against the floor. Grabbing for air, her hands found the bars. They were as cold as ice. All she felt was pain as she landed against the red cell. On the floor of the last cell she saw the woman's hair laying in clumps as she screamed. It echoed in her mind like spikes being driven into her brain. And suddenly she watched her lunge for the bars, her hands grasping Terra's. Her eyes stared into her soul, like a magnifying glass in the sun, her gaze like fire burning into her mind. Her hands were warm against hers, almost hot as she gripped her. Breathless, Terra stared back at the woman. Trying to pull her hands away from the bars, she felt the woman tighten her grip against hers. Gasping, the woman leaned closer.

Finally, she understood. Because deep within the cells of the silent tomb of lost souls, was a part of herself. She felt herself struggle to breathe as she stared into the eyes of the woman. She was not a stranger. She was not just another woman. The red cell was emptier. And for the first time within the Gray, she heard sound, but only for a moment. As the woman in the cell, that desperate screaming woman with Terra's long red hair, and deep green eyes, grabbed her dress, she pulled her against the bars and peered deep into her. Her gaze pierced Terra's soul as the woman screamed.

"Save us!"

And just as quickly everything grew silent again. The floor shook as a deep red light began to flash and cells began to open in the hall. There they stood, each rigid, ready for their final walk. Their eyes were empty now. They were nothing, but empty shells marred by tears. But the trails were dry as each of them stepped forward into a line as the cells opened. They waited. Staring ahead, like silent machines. The lost souls waited. As the light turned black each of them turned towards the rising gate and began to march out of the tomb. Running into the line, Terra crept along with them. Each step she echoed. Each movement she copied as she slowly made it out of the tomb. As she stepped back into the smoke, she felt her lungs begin to ache, but slowly she moved forward, blending into the line of emptiness. She felt the tears come to her eyes as she remembered the woman in the red cell. Locks of her hair lay on the floor in clumps, her eyes growing darker, and her skin was torn, red from blood. She was tortured from memories, lost moments, and hope. *How could you keep even a shred of hope in the tomb of the lost? Wouldn't hope be the biggest torment of all?* The woman was living in the delusion that there was a way out. And as the tears began to glide down her cheek again, Terra realized. That woman.... was her.

Falling against her tree, Terra began to climb. Cradling herself in the branches she watched the lost disappear into the sea. Exhaustion filled her as she watched them and saw the door that wouldn't open. *It had to be the answer. Somewhere there was a key, the key to save herself.*

With a gasp, Terra shot up from her position on the floor. She felt her hair matted against her face. The blanket she had curled up in was crumpled against the wall, the table beside her was tilted to its side and pain shot through her ankle. What happened? Gasping for air, she looked around her living room, hadn't she just cleaned? What time was it? How long had she slept? There was no light filtering through the soft brown drapes of the living room. In the corner she saw her phone blinking with missed messages as she struggled to stand. Looking down to the sofa she watched a little gray mouse scurry off the cushion to hide against the wall.

"Oh my God! Did I sleep with a mouse last night? Wait is it still night? How long did I sleep? What happened to the living room? It looks like I was robbed!" She exclaimed into the air. Stumbling to the phone, she grabbed it and read.... 4:32 a.m..

"Are you serious? I missed an entire day? Oh my God! Autumn!" She had missed her!

There was no doubt that her phone was going to be full of nasty messages from her mother. Had anyone even tried to contact her or tried to wake her up? Where were all the well-wishers? Where were her friends after all of this? Grabbing a cup from the counter, Terra poured a cup of coffee from the pot the night before and threw it in the microwave. At least she had remembered to turn the pot off, she thought to herself.

Quickly, she opened the door to stop the loud beep of the machine and plopped back down on the sofa. Maybe there was something on her phone; after all, it was blinking. Scrolling down, she saw just one message from Sheila.

"I'm going to give you a couple more days. You didn't answer the door when I came to check on you. You better be doing more than sleeping! The time to sleep and cry is OVER!"

Terra never understood how rude her mother could be. Just because she had been through a couple of divorces didn't mean she knew how to handle the death of a soul mate. *It was a completely different thing, wasn't it?* In a divorce, the man is still alive. He might have betrayed you, but you knew there was hope. You could still see them and hear their voice. It was possible to find closure and peace, knowing they were going through the same thing. When you divorce, you hate. When someone dies, the only thing you can do is long for the arms of the one who had held you, loved you, and protected you. But they are not there to offer any kind of explanation. They are no longer there to answer your questions. You don't know why they had to leave you; they are just gone.

When the one you love dies, you look for signs of them in the shapes of the clouds. You look for them in the shadows of the room. It is then that you hope ghosts are real and that some form of them will come back to visit you. You long to hear their voice in the wind. You hope for them to visit in their dreams. But Terra hadn't seen anything. She hadn't felt anything, just longing. And her dreams were only filled with the terror of that strange place she kept going back to.

Looking around at her living room again, she knew that she hadn't been robbed. The doors were locked, the neighbors were close by and the large bruises on her ankles proved that she had done all of this while she tossed and turned on the sofa they had shared. She felt the cup growing cold in her hands as she lifted it to her lips. Terra had always waited too long to take that first drink. It had always drove Darren crazy. It didn't matter now. None of it did. Sheila had told her to reinvent herself, but why would she do that? She was already everything that she wanted to be.

Except for that mouse. She couldn't believe there was a mouse scurrying around in her hair all night and apparently all day. Shaking her head, Terra remembered Darren always telling her that even if it was cute, if there was one mouse, there were many, many others. What if the mouse was Darren? She thought to herself. But no, that was silly to think something so ridiculous. He hated mice. She hated mice. They might have been cute, but they were still creepy, trouble causing rodents. How was she going to get rid of it? Terra couldn't imagine killing the little thing, but she was terrified to get too close. What exactly was she going to do? That was something she had never had to deal with on her own. She couldn't ignore it because they would just keep coming, more and more mice, until the entire apartment was covered with them.

Again, she knew she was being ridiculous, but it still had to be taken care of, somehow. Maybe she did need to make some changes. At that moment she felt helpless. That was the last thing she wanted to be. She hated the idea of having to settle for some man just to take care of silly things like a mouse in the apartment. She knew she needed to be strong. Maybe go back to college, maybe get a career. She knew she wanted to rise above her tiny apartment. There was a lot that she wanted to change, a lot of dreams she still wanted to catch.

"First things first, a shower...." she stated to the little mouse in the corner. "No, wait, how about a long bubble bath, some nice music, and a glass of wine. It's still dark outside, I can do that. We will just call it my morning juice." She laughed to herself as she tossed her cold coffee down the drain. "Who is going to tell me no, right? Maybe with a little music, I can stop talking to myself, that might be a good thing. I don't want anyone to think I'm crazy, even if I am. But I can walk around my apartment naked.... at sunrise.... with a glass of wine. That seems PERFECTLY normal." She laughed heading towards the remote.

Flipping through old cd's she picked one and threw it into the system that was obviously a reject from the 90's. But like Terra, it was still around. She still hadn't managed to get the hang of some of the new modern technologies of iTunes, playlists, and whatever else was out there. She was used to the old ways. There was just something about a cd. If she had her way, she would have a record player, but she hadn't managed to find one of those that she liked yet. There's an idea, I'm going to get cleaned up, get out of this house, and go find a record player. I might be crazy, so I might as well have a little fun with it. Wait, what stage of grief was this? Was it the admitting that you are crazy stage? She was sure she hadn't heard of that one yet. Grabbing her phone, she sank into the warm bubbles and googled the stages of grief. Looking down she read the seven stages of grief, (modified Kubler-Ross model).

Let's see, Shock, initial paralysis at hearing the bad news. Well, I did that. Denial, yeah, I did that too. Anger, well, I've had my moments. Bargaining, maybe a little. Depression, obviously... I just slept for a day and a half. I'm sure that's not normal. Testing and acceptance.... maybe, maybe not. Oh, and it says here that it's not linear, you can hop around the different stages. That's great. She told herself as she dropped her phone to the floor and dipped deeper into the tub, letting the actual mouse nest of her hair float around her. This was going to be an interesting day.

Maybe she should get a cat... but then again that seemed a little bit cruel. For now, she would just have to focus on getting out of the tub, and getting out of the apartment, and out of her own head. Feeling the sun on her face could be a good thing.

After dragging herself from the tub, she stood outside of the bedroom door trying to gather the courage to find her clothes. Why did she have to put her suitcase in the bedroom? Quickly she opened the door, ran in, and grabbed it, dragging it into the living room as she slammed the door shut behind her. Gasping, she stood with her back against the door. She knew she would have to figure out how to face that room. A little bit at a time, but today she had to get out of the house. She had to take little steps, one day at a time. Now where had she hidden the extra money from selling the car? Hopefully, the mouse hadn't found it.

Going into the closet under the stairs she pulled out the little metal box and grabbed the money out. This would have to do for a little while. There was more than enough left, but she would need to get new clothes, something that wouldn't remind her of Darren. Everything reminded her of him. And how was she going to get through this if she was constantly thinking of him? Maybe she should call her mom. Maybe she was right and they could go out together. They could have a girl's day. And if she was mad at her mom, then it might be easier to get through the day. Going out alone, might not be the best idea, not yet. After all, she was always mad at Sheila for something, especially since she was keeping Autumn away from her.

It would be nice to see her little girl. There's no way she would try to exclude her from a shopping day, right? Terra knew that she had no right to keep her from her. She knew that her mother meant well, even if she didn't agree with how she did things. It was still early, though. After sending her a text about her idea, Terra stepped outside into the early morning light. She would just have to keep herself busy until they arrived.

Stepping out into the first light of the morning, Terra closed her eyes and took in the fresh morning air. Darren had been sick for a while and he had always told her that she needed to get out of the house more. She just hated the thought of leaving his side. Today was different. She felt the concrete sidewalk under her feet in a new way. Everything seemed fresh and renewed. The dew glistened like diamonds on the grass as the light began to dance across it. Maybe she could start with just walking up and down the sidewalk from her apartment to the car. Terra didn't want to go far from the apartment. She felt safe there.

"Terra!" She heard a yell from across the parking lot.

"Umm... yeah?"

"Hey, I meant to come and see you at the center. How are you feeling?" Greg asked as he cautiously approached her.

"That's ok, I really wanted the time alone."

"I wanted to apologize again. I really didn't mean to be like that... the night Darren died. I guess I had too many drinks... and you seemed so sad" he stated as he kicked his feet against the grass. "I really want to be here for you. It must be hard. I can't stop thinking about him. It has to be worse for you."

"You know... that makes me feel bad. I never really thought about how this has affected you," she answered, trying to sound sympathetic. "I just can't get over what... you... tried... to-"

"I know, Terra, I'm so sorry. You probably shouldn't forgive me. I just keep thinking about everything you have been through with all of this. And I know what I went through when Moriah ran out on me and our baby... I just hope that maybe someday... you can forgive me and let me just... be... your... friend," he said, trying to take her hand. "All I want is for you to be safe. You don't have to go through this alone."

"But I am alone, Greg! How can I really trust you after that? I know that you've had a hard time with Moriah for a while. It's not like she ever really loved you. I don't know what she was doing, but she obviously didn't love you."

"OUCH! You hit a little below the belt on that one, don't ya think?"

"Well, you deserve it! What do you expect? You were his best friend. The one I should be able to turn to. We took care of you when all of that was going on with your wife. We gave you a place to stay, helped take care of your daughter... We did that for a year, Greg, what the hell?"

"I know, listen, I said I'm sorry. People do stupid things when they're drunk. I thought that you wanted me. I thought you had been watching me for a while, and Darren kept telling me how he couldn't satisfy you, how he couldn't take care of you... that he couldn't make love to you... I just took everything completely out of context... and that's my fault. But that doesn't mean I don't care. I promise you, that will never happen again."

"I don't want to trust you... But I can kind of understand where you are coming from with that. You guys basically lived with us for a while. We did so much for you. And that... was just awful. I'm not a cheater, even if he couldn't take care of me as you put it. There's just no possible way I could do that to him."

"I know that now. I didn't even see it as cheating. I saw it as just helping a couple of friends out. I thought that at least I was someone that you could both trust. Keep it in the family, ya know?"

"Yeah... ok, I guess I can try, but if you ever, I mean EVER try to force yourself on me again. You will regret it. I'm not sure what I will do, but I promise you... you WILL regret it."

"Okay... I understand. I appreciate the chance. Can I walk with you for a few minutes?"

"Yeah, but I'm waiting on Sheila and Autumn. We're going out. I need to get out and do... things." She hesitated.

"Absolutely."

And so, they walked and talked about Darren and how he had always been there to watch over her, even if she never left his side. Glancing back at the apartment door, for just a moment she thought she saw him. It was like a whisper, smiling watching her walk-in front of the apartment. And just as quickly it was gone, like a mist. A comforting illusion. Staring at the door, she felt her heart cringe at the thought of being alone. She had never really been alone. She dreaded the apartment. It was the last place she wanted to be but, looking at the world around her was even harder. Darren wasn't there to appreciate the beauty of the early morning sunrise, the glistening of the dew, or the soft summer breeze that caressed her hair. Even with an old friend by her side, it wasn't the same. Trying to trust Greg was even harder.

As he left, she watched as the clouds drifted softly across the sky like wisps of cotton candy. It was full of soft pastel colors, and the scent of wildflowers surrounded her. The world was so full of beauty, and she had spent years ignoring it. She had kept herself so busy that she had forgotten the little things, the little moments, the beauty in nature. Terra had always been a fan of walking through the woods with a camera and trying to capture the little overlooked details of nature. She had always loved bugs and flowers. Summer was almost over now, and it had seemed to have flown by so quickly. This was the first morning that she had taken the time to feel the warm summer sun on her skin Thinking back, she couldn't remember the last time she had enjoyed it. She had always been by Darren's side. She had missed it. But soon Fall would arrive with its warm colors, beautiful leaves and crisp nights. It had been years since she had enjoyed a hot cup of apple cider and a warm fire. Silently she vowed that this year would be different. The next hour flew by and finally, Terra watched Autumn jump out of Sheila's car. She ran to her, her hair flying behind her as she crashed into her mother's arms.

"Mommy, I missed you so much! Are you okay? Are you done being crazy? Grandma said we were going shopping! I can't wait!" she squealed, wrapping her little arms around Terra's waist.

"I'm going to be ok, and no I'm not crazy, although I'm sure your grandmother tried to convince you that I was!" Terra giggled. "I can't wait to spend the day with you. We should go get ice cream for breakfast!"

"WOW, we can DO that?" Autumn giggled. "Grandma won't let me do ANYTHING fun! I have been so worried that you would never come home!"

"I'm home now, baby. We are going to be together now," Terra whispered as she held her little girl tightly against her. "Hurry, let's get out of here, before Grandma decides she wants in the apartment!" Grabbing Autumn, the two of them ran giggling towards the car and quickly hopped in. "Let's get out of here, Mom. I need some retail therapy. Wherever you want to go, if it's not depressing, and not local. Maybe we could go to the mall. That's about an hour away, right? I desperately need a change of scenery."

"This is some rather unusual behavior out of you, Terra. You never seemed to want to do anything like this before. Are you just trying to pull my chain? Because if this is a joke, it's not funny," Sheila glared, gripping the steering wheel tightly.

"I'm not joking, Mom. I'm trying to do something different. Maybe you're right. I don't really want to sit in there and be depressed. And I really don't want to be in that bedroom alone, not yet. I need some time. And because of that, well, I need new clothes. I need to stop thinking about him, each second of the day. I just can't do it anymore. I hate crying all the time. I need something that doesn't remind me of him. I took down pictures; I packed away what I could of his things and I closed the bedroom door. I cannot survive this without a little change, or a LOT of change. I don't know what to do, and you are the only one that has made any suggestions, so I might as well give it a shot."

"That's different, but hey, I'm all for it. You have NEVER taken my advice before, not even a little bit. So, I'm going to savor this moment. It's about time you started listening to me. No daughter of mine is going to sit around acting pathetic. No man is worth it," Sheila grinned in surprise.

Terra bit back her words as she smiled and returned her mother's grin. Sheila was wrong about him not being worth it. He was her soul mate. Darren was not just a random man that she was trying to get over. Crying over losing the love of your life, wasn't such a bad thing. She couldn't help but think that maybe she had already found her love. She had already had her happiness, but he was gone. Would she ever feel that way again? Was it fair to ask for another soul mate? Was it fair to ask for another chance?

"Well, Mom, let's go. Oh, and we need to get ice cream for breakfast," she stated forcing a laugh. Deep down she knew that it was going to be a lot better to get away from things for a while. Looking back at Autumn's sweet smile, she felt a strength she had never felt before. It felt like a blanket of courage. She knew that she had to conquer this mountain for her.

The next few hours flew by as they drove out of town to the mall. With the radio loud with pop songs and the windows down, Terra almost forgot about her sorrow, almost. Together her and Autumn ran through the bookstore, visited the coffee shop, and headed for the wide assortment of clothing stores. She grabbed a couple of small things to help hold her over and then she saw it. She saw just a corner of emerald green fabric. As she got closer, she saw little daisies scattered throughout the soft challis fabric. Its thin delicate straps reminded her of walks in the summer sun.

Terra couldn't help but picture walking in the park with flowers in her hair, letting the warm summer sun caress her skin. Paul.... his smile flashed across her mind like a gentle kiss in the rain. She felt her cheeks getting warm as she thought of the last time she had seen him. Quickly she buried her gaze in the racks of clothing as she clutched the emerald sundress. The last thing she wanted was for Sheila to see something like that. There was no doubt she would ask questions. She always tended to ask too many questions. It wouldn't be possible for her to ignore her cheeks turning scarlet red. The more she thought about Paul, the deeper her smile began to get. Maybe she could just blame it on the little dress? Still she hid her face in the racks. Shaking, she lifted out a soft pink blouse and a red pair of pants.

As her hands shook with her new treasures, she searched for a white top to match, and maybe a jacket that would be perfect for those crisp fall nights. It had always seemed like a rule for red heads to never wear red, but she had never cared for rules. Red was by far her favorite color, and it wouldn't hurt anything to wear something red. Of course, the more she thought about Paul, the more she matched the bright hue. She missed him more than she cared to admit to even herself. Finding a few other things, Terra headed for the cashier. She felt ready, ready to face the world. She was ready to live again. It felt crazy to think that adding a few new pieces to her wardrobe could make her feel more confident, but for the first time in her life, it did.

The last thing she wanted was to take life for granted. The world around her was beautiful, vibrant, and full of opportunities. She saw everything with new eyes as she looked around as people rushed through the halls. As she grabbed Autumn's hand, she saw so much hope glistening in her eyes. Her little girl deserved to have a happy and fulfilled mom. And she knew that it might be a lot of hard work, but she would find a way to be everything that lovely little lady would ever need. She wanted to be a good role model for her. She wanted her to know that you can be strong. You can find a way. You can live a fulfilled life and not have to rely on other people to make you happy. For the first time in a long time, Terra couldn't wait to get home. She couldn't wait to open the curtains, crack open the windows and let the light and fresh air brighten their apartment. Maybe they could fill the rooms with new memories, happier memories. She wanted so much to forget all the sickness they had witnessed. She wanted to forget the memories of death and replace them with life. A beautiful life.

"Mom," Terra asked timidly as they headed back to the car, their arms full of bags. "Maybe we could stop by one of the discount stores, maybe we could find a few new things to brighten the apartment."

"Really? How are you going to do that? You have always used browns and blues. You would have to redo everything!" Sheila scoffed at her daughter.

"I don't know about all of that. I was thinking maybe just a couple pillows and curtains. I could take out the blue and maybe add something different. I was thinking maybe red or yellow? I always really liked those colors. It would be a lot different. Maybe it would be more my style, I don't know. I just think that freshening things up would be nice."

"Okay, if THAT'S what you want to do!" She answered sarcastically. "I'm beginning to think that you are taking this a little too far. You can't completely reinvent yourself in one day!"

"That's not what I'm trying to do! I just want to live a little! I'm just trying to find a way to get through this!" Throwing her bags in the trunk of the car, Terra settled into the passenger seat. "I thought this was what you wanted!"

"It is, darling. Just be careful, not too much too soon. Although a couple of throw pillows wouldn't hurt. I just want you to be ok! You seem to be making great strides, but I really want to make sure you are ready for all of this and not pushing yourself too hard. I'm normally the one to push you. I'm not used to you pushing harder than me. Did you get tired of crying or something?"

"I don't know, maybe. I did miss an entire day, slept right through it, and honestly, I want to forget that any of this ever happened. That's not possible, though. Maybe I'm being silly, but I don't want to go into that bedroom again. I need to know that I'm still alive. And if a little sundress, and a splash of color in my apartment will help with that, then who are you to disagree? I can't live in a museum. I must be strong for Autumn, I really, really.... don't know what else to do," Terra whispered. She felt tears start to run down her cheeks like salty pebbles scraping down her face. Her hands dashed up quickly to cover tears. "I have to get through this."

"You know what... why don't we have a sleepover at mommy's house tonight!" Sheila blurted out with more cheer in her voice than Terra had heard in a long time. "Wouldn't that be fun Autumn? We will stay up, do our nails, we can dance in the living room, eat ice cream, and annoy the neighbors with our loud singing! What do you think?"

"ICE CREAM!!! That sounds great, Grandma!!" Autumn squealed from the back. "LET'S DO IT!" Sinking down further in the seat, Terra grabbed her mother's oversized sunglasses and closed her eyes. It was going to be a long night.

7

Pushing her hair back into her little black ball cap, Terra headed for the center. This was her first time back for outpatient therapy. She had barely slept the night before. Making it a priority, she grabbed whatever she could to wear. The thought of being late always tormented her, so here she was arriving in an oversized black sweatshirt, a pair of knit shorts, and boat shoes. She was comfortable and looked the part of a lonely, widowed, single mom. With her head down, she shuffled inside barely noticing as her shoulder peaked out from neck of the sweatshirt. Terra hadn't even worn makeup in weeks. It was supposed to be a group support session for people in the community. It was hard to tell what kind of people she would run into, and the last thing she wanted was to be noticed. She completely expected to sit in the corner and watch everyone else share their misery. After all, misery loves company. Grabbing the chair closest to the corner she sat, holding her hands in her lap. A deep sigh escaped her lips as she watched the others entering the room. One by one they took their spots in the circle as she picked at the corners of her nails, trying to take away the polish from a few nights before.

"Terra....," a familiar voice whispered behind her. "Is that you?"

"Paul...," she whispered as his hand gently touched her shoulder. "How have you been?"

"Well, I've been wondering about you, actually," he stated taking the seat beside her. "I wasn't sure how to reach you? Or if you wanted to still talk to me?"

"Well, I wasn't sure what to do. I'm still not sure what to do. I just don't want to jump into, well... I don't want to bother you, I guess," she stuttered, trying to pull away the tendrils of hair that had fallen into her face.

"Are you afraid of me, Terra?" Paul asked, as he gently tucked a piece of hair behind her ear.

"I wouldn't say that...., " her voice trailed off.

"Maybe we should talk later, if you have a minute."

"I'm not in a hurry... What are you doing here anyways?" she asked as her voice rose.

"I still come to sessions, sometimes. They can help. Even if you are just listening to other people and how they are coping with their problems. At least, it helps me to keep things in perspective," he winked.

"I'm glad you're here, Paul. I missed talking to you," she muttered, wishing she had prepared herself a little better. "It's nice to see a friendly face."

Sitting quietly, Terra watched the others share their stories. Each one had a different perspective, a different way that they viewed life. For some, it was all about success after sorrow. For others, it was about finding love again. But for her, the only thing she thought of was how short life really was. How quickly life can be taken away from you. How each moment was a blessing. Glancing over at Paul, she saw him fidgeting, trying not to look her way as he focused on the others. She could tell, that for him, it was about love. He talked about finding a way to love and forgive. He hoped that maybe one day, he would find a way to open and really love again. Terra couldn't help but be a little frightened as she listened. Many of them had been working through things for a long time. Much longer than she had anticipated. Years had gone by for some, and they were still dealing with the same issues. It was apparent to her that each day was going to have its own struggles. But she was inpatient. She kept listening, hoping for a quick fix or a miracle cure. There was nothing. At the end what she felt the most was peace. At least she knew that she wasn't alone, after all.

"Do you want to get out of here?" Paul asked as held his hand out to her.

"Umm... sure, I guess," she mumbled as she took his hand. She felt her heartbeat quicken at his touch. It was as though nobody else existed in that moment.

"Can I buy you a cup of coffee?"

"I don't know, I didn't really expect to run into anyone I know. I was in a hurry. I didn't even brush my hair."

"It doesn't matter," he giggled. "You look beautiful."

"Not today. This is my I-slept-in-this look," she tried to laugh, looking down at her feet.

"People go to the store in their pajamas. I think you will be fine," he answered, squeezing her hand. "Or do you not want to be seen with me?"

"No, it's not like that! I don't want you to be seen with a complete mess!"

"You're not a complete mess, and I just want to slow

down and spend a few minutes just talking with you."

"Actually, my mom is babysitting today. I would enjoy spending more than just a few minutes with you. Maybe, you could follow me home and wait for me to change into something more... you know... presentable?" Terra snickered as she peered up at him. "Unless you are uncomfortable with that. You don't have to come in. It will only take me a couple minutes to get dressed. You could just wait out in your car, or truck or whatever you have," she rambled. "I don't want you to be uncomfortable."

"I wouldn't be uncomfortable. I will do whatever you ask of me. To spend a few moments with you is more than worth it. At least, then, I will know how to find you," Paul answered, squeezing her hand. "Let's do this. There's just one little problem. It's raining and I parked at the edge of the bike trail. Can you give me a ride? "

"Oh my, it wasn't supposed to rain today. I left the top down....," she laughed looking through the window. "That looks bad, too.... Well, come on, I guess we can pick up your car later."

"Lead the way!"

Soaking wet from the rain, Terra headed towards her tiny apartment. His hand rested gently on hers, as he ran his thumb back and forth against her skin.

"I can't believe I'm taking you to my apartment," she laughed almost to herself as she gripped the steering wheel. "I must be crazy. I barely know you."

"Well, why not? I care a lot about you. And it's just for a few minutes, right?" He answered, taking his hand from hers. "If you're uncomfortable, I can wait in the car."

"That won't be necessary. I would really like for you to come in for a few minutes," she gushed reaching for his hand. "I really like you. I just don't want to do anything.... stupid. I'm a widow, and I'm hurting. It just seems too complicated. I don't want to get into something, and it not be real. It just seems so soon. I really want to spend time with you. I keep thinking about you. I remember the way you touched me, the way you kissed me. I want you. I just want to make sure it's real."

"You don't have to have this figured out, Terra. It's ok to not understand everything. It's ok to hurt. It's ok to not know for sure what is happening. Does anyone ever really know what their hearts are telling them? I know you're confused. I know that you are hurting. You would have to be. What you are going through can't be easy. But believe me when I say that I will risk the pain, the heartbreak, and the misery if I can spend just a few minutes in your arms. You are like my heaven, and I will be as patient, as understanding, and as helpful as I need to be for just a chance with you."

"Are you sure about that, because I'm not even sure of who I am anymore."

"I've never been more sure of anything in my life."

Terra's breathing began to become heavier, as she pulled up beside her apartment. The rain was heavy and she could barely see the door just a few feet away. She felt her eyes meeting his as she glanced over at him. Had he even looked away? His gaze was unassuming, gentle, and comforting as she shut off the car and let the rain pound against the windshield.

"I know that you are really looking for something new, something real. And I'm so afraid of hurting you. I want to spend time with you, I want to get to know you OUTSIDE of the crisis center, but I can't promise you anything. I'm just not ready."

"I understand that, Terra. You keep saying that you like me, and that you want time with me. And that's enough for me. I'm looking forward to getting to know you outside of the crazy house," Paul answered turning to face her. "Would you like for me to wait in the car?"

"Actually, it might take me a few minutes. Would you mind coming in? There's still a fresh pot of coffee if you would like a cup. I just don't want you to have to wait out here in the rain."

Opening the door, he took off his jacket and ran to open hers, holding the jacket above both of their heads as they ran to the apartment. Stepping inside, she turned to lock the door behind her as his hands grabbed her ball cap and tossed it to the floor. As he walked to her, she felt so small and insignificant, he towered above her, his eyes were powerful as he looked down on her small frame. Slowly, his face crept towards hers, his lips were warm and sweet as he pulled her body close to his. She felt a gasp escape her lips as he caressed them with his. She felt her body melting into his arms as his face brushed against hers. It was like she was being wrapped in sunlight. She could feel herself surrender to him. At that moment, nothing else existed. Nothing else mattered, only Paul, only his strong hands holding her close to him. The only thing she felt, the only thing she could taste, the only thing she heard, or saw, was him. Slowly, she felt him pull away, his eyes full of longing.

As she rested her head against his chest, Terra felt his hair tickling her cheek as she listened to his heartbeat. It was an old habit. She had always managed to find a way to listen or feel Darren's heartbeat as he rested. She had always been a little worried about him. Running her hand up his body, she rested it in the thickest part of his hair and began to twirl it around her fingers. It was as dark as coal with just a few silver pieces thrown in.

"You're so sexy...," Terra stated as she lifted her head to meet his eyes. "I think you're crazy to want to be with me."

"I thought it was pretty well understood that we are both crazy," he giggled. "You're perfect, Terra, don't be ridiculous."

"You haven't even seen me anywhere close to my best! When you met me, I was an absolute mess. My hair was matted up. My clothes were wrinkled. I'm sure my eyes were swollen from crying. I had no sense of humor. And, I had just had some kind of episode."

"Well, at least you know you can't scare me away!" He laughed as they both sat up. "If that's how you feel, though... I would like to take you out for coffee, dinner, or something, maybe a real date. I probably should have done that before kissing you."

"Honestly, I'm not sure the awkward first date where we don't know what to talk about is really required," Terra giggled.

"No, I guess not! That's okay, I won't miss that part. Maybe we can skip to the fourth or fifth date where you agree to be my girl," he winked at her.

"Ummmm.... maybe," Terra answered flatly as she rose and headed for the hall closet. "I'm just going to get dressed." Quickly she grabbed her new dress and headed for the bathroom. She had managed to get used to avoiding her bedroom quite well. But she knew that one day soon, she would have to face it again. She missed her bedroom. She missed privacy. Maybe she could buy a new mattress? Of course, she didn't exactly have enough money to handle a purchase like that. But it would be nice to have something fresh and new, a mattress that wasn't molded to Darren could be a good thing.

Looking at her reflection she had so many memories with Darren. Each morning he would watch her brush her hair, wash her face, and the rest of the morning routine. He would stand behind her in the doorway and just smile at her. It had been the thing that had always annoyed her the most, but now... now she really missed seeing his face standing there waiting for a kiss. And now, she couldn't help but feel guilty because in their living room was another man. A man that she had only just met. Paul had just asked her to be his girl. What did that even mean? Did he mean girlfriend? Did he want to be a couple? For a moment she imagined herself always being by his side.

She adored Paul, or at least what she knew of him so far. He was such a genuine and tender man. Even in mourning she knew that was something that you don't see every day. But how could she go from loving a man so unconditionally and so deeply, to being a widow, to belonging to another man so quickly? She knew it wasn't possible. She knew it wasn't fair to Paul or even to herself. Why did she have to find this perfect man so quickly. Was he going to end up being just a rebound, someone to fill the void?

Splashing her face with water, she couldn't imagine hurting him. The last thing she wanted to do was say no, but was it fair to say yes? Hopefully, he would understand that she just wasn't ready to commit. As she gently placed the emerald daisy dress over her shoulders, she knew that she would need to talk to her therapist. She didn't want to lose Paul, but she also didn't want to mess everything up. Relationships can be delicate, and if you are not whole as a person, then it is destined to fail. She had been in enough therapy and read enough books to know that you cannot rely on another person to take care of you, to complete you. You must be able to rely on yourself. You must know what you want and not need anyone else to fulfill you. Wanting someone in your life and needing them in your life were completely different things. There was strength and solidarity in knowing for yourself that you can survive on your own. Grabbing her favorite products, she began to tidy up her hair, letting her waves fall softly around her face. Paul had never seen her hair fixed the way she liked it.

Glancing around the tiny living room, Paul felt a little guilty. There was a blanket and pillow sitting on a chair in the corner. A couple of old coffee cups were scattered on the table from days of neglect. There were no pictures on the wall. There were no knick knacks or memorabilia. It didn't look like a home; it looked closer to a small hotel room. It was a disorganized type of clean. Unusual things sat in corners. And he saw that the trash can was full of take out and drive-thru bags. Standing up, he grabbed the old coffee cups from the table and took them to the sink. Grabbing the trash out of the can, he tied it up and quickly washed the cups. He heard her in the other room stirring around. Smiling to himself he grabbed the sponge and began wiping down the counters. At least he could help her with a few things. It was obvious that she had basically confined herself to only a couple of rooms. He only imagined what memories were held. He saw old blue pillows and curtains tossed in the corner. Deep scarlet curtains hung in their place. The new pillows were scarlet lace with a warm golden color underneath. Looking down, he saw another one covered in long fur. They seemed like her, beautiful, modern, and classic all at the same time. He couldn't blame her for wanting change. Sometimes making changes in your environment helped you find yourself again. Self-expression had always been something that helped him.

There were similarities between himself and Terra. From the looks of the place, she, too, had avoided her bedroom and the kitchen of her tiny apartment. It was tough living on the sofa. He remembered what it was like for him those first few weeks alone. Everywhere he had looked in his home was another memory of betrayal. Each moment had been etched into his mind. He had seen another man holding his wife and that was more than enough to poison his view of their home. How many places had they been together in their home? He had scrubbed every inch of it, trying to get rid of any sign that they had been there. The countertops were cleaned because what if they had made love there? What if they had on the floor, their bed, in the shower? He hadn't been able to stand looking at the place. And when he put it up for sale, he asked for a little bit more so he included all the furnishings, all the pots, pans, dishes, and even towels. Paul didn't want any of it anymore. And of course, he had allowed Patricia to purchase it for her and her baby.

After all, he just wanted a fresh start in his new place. It had only been a few days since she had moved back into the old house. He couldn't help but notice that she moved in alone. Her lover had abandoned her after a few months to raise their baby boy alone. He had almost felt guilty for allowing her to be alone, almost. Every time Paul had felt a little sympathy for her situation, he was reminded of her plan to use his money to support her lover. His journey to freedom had been full of obstacles. At one point he had even considered giving her a second chance. Each time they would speak, and he tried to make peace, he was reminded not only of her betrayal, but all the many times that she had dismissed him. Patricia had always complained when he would have to go to a meeting. She acted as though she expected him to always be home with her. When he was home, she had always made a point to remind him that he didn't make enough money. He didn't buy her enough gifts. He never took her anywhere. She complained even when he took her on vacations, bought her beautiful diamond jewelry, and made an extra walk-in closet just for her shoes. Still, she claimed that he never got her anything, and never made her a priority.

Wiping off the counters of Terra's little abandoned kitchen, he could tell that she too, loved to cook. A beautiful array of spices sat on a carousel spice rack, many of them had been well loved and some of his favorites were almost empty. Paul couldn't help but smile as he peeked in the cabinets. She had a variety of pots and pans, and on top was a cast iron skillet. It had to have been older and well-seasoned. Maybe he could make her dinner sometime. He hadn't had the opportunity to cook for someone or with someone for a long time. Patricia had hated to cook. The idea of having someone to cook with was tantalizing. Of course, it could also be bad. What if they only ended up fighting over what spices to use or how hot to have the skillet? Regardless, he wanted to show

Terra his new house, maybe even tonight.

Hearing the bathroom door creak open he headed back to the living room. And there she stood; he had never seen her look more beautiful. The narrow sliver of sunlight that had escaped through the curtains seemed to rest on her perfectly. Her soft red waves fell down her back as the sunlight kissed each lock of hair. Her green dress was covered with daisies, just like the one he had brought her at the center. Looking at her, he felt his heart melt. Here she was, a woman who had lost so much. She had lost all her plans for the future, her security, and the man she loved. Now, she stood before him like an angel from a dream. Walking to her side, the only thing he thought of doing was caressing her lips with his.

"You look beautiful..." he whispered.

"Don't act so surprised," Terra giggled, "I do clean myself up every now and then."

"I never doubted that. I just never could have imagined you like this."

"Don't be silly, Paul! It's just a sundress. I wear them all the time," she laughed nudging him gently on the arm. "It's really not a big deal. You are just used to seeing me in ratty hair and pajamas."

"I've seen you in other clothes, a couple of times. Just never a dress, I don't think. If I did, I don't remember."

Laughing, she wrapped her arms around his neck and pressed her body against his playfully. "Are we going to go somewhere or are you just going to stare at me?" she teased.

"I have an idea... let's go somewhere, while I stare at you!" he laughed as he grabbed her hand and headed for the door. "I want you to see something."

"Really, now? What do you want me to see? I think I have seen a lot of you, and I grew up in this little town so I don't see what you could possibly surprise me with."

"Well, you haven't seen my truck, yet!"

"OH, your truck. I wasn't expecting that! Don't tell me that you are one of those hunting, fishing, beat up truck kind of hillbilly guys, are you?" she laughed.

"No, I'm not actually, but I still have a truck! And what exactly is wrong with our hillbilly redneck neighbors?"

"Nothing, I guess. I just never got into any of it. I enjoy going out and looking for animals, I just don't want to shoot them, personally. I like going out to the river and watching the water, but staring at a fishing pole for hours... not so much," Terra replied. "I guess I'm a little weird because everyone else LOVES it around here. I don't judge them for it. We all like different things. Of course, I never really felt like I belonged here anyways."

"I pretty well agree with you on all of that. It's not my thing either. My truck though, well, I just like it," he laughed. "I guess I always envisioned putting blankets in the back, and having a tail-gate date, complete with stargazing a couple glasses of wine and a picnic. It just... well, it has never actually happened."

"Well, you never know, maybe one of these days, it might."

"Well.... maybe we could just start by getting you out of your apartment."

"Why? Is there something wrong with my apartment? I thought you had enjoyed your time here," She winked, throwing her arms down to her sides she took a couple steps back.

"Of course, I have. I just thought you might want a real

meal. From the looks of your trash, it's been a while. "

"You might have a point there," she sighed.

Grabbing a long white sweater from the hall closet, Terra took his hand and together they drove back towards the center. It wasn't August anymore and now the air had started to become a little cooler in the evenings. She couldn't help but wonder where he was planning to take her or if he really had a plan at all. In the back of her mind, she felt the struggle. She loved being around Paul, but it was hard to not think about Darren.

It was hard to not think of everything Sheila had said about him. Were there really rumors of him cheating on her, using drugs, and him just not wanting to be home because she was too boring? Or was it all something she had made up to try to get her to move on a little faster. Their little town could be overwhelming with gossip, but more often than not, there was some level of truth to even the harshest of rumors. What was the truth? Would she ever really know? What if somewhere out there, there was another child that he had left behind? Another woman lost and alone. Could that be a possibility? Did it matter? Was she going to let a little gossip overshadow the love she had for him?

Despite everything, Terra wanted to know. Maybe it would give her some sort of closure, even if he could never defend his actions. Would that make her feel better, or worse? Looking over at Paul, she couldn't imagine not caring for him. He had been so sweet to her. Did he have something to hide, too? Or was he just trying to see if he could prey on a widow's emotions. If that was the case, he was doing a good job. He had her attention, but was that a good thing or a bad thing?

"What are you thinking?" Paul asked as they pulled up beside his truck. "You look like you're somewhere else?"

"I don't know, "she sighed as she threw the car in park. "I guess I'm just thinking about all of the rumors about my late husband. And thinking about other things that my mom said. I just don't want someone to take advantage of me, I guess. You don't seem like the type of guy that would do that, but I'm a little scared." Getting out of the car Terra leaned up against her little car. "You know, I don't have much of my own and I've always depended on someone else to take care of me. Look what that got me, a dead husband, a tiny apartment, and a car that my mother gave me. We didn't have insurance money. I had to sell a lot of stuff to pay for his funeral. I'm still selling stuff. I'm going to have to get a job, a career, or something. I don't think I can handle someone playing games, ya know?"

"Terra, I promise you; I am not one of those guys. I'm not going to take advantage of you. If you need space, I will give you space. If you need time, well, I hope that you can still be around me. I really like being with you. You are a breath of fresh air, especially around here. And because of that, I hope that you will allow me to be a part of your life. Even if it's just a small part for now. I'm tired of all the women around here. Either they are slutty and sleeping around with every guy in town, or they are doing drugs. There is no one out here like you. You have an honesty about you. You have virtue. And what rumors? I haven't heard a peep about your husband. Of course, I never have asked much about him, but I can imagine if there was a rumor going around about a man who had left a widow behind, I would hear it and I would remember," he stated leaning up beside her. "And there's nothing wrong with getting a little help sometimes. That doesn't mean you have to depend on that person for your happiness. You need to find that on your own. If you can't find your own happiness for yourself, then you won't be able to find it in anyone else."

"I don't know how to find it, Paul. The only thing I have done in a long time is take care of someone else. I don't even remember what I really like anymore."

"I bet you do. It's the little things, Terra. The little changes you make not only for yourself, but for your daughter. It's the changes in the apartment, the way you dress, and what you do with your time. All of that starts to happen on its own. "

"It doesn't really feel like it. I am so afraid of jumping into something too soon. I don't want to ruin this. I think that this could be so much more than what it has been between us. I don't want to destroy our chances because I'm still hung up on Darren. "

"I'm a lot more patient than that. And you are going to be hung up on him. He was your husband. It's not like you caught him cheating, honey. He died. That's a whole different set of emotions that you must come to terms with. Believe me, I don't expect you to be ok overnight," he stated putting his arms around her. Standing there for a minute, he watched a single tear sneak from her eyes as he held her against him. "It's going to be ok; I promise. I won't give up on you. You are a good person, and honestly there doesn't seem to be many of those left." Pulling away, he looked down into her eyes. "Can I still take you out to dinner? We could go for a short walk, whatever you want to do."

"Can I get a rain check on that?" She asked pulling

away from his gaze. "I mean a serious rain check. I think I need to clear my head a little. I feel really confused right now. My head is just swimming with memories of him and now thoughts of you. It doesn't make sense," Terra stated, shaking her head a little. "I really want to go and spend the rest of the day with you, I really, REALLY do. But honestly. I really need to clear my head."

"How much time do you need?" he asked, stepping towards his truck. "Do you want me to leave you alone, or should I call you sometime?"

"NO! It's not like that. I was thinking tomorrow evening, maybe? Is that possible?"

"It can be, but like you said, I want to make sure you have time to clear your head," Paul stated dryly.

"You seem irritated," She winced.

"I mean a little bit, yes. I want to show you more about me. But I do understand. I will respect your boundaries. All good things come to those who wait. Just understand that I want more than just your body and what it can do for mine. Sex is cheap, Terra. Don't let that be how you cope with your loss. You are better than that. I want to spend time doing things with you. I can get sex anywhere. I want to share things with you, not use you. But yes, if you want, I can pick you up tomorrow evening. Let me know if you change your mind again."

Terra watched quietly as he climbed into the driver's side of his black truck and quickly drove away.

8

"Mommy! WAKE UP!" Autumn screamed from the apartment door. "You've been sleeping all afternoon, you need to wake up, MOMMY!" Running to Terra's side, her little arms began to shake her wildly. "Uncle Greg is here!"

"Oh, man.... what is he doing here?" Terra stuttered from under the blanket. "What time is it, baby girl?"

"It's already ten o'clock! I've been awake, by myself, forever, Mommy!"

"Stop shaking me, AUTUMN!"

Giggling, Autumn ran to the door, as Terra sat up on the couch. It had been another long restless night. And here she was still in her new sundress. She wasn't sure she had even taken her shoes off. Brushing her hair out of her face, she pushed the blanket to the side and grabbed her pillow. "I see you have taken over my spot on the couch, pretty lady," Greg laughed from a few feet away. "How have you been feeling today?"

"I don't know, I guess I'm ok. There's not much to report really," She answered politely as she stared back at him.

"Ok, huh? Are you ready for company? Here I brought you coffee. I had a feeling you might need it," he said handing her a cup of steaming hot liquid. "I honestly expected this place to be a total mess. I thought I might take my spot back on the couch to help you for a few days."

"I don't really go into my bedroom, Greg, too many memories." She mumbled taking the coffee from his hand. "I don't really think I need your help. I'm used to taking care of this place on my own."

"You might be, but things are different now. You just got back from the crazy house, after all. And now apparently you're sleeping in my spot," he laughed.

"That place isn't for crazy people; a lot of people go there."

"Maybe, maybe not..."

"Trust me, it's not."

"Fine, so how are you really doing? Have you just stayed in the apartment the whole time you have been out?"

"THAT'S right, Mommy doesn't leave," Autumn chimed in sitting beside Terra. "Grandma says she needs a man to take her out!"

"She would say something like that! But that's the last thing I need, baby girl," she answered giving the little girl a hug.

"Well, she's right, you can't just stay here all the time, moping around. That's what Grandma says."

"Well, if that's what Grandma says, maybe I can help out a little and get your Mommy out of here. What do you think, Miss Autumn?"

Reaching over, Greg put his hand on Terra's shoulders and squeezed her gently. Shrugging it away, Terra stood up and without a word excused herself to the restroom. She couldn't believe he was there again, so soon. He certainly had guts. "Autumn, why don't you go upstairs and play while me and Uncle Greg talk, ok?"

"But, Mom!" she whined. "I want to visit with Uncle Greg! I don't have Daddy around anymore, and you are always mopey and sad. I want to play. I don't want to be sad. When is he coming back anyways? Why did Daddy leave us?" her voice raised as she sobbed.

"Honey, Daddy can't come back, we explained that to you. That's why I'm sad. I miss him," Terra stated trying to wrap her arms around her five-year-old little girl.

"Grandma said he left because he doesn't love you," she stated, pushing Terra away. "What did you do to him, anyways, for him not to love you?"

"Autumn, that's not what happened. Your daddy can't come back, baby.... he died," she answered trying to pull Autumn back into her arms.

"NO! That's not possible. That's what I told GRANDMA when she tried to tell me that. You ran him away from us. He is too young to die," she screamed, running for Greg. Throwing herself beside him, she grabbed his arm. "YOU tell her the truth, Uncle Greg! Daddy isn't dead, he just ran away from Mommy."

"Oh, little darling, I wish that were true, but it's not," he stated squeezing her tightly. "I'm sorry but your daddy died. He had been sick for a long time. Your Mommy is going to be sad," he whispered looking up longingly at Terra. "We don't want her to be lonely. That's why I'm here. I want to comfort her. Maybe she will let me come around to help her."

"I don't really need your help Greg," Terra answered

abruptly. "I'm going to go get dressed. Maybe you can try to fix whatever Sheila has told her. And that's all I want you to do." Grabbing some clothes, she went into the bathroom and slammed the door behind her. Turning the water on, she began to sob. Tears poured down her face as she tried to splash cold water on her warm cheeks. She felt her heart racing at how Autumn had spoken to her. She had never known her daughter to be so rude, so obnoxious. What Sheila had done was wrong. How could she lie to her daughter, turning her against her own mother? Now she just stood there struggling to hold it together. She hadn't cried in front of her little girl and she didn't plan on starting now. Yes, of course, she had been sad. Of course, she had been sleeping a lot. But to hear this from her little mouth hurt more than anything.

Terra felt her body shake as she fought to regain her composure. Quickly she wiped off her face and threw on a pair of denim shorts and a tank top. What was she supposed to do now? Opening the bathroom door, she was ready to handle Autumn. But when she stepped into the room, she found her asleep on Greg's arm. Her little eyes closed, her arms wrapped around his.

"Come sit down, I want to talk to you," Greg pleaded.

"What could you possibly want to talk to me about?" she answered as she folded her arms across her chest.

You know I have always liked you. I didn't mean to scare you, or hurt you. I'm so sorry. I didn't mean it. I saw how he looked at you. I saw how lonely you looked when he told you that he loved you. I saw all of it. It just made me want to take care of that loneliness. We all had been drinking. I thought it would be ok. I'm sorry. I don't know what else to say. I promise, it won't happen again," he sobbed looking up at her. "You said you would give me a chance, but it doesn't seem like you are. We are both going through this. You know you can rely on me. I never meant to hurt you."

"I don't know, I'm trying Greg, but I just woke up after a long night. You know I don't do well in the morning."

"I know I did and I just want to promise I will never do that again, not without you asking me to. Can you just come here and sit beside me? You know Darren talked about you all the time. He talked about, well, things he probably shouldn't have. He made me want you with every word he spoke. I just felt like I was watching him take you for granted. I knew he wasn't taking care of you. I never saw him really kiss you, hold you, or anything. A woman needs to be made love to."

"I was lonely, but I was ok... what kinds of things did he say about me. And what makes you think he was taking me for granted? Darren loved me..." she whispered, stepping closer to avoid waking Autumn.

"He may have loved you, but he didn't respect you enough to not tell me about how sweet you were to taste.... he said you felt amazing."

"Why on earth would he tell you something like that?"

"I don't know, but he did, all the time. He told me lots of details. He even asked me if I had thought about screwing you for him, after he started getting sicker. I told him no, but he kept asking. He wanted to watch me do things to you that he couldn't do."

"OH MY GOD!" Terra shouted. "You have to be kidding. Why would he want something like that? That's disgusting. He was supposed to love me, protect me..." she sobbed into her new red pillow to muffle the sound of her anger.

"After a while, all I could think of was being with you. Then we were all drinking and I saw the pain in your eyes. I just wanted to help. I hate seeing you hurt," he answered, sliding his arm from Autumn's. "I just want to help."

"Greg, that's not helping. That's perverted. I thought this conversation was over. I just want you to slowly earn back my trust. One. Day. At. A. Time. Can we do that?" She answered throwing the pillow to the floor. "Have you heard any of the rumors about Darren? I mean since you are over here confessing things that I don't need to know? Did he cheat on me? Was he doing drugs?"

"I honestly don't know.... I do know that he talked about other women sometimes. I never understood why or how he could look at other women when he was neglecting you. He came to work laughing once that you had dressed up in a little sheer number and waited for him to come to bed. He thought it was funny that he rejected you. I never understood that. I guess he told you that he was tired and had a headache when honestly, he didn't. He just wanted to see how you would react."

"He told you about that night?" She whined as she stood to her feet. Terra slowly began to pace across the living room. "I spent three days planning that night. It was his birthday. I had lit candles and picked out the sexiest little thing to wear. I waited for him half the night to make love to him. When he said no, I thought it was because he was tired and sick. I thought he was sobbing as he fell asleep. Apparently not...?" she muttered almost to herself. "How do you know that?"

"He told me. I'm sorry, Terra, but not everything about him was good."

"But he's dead. Why is this all coming out now? Now, when he can't answer. He can't defend himself? I don't know what to believe anymore, Greg." Without saying another word, Greg wrapped his arms around her and started humming. "It's ok, it's going to be ok." Rocking her back and forth, he held her as she sobbed. Her body was tense and warm. Tears ran down her face like a raging river as she pushed him away. "Here I will let go. It's ok. I'm sorry, I'm so sorry, but maybe you need to find a man that will appreciate you more than all of that. He didn't appreciate you. He didn't love you anymore, not after you had the baby. I don't know why. I don't understand it, but something changed in him. He wasn't the boy I grew up with, not anymore."

Pushing away from him, she flung the bedroom door open. Running to the side table she grabbed the drawer and emptied it onto the bed. Dust flew everywhere as the contents spilled over the stiff white blanket. She saw matches from the bar beside the car lot, an old zippo lighter, and a couple of business cards that had flown out of his wallet. Then she saw it, a little box of wood at the end of the drawer. Yanking at it, Terra quickly pulled it apart. And there it was, a little shred of paper with a girl's name and a house key.

"That's it, I'm done. I'm done mourning and worrying about what everyone else thinks. I'm done being sad. If he really loved me, he would have taken better care of himself. He would have been here. He would have been WITH me. He wouldn't have been talking to his buddies about rejecting me. He wouldn't have this other woman's name, number, house key, all of this crap!" she screamed stomping passed Greg to the freezer where Darren had kept his extra cigarettes. Grabbing a pack, she ripped it open and stepped outside. Lighting it up, she inhaled the nicotine and let it fill her body.

"Terra, you're not a smoker. This isn't you," Greg followed.

"What are you going to say about what I do or don't do? The only thing you know about me is what he told you," she stated as she brought the cigarette back to her lips. "I can't believe this. I can't believe he would do this to me."

"I don't think he knew what would happen. I'm sure he loved you, he just...."

"SERIOUSLY! You just said he did all of this, told me the things he told you and now you are going to tell me that he loved me," she questioned, shaking her head.

"I don't know what to say, Terra! What do you want me to say? You asked me questions and I answered you! What did you expect?"

"I expect to find out that my husband loved me. I expected to find out that he was loyal to me!"

"Well, I'm sorry but you need to calm down! What would your therapist say?"

"I don't know. I don't really care. Just how am I supposed to deal with this? I guess finding a girl's number and a key doesn't really mean anything does it? But putting all the rumors together, that makes for a picture that is a little less than I expected." Throwing her cigarette down, she headed back to her bed. Grabbing the items from the drawer she swiftly threw them all in the trash. The room was dusty and hadn't been touched in months. But now, she was ready to reclaim that part of her life. Grabbing the blankets, she threw them into a trash bag and tossed them into the living room. I guess there was more that needed to be changed. Who was this woman and why had he told his friends intimate details?

Who was this man that she had been mourning? It didn't seem like the same man that had cared for her. Darren had cherished her. He had adored her. He was always bringing her flowers and gifts when he was late. Hadn't he confessed his love to her that night before he died. He didn't want to die. He hadn't wanted to leave them. What exactly was she supposed to do with all of this? Grabbing the sheets from the bed she saw something brown under the mattress. Quickly she stopped to investigate what it was. Once again, it was something secret, something she hadn't known existed. Pulling out the brown leather journal, she began to thumb through the contents. It was full. It looked like he had been writing in it for quite a while. Maybe it would give her some answers. Gently she held it to her and sat down on the side of the bed. Could she really read it?

"Maybe not today, but soon," Terra mumbled to herself.

"What did you find?" Greg asked, stepping into the bedroom as he closed the door behind him. She watched his hand drop to the knob and turn the little lock.

"I took Autumn upstairs to her room. She's out cold. No doubt, she will be asleep for a while," he whispered.

"What are you doing? Why did you lock the door? I normally leave it open," she asked placing the journal beside her as she stood up trying to push passed him to the door.

Without a word, Greg grabbed her shoulders and began pushing her towards the bed. Lowering his mouth to hers, he smashed his lips against hers. His hands ripped her tank top away from her body as he pushed her down against the mattress.

"Greg! Stop! Please, don't do this to me!" she screamed from behind his hand. "Stop! " Terra felt her eyes swell with tears as she looked down at her top, lying in shreds beside her.

She felt his hot breath against her neck as she struggled to move against him. Her hands pushed at his cold iron shoulders as he shoved his body harder against hers. Terra felt his fingers dig into her as he forced her into the mattress that her and Darren had shared. It was the mattress where they had made love. Her tears welled up like fire as she remembered the last time she had laid on that mattress. Rage encompassed her as he dug his fingers into her legs, filling her with pain. Her head flung back as he pushed her farther down as she fought against his grip.

Leaning up he unbuckled his pants and yanked at her shorts as she tried to roll away from his grasp. Kicking at his chest, she felt nothing but air as his fingers dug into her feet as he pushed her legs against her chest. Grabbing them he flipped her over as she gasped in fear. Pushing her face against the bed, he grabbed her hips and pulled them towards him. Clawing at the mattress, Terra tried to find traction to pull herself away, but he was strong and only gripped her tighter. Grabbing her hair, he yanked her head back. She felt her long red strands ripping from her scalp as she screamed. But she was no match for Greg's intensity as he pried her body open forcing himself inside her. Her face was covered with tears as she felt the hot searing pain of his betrayal as he took from her what she had only given to a few in her life.

Continuously he pounded his body against hers. She heard him moaning as he held her down. Terra tried to lift her head enough to catch a breath and let out a scream, but just as quickly as she lifted her mouth from the pillows, he forced her back down.

"You don't know what's good for you, Terra! Your husband was an asshole, he wanted me to FUCK YOU, so if that was what he wanted then I am going to honor the wishes of the dead. Like it or not, I'm going to FUCK the hell out of you. You are just a crazy bitch anyway. I tried to do this the nice way, but no... you wouldn't do that, so I'm just going to take it from you," he laughed as he slapped her ass.

Pain shot through her body as he ripped through her flesh. She felt his anger as he continued to smack her ass, then her back, and then the back of her head as he continued to hold her down. Again, and again he hit her and pulled at her hair each time she slid away from his painful thrusts.

"Somebody, please help me! Please stop, Greg! I don't deserve this!" She screamed for a moment as he let go of her long enough to slap her ass again.

"Don't you say another word! You can't tell me no! This is a dying man's last wishes. That's right, he wanted me to fuck you. He asked me to for months. You have no right to withhold this from me. He was right, you are a delicious piece of ass! I should have been fucking you for months," he laughed. "Not only that, but since you won't stop crying and screaming. I'm not just going to take your little pussy, but I'm going to shove my dick right up your ass. I bet you will love that! From now on, you're my little fuck toy, and that sweet pussy of yours, BELONGS to ME. And I'm going to come back to fuck it any damn time I want!" he snickered. She saw his face in the mirror in front of her. His teeth were clenched together and his eyes looked dark and evil. "And what I find even more funny, is that you can't do anything about it! You won't be able to prove anything. After all, you just got out of a fucking mental hospital."

Screaming into the mattress one last time, Terra's body fell limp as he hit her again. Every muscle in her body ached from trying to resist him. Still, he continued to torture her. She began to wonder if he would ever stop. Her eyes glazed over as she tried to imagine herself somewhere else, anywhere else.

Hearing a man's voice from inside the apartment, Paul hurried to the door. Grabbing the handle to Terra's apartment he noticed that it was cracked and headed inside. He had hoped to surprise her with flowers. They were lilies that he had discovered along the side of the road, the last ones of the season. Heading into the living room he heard noises coming from the bedroom. Flashes of catching Patricia with another man taunted him as he got closer to the door. It couldn't be, Terra was nothing like Patricia. Taking a deep breath, he grabbed the knob of the bedroom door, he tried to twist it open, but it was locked. As he leaned down to try the knob again, he heard a muffled cry. He heard her sweet voice begging someone to stop, and then he heard a man's laugh. Stepping back, he threw the flowers down and launched himself at the door.

As it collapsed into the room, he saw her red hair covering her face. Her top lay in shreds on the floor and a man was ripping into Terra's flesh. Paul saw blood running down her thighs as she laid there helplessly. Her face was red, covered in tears. Her arms shook as she gripped the mattress her eyes glazed over.

Grabbing his arm, Paul yanked him away from Terra and landed a right hook against his jaw. "What do you think you're doing to her!" Paul screamed as the brute hit the floor. "I don't know who you think you are, but don't ever come anywhere near her again!"

"Who the FUCK are you to tell me what I can and cannot do?" Greg taunted as he pulled himself from the floor. "I can do whatever the FUCK I want. Her husband gave her to me."

"I think that Terra should have something to say about that, don't you think?" he smirked as he landed another punch against his jaw. "She is not the kind of girl a man gives away."

"Like I said before, who the FUCK are you?"

"I'm a friend," Paul answered, staring straight into Greg's eyes. "Get the HELL away from her." Shaking his hand, he clenched his fist again and landed another punch against his nose. Feeling the flesh break against his hand, Paul felt his breath quicken as his anger grew.

"What are you protecting her from, exactly?" Greg laughed. "I bet you are just mad because I fucked her first! You are probably one of those crazy people she was in there with. She's not herself. She can't say no."

"You know what, I am one of those crazy people, and guess what that means? That means I can beat the living hell out of you and declare temporary insanity," Paul screamed as he grabbed the other man's shoulders. "Get out of this apartment, stay away from her or next time...

you might not survive."

Pushing Greg's half naked body out of the apartment, Paul threw the door shut and locked it behind him. Quickly Paul headed towards the bedroom. She hadn't moved. Her face was swollen with tears, her eyes were glazed over. She looked empty as her body lay there against the bed, trembling.

Running to the bathroom, he grabbed a couple of washcloths and began to clean the blood from her legs. He felt her flinch against his touch. Gently, little by little he cleaned her up and found clothes to dress her. He had seen toys out in the living room. There was no doubt that her daughter was close. She didn't need to see her mother like that. Wrapping a blanket around her, Paul carried her to the couch and held her close to him. Patiently he waited for the shaking to stop. She was cold, in shock and in an unbelievable amount of pain. Weakly she tried to push away from him. Her breath still came in trembling gasps as she cried. Still he pulled her tighter, rocking her, cradling her body in his arms. Closing his eyes, he gave her all his warmth and all his love as his tears met hers. And then, finally she stopped fighting against him, and wrapped her arms around his chest as he held her.

"Thank you, Paul" was the only thing she said as her eyes filled with a different kind of tears.

9

The Gray......
Here she found herself
again...
deep within
her own sea
of hopelessness.
Her pain
her sorrow
surrounding her like a thick fog
of emotions, dwelling.

The tree clung to her body as she awoke in its embrace. The sky was thicker this time. Looking around at the familiar oil waves, the people heading for the shore to lose themselves in the depths of its despair. This time she felt the temptation.

She felt her body longing for rest. Terra had fought a good fight, but what was left for her. The man she had loved betrayed her. Closing her eyes, she felt the heat. She felt the thickness of the smoke and fog entering her lungs. She saw the bruises on her body. The scars on her legs had grown deeper. Blood seemed to drip from her pores as the tree clung to her. Pulling away from its thorny embrace, she felt her dress rip, leaving its innocence behind her like a flag of surrender.

Slowly, she stepped forward into the Gray. This time she did not notice the glass shards upon her feet. This time, she couldn't feel rocks against her body, the smoke upon her skin or the breathless emptiness that surrounded her. Why was she still fighting? What was she fighting against? Was it really worth all of the pain, the misery, and the sheer torture to keep going, to keep fighting? So steadily she stepped forward towards the black waves. But unlike the others she walked forward willingly. She saw the emptiness in their eyes. Their bodies were vacant. Mindlessly, they walked forward. Ahead of her she watched them fade into the depths. One by one she watched them stop before their feet touched the oil. The closer she got to the edge, the more she smelled it. Sulfur, pure sulfur surrounded her. The smoke seemed to push her further now. She was almost there. Stopping for a moment, she looked out through the vastness of the depths of the black and the little door that you cannot see. It stood there. She saw it more clearly now. The little window was glowing blue and green. It stood like a beacon of hope for the hopeless, the worn, and the weary.

Was that what she had become? Was she as lost as those who walked blindly into the waves? Looking around one more time, she stepped into the darkness, into the oil, into the black depths. Then she took one step, then another and she felt the darkness begin to cover her. It would be over soon. Closing her eyes, she stepped forward again. The depths felt warm and soft like a blanket that was slowly swallowing her. In the gray sky above her she saw streaks of lightening in the distance. They arched across the sky echoing each thought that crossed her mind. Each moment, she felt herself go deeper into the waves. It was beginning to cover her. Around her, she watched the others go ahead of her. She saw their startled faces as she saw each of them awaken, a moment before going under. She saw their fear, their anguish, and their sorrow as they took that final step into the depths. As they bumped into her blindly, she felt herself stop and a little voice from behind call to her.

"Don't do it! You're not one of them!" a little girl cried from the shore. "Don't give up! You still have a chance!"

This was the first time she had heard anything so clearly within the Gray. But there she stood; a little girl covered in black. Her pigtails were covered with soot. Her face was full of scars. Turning to face her, she watched the oily water swell around her. This had never happened before. It was reaching for her, like hands of darkness that were not willing to give her up.

"RUN! It's coming for you; you have to RUN!" the little girl screamed.

Picking up her dress, Terra lifted her feet and pushed away from the oily depths. Each step she took, the waters seemed to follow her. It pulled her back in every direction. Then she remembered. Beside the door the rocks were whiter, maybe the depths couldn't reach it. Changing direction, Terra headed for the little gleam of hope. The little window in the distance. Along the shore she fought, going sideways against the crashing waves. She saw the fires burning harder in the distance. The lightening grew fiercer as she got closer. The little girl was following her to the door. She was running towards her. Quickly, as she got close, Terra dove for the white rocks on the edge and grabbed them with her fingertips. She felt herself scream as the little girl reached for her, pulling her into the glass sands of the shore. Slamming their backs against the door, both gasped for air just in time to watch the oily waters swell again to swallow the last of its victims.

"How can I hear you, little one?" Terra asked as she regained her breath. "Where did you come from?"

"I have always been here. The only ones who can hear each other are the ones who still have hope. The rest of them are blind. They are numb. They are just empty shells. Each day I come here to see if just one of them will hear me. Nobody ever has, not until today. I knew you would hear me."

"I have never seen the sky light up or the water swell like that. It didn't want to let me go," Terra answered.

"No, of course not," she stated dryly. "Come on, we have to get out of here before the next wave."

"Where are we going?" Terra questioned with her hand on the knob of the door. "Hey, do you know where this door leads? Has anyone ever found the key?"

"NO, silly. You are the only one that has ever noticed it besides me, of course. I have never found the key. I have been searching for years. Sometimes I just sit here and look through the window, wondering what that world feels like."

"It looks beautiful."

"Well, if we were meant for beauty, we wouldn't be here. Come on, we have to go!"

Grabbing her hand, the little girl started to drag her away, behind the door, passed the gates, passed the rocks, and passed the smoke. And so, it stood like a black cave, there was a house made entirely of rock. The rock glowed black, reflecting its surroundings. It blended into hillside like a blanket. As they stepped inside, Terra felt the ground tremble as she fell to her knees. This place was like glass. It was cold to the touch, smooth, and reflective. In the floor, she saw her reflection. Every scar was a memory that was etched on her face. Her dress was almost completely gone now. It lay in tatters around her like bandages glued to her skin. The little girl rushed past her to a carved-out portion along the edge. It was shaped like a bed, and quickly she scurried in, hiding away from the world.

"Quick, come here. You HAVE to hide," she whispered firmly.

"I'm coming!" Terra answered trying to keep her voice quiet. "Hey what should I call you, what's your name? How long have you been here?"

"Well, if you really must know. My name is Autumn. I've been here for five years, and I'm ten years old. I have seen them come and go. I have waited years for just one person that I could talk to. I just want one person to not go into the depths. Maybe you can help me, find my way out.... of this Gray."

***

Startled, Terra sat up from her position on the couch. As her pillow and blanket flew to the side, she ran to the bathroom. Holding her hair back, her whole body started heaving into the toilet all the food she hadn't ate that day. Beads of sweat glistened on her forehead as she collapsed to the floor. Holding onto the toilet she began to sob. This was the strangest thing that had every happened while she was dreaming of the Gray. How could Autumn have been there?

And that's when she remembered the events of the morning so far. She remembered why her neck was sore. She remembered why her bottom felt bruised and torn. The pain shot through every inch of her body as she leaned up against the cold bathtub. Terra's eyes closed as she began to sob uncontrollably. She couldn't control the cries anymore. Moans escaped her lips as the tears ran like rain down her face. They hit her chest as it heaved up and down from the trauma. How could she have trusted him after what he had tried to do to her, and now what he had done. Did he lie about Darren? That paper with the name on it and the key, could have been anything. But she had found his journal. What would it reveal? The pain in her heart, and in her mind was almost as strong as the pain in her body as she cried out into the air.

"Terra, I'm here," Paul gasped as he stormed into the bathroom holding a glass of water. "It's going to be ok."

"NO! NO, it's not. It's not okay. Nothing is ok anymore." She sobbed into her arm. "I didn't deserve that. I don't deserve any of this."

"I know you don't. I know it doesn't seem like it, but it will get better," he whispered as he joined her on the floor. "I promise, I will help it get better, somehow."

"It's too much. I don't know what to do anymore. I just want to give up. I just want to die. I can't take anymore. It's not worth it, Paul. It's just not worth it."

"Yes, it is, Terra. I know it is. Listen to me. I've been where you are. I mean the same things didn't happen to me, but I wanted to give up. I wanted to die. Hell, I tried to die. Believe me, it gets better," He answered as he took her into his arms. "Don't be like me," he whispered in her ear. "PLEASE...don't be like me. You are better than me. You are stronger than you think you are."

"I can't do this, I'm not strong enough. I'm so tired of fighting."

"You have to listen to me. You have a beautiful little girl to think about. Your life will get better, you just must get through this rough patch. I know it doesn't seem like it will ever end but believe me it will."

"ROUGH PATCH! I don't think this is just a rough patch! My husband died, my mother is pushy and psychotic, people are judging me for being at the crisis center and then I'm raped by my dead husband's best friend. This is more than just a patch. This is the definition of crazy! My life doesn't make sense anymore. I keep thinking it's going to get better, and it never does. Then I keep having these dreams... there's this place.... and it's always the same... but different. None of this makes any sense," she screamed through her sobs. "Where is Autumn? Is she here, or did my mother stop by and take her again?" Pushing on the side of the tub, Terra tried to pull herself up.

"Do you want me to help you up?" he asked reaching down for her.

"No, I can get up by myself." Pushing on the side of the tub again, her body shook as she finally stood. "It hurts so bad, everything hurts!" she cried. "Maybe I should call the cops.... but I can't.... because then you would get in trouble."

"I think I got to him before he finished, I think, I hope, I don't think there would be any evidence. I'm sorry, Terra." He answered trying to pull her into his arms. "Is there anything I can do to make it better, anything at all?"

"NO! Nothing is going to make it better, Paul. There is nothing you can do," she snapped as she pushed him away. "Did Sheila come and get Autumn?" Terra asked trying to pull herself together.

"Yes, your little girl came downstairs after a while. She asked who I was and I told her I was a volunteer at the crisis center. I told her you weren't feeling well, so she called your mom to come get her. Considering the circumstances... I thought you would be ok with that. I'm sorry if I was wrong."

"OK!" she stated as she tried to walk into the kitchen. Grabbing the cigarettes again she headed outside, lit one and stuck it her lips. "I hope you beat the hell out of him..." she stated to Paul as he walked up behind her. "That bastard deserves so much more than just a beating. You should have heard some of the things he said to me. It was awful."

"I can only imagine. He didn't seem right. Believe me, I haven't been that mad in a while," he stuttered. "I threw him out of here."

"Did you tell anyone what happened?"

"No, I just told her you weren't feeling well. Your mom didn't even come inside."

"She never really does. This place isn't good enough for her," Terra stuttered as she headed back inside. "I'm so tired of this place, Everywhere I look there's another crappy memory. Hopefully, I hear back from the social security office soon. I'm supposed to get some type of survivor benefits. Then maybe I can get out of here," she said more to herself than to Paul. "I have to get out of here. Maybe I need a big scary dog that hates men."

"Well, hopefully, the dog won't hate me," Paul answered from behind. "Are you allowed to even have dogs here?"

"I don't know, but I need something. What if he comes back?"

"I don't think he's going to come back. I was pretty hard on him."

"I hope you're right... how bad are the bruises? Can you see them? Because my whole body hurts. It's like a thousand knives stabbing all over my body," she gasped as she sat gently at the dining room table. "I guess you probably won't want to take me out tonight. I don't think I can be much fun right now. I can barely sit down."

"I can't see the bruises when you have clothes on. But I know where they are," he stated, taking a seat beside her. "You don't have to be fun for me to want to take you out. I know you're not going to be able to do much for a while. That doesn't matter. Maybe I can go get you something to eat. Or maybe it would do you some good to get out of here."

"Maybe..."

"Not to be rude, but you have to give me something to work with here, Terra," He answered as placed his face in his hands. "I don't want to be around if you don't want me around. I know that you are going through a lot. I know that you have been through a lot, but I'm here. I'm trying to help. My hands are busted up from knocking the shit out of that guy. Who the hell was he anyways? How did he get that close to you? Honestly, I thought the worst when I saw you bent over the bed. The last time I saw a woman in that position when I wasn't involved.... well, it was when I caught my wife cheating and honestly, I went off. Maybe I got a little angry today, but I have every right to." Slamming his fists against the table he stood up and walked into the kitchen trying to breathe. He didn't mean to be rough on her, but she needed to let him know something other than just trying to avoid being seen in public with him.

"Paul, I didn't know...you never told me what happened."

"Well, it doesn't really matter does it?" he answered walking back to the table. "Who the hell was he, Terra?"

"Well, he came in while I was asleep. He was friends with Darren. Autumn calls him Uncle Greg," she stuttered, trying to understand his anger. "I don't understand why you are so angry, Paul. I'm not like your ex-wife. I didn't want anything to do with him." Reaching her hand out to him, she tried to touch his hand, but quickly he jerked away. "Hey, I'm not like that. Obviously, I'm not. Look at me! Look at what just happened to me. How could you be so angry with me right now?"

"I'm not angry with you. I'm angry with myself. I should have never left you alone. You are vulnerable and right now you are weak. To hell with what I did, we should still call the police!"

"I'm not weak. I have never been weak. I can handle myself. I took care of my husband and my daughter for a long time. I don't need you to take care of me and I'm not calling the cops and dealing with that whole thing. The last thing we need is more drama!"

"No? Then explain today."

"What do you mean explain today? I was raped by a man who was supposed to be my friend, who stormed into my bedroom, locked the door and no matter how hard I fought against him..." she whimpered as she stared into his deep brown eyes. "What was I supposed to do?"

"Listen, I know it's not your fault. I know you're not weak, but I feel responsible, especially after how hard I beat him." Looking down, he showed her his knuckles. They were black and bloody. His hands were swollen. "I can't remember how many times I actually hit him. I got angry. I have a problem, apparently. I try so hard to be nice. I try so hard to be good and help people. It never seems to matter. I'm always the one left standing alone."

"I'm not going to leave you standing alone! That's not who I am. I care about you, and I want to be with you.... anger problems and all. You don't have to try too hard with me. I am not perfect and I don't want you to be either. The only things I want are your honesty and your patience. I'm taking it slow because I want to make sure it's right. I don't want a relationship that is just a bunch of co-dependent trash wrapped up in a nice little package. I want the real things. Hell, I thought I had the real thing, but I keep hearing more and more trash talk about Darren. I have no way to find out what is or isn't true."

"Co-dependent trash? Is that what you are afraid of?" he laughed under his breath.

"Well, yes, I guess so. I am vulnerable and in a lot of pain, but that won't stop me from being strong and independent. I don't want our relationship to be doomed before it starts. Isn't that the logical thing to do?"

"Logical, yes. Realistic, I don't know," he questioned

quietly. "Maybe if you are so tough... strong and independent, why don't you get rid of that little mouse that keeps scurrying under the stairs?"

"The mouse! It's back? I forgot all about that little thing. Why? I bet you think I can't do it, don't you?"

"I don't know, maybe you can, maybe you can't.... why don't you show me?" he scoffed.

"Fine," she answered.

Stomping into the kitchen, Terra grabbed an old coffee can and punched a couple holes in the lid and returned to sit quietly beside Paul. Quietly, they watched the little mouse for a few minutes. They watched it come out from the hall closet for a moment and then go back in. The next time it stayed a little longer. They sat there for a few minutes watching, until slowly Terra stood up and each time the mouse went back under the stairs, she would take another step forward. Holding as still as possible, Terra waited. Finally, she watched him come close enough to where she was that she tossed the coffee can on top of him. Walking over to him she grabbed the lid and scooped the little mouse up into the can. He was safely sealed in.

"Well, I guess Autumn has a new pet," Terra proclaimed happily.

"I guess so," Paul laughed as he scooped her up in his arms.

"Ouch...." she cringed. "I was trying so hard to be strong, that I completely forgot what happened."

"I'm sorry. I was trying to be careful."

"It's ok. Hey, maybe you should get me out of here. I think this place is making us both agitated," She laughed. "Just make sure that I don't look like I've been run over by a truck."

"Just take a few minutes, you can't see anything with what you're wearing. But you need to be comfortable. I'm sure you have something?" he answered as she headed to the bathroom again. "Do you want to go out somewhere public or private, like a park or a picnic...."

"I don't know, maybe both?" She answered as she peaked her head around the corner. "Why? What do you have in mind? I might need to get a cage or something for the mouse, at the very least. Maybe food?"

"Okay, well, why don't we just see what happens? It's not my usual thing, but we can give it a try."

10

As Paul pulled into the driveway, Terra glanced up at the old brick home nestled into a hidden historical part of their little town. It was beautiful. It was a gem of serenity basking in the moonlight. She saw the lilies framing the front of the house as the moonlight reflected against the river close by. She only imagined how beautiful the views were from the second-floor windows. As they stepped up to the large red front door, Terra took a deep breath. Just for a moment she closed her eyes and imagined herself having a place so quiet, so peaceful. The door was framed with two beautiful topiaries, perfectly set on either side. Glancing over at Paul, she saw his eyes fill with pride. He had a smile that she hadn't quite seen before. It was evident that he loved this place. She couldn't help but watch him glance along the yard, the flowers, and even the small quirks that such an old home was bound to have. Slowly he opened the door and waited for her to step inside. As she crossed the threshold, she was embraced with warm golden walls, dark hardwood floors and a rich burgundy oriental rug. She hadn't seen one like that in many years. It had to have come with the house. With each step, she found a new discovery. Everything seemed to glow with warmth. This place had always been loved. It wasn't one of those older homes that had been abandoned, or left to rot. It had been appreciated by its previous owner and now obviously by Paul.

Glancing down at her shoes, she felt her body begin to get a little weak. It had been a long day. So many things had happened. She had never really felt this much confusion, this much pain, this much turmoil in one day. Today should have been beautiful.

"I really love it, but I'm starting to feel tired. I really don't want to go home," Terra whispered.

"You know you don't have to go back to that apartment. I honestly wouldn't blame you if you didn't. You are more than welcome to stay here. I would love to have you with me, tonight."

Reaching for her hand, he headed towards a pair of French doors. She saw the moonlight dancing across the water as she stepped onto the brick patio. She saw the stars glistening against the night sky as she sat gently on the plush cushions of his wicker outdoor sofa. Around them she saw the twinkle of fireflies as they danced among the leaves of the weeping willow. Quietly, she watched him light a small fire in the fire pit. She adored his intensity as his hair fell into his face. Brushing it away, he grabbed a small blanket and wrapped it gently around her for the second time that day. As she leaned up against him, the only thing she felt... was safe. She couldn't help but rest against him, wishing the pain that she felt would disappear. Honestly, she wished she hadn't even woken up that day. She wished none of it had ever happened.

Terra didn't know what to think anymore. She didn't know what to feel. There was an emptiness in her heart that she had never thought she would know. Feeling his arm around her, she took a deep breath and closed her eyes. She felt hot tears starting to form as she remember how Greg had betrayed her trust. She still felt his hands gripping her, his fingers digging into her flesh as he.... well, she couldn't bear to even allow herself to think about what he had done. How much would she have to go through? How much torture could she endure?

"Sweetie..." Paul whispered, as he tickled her ears with his lips. "I know it's been a really long day. I know you're in a lot of pain. I'm here if you want to talk about it."

"I don't want to talk about it. I don't want to remember. I don't want to admit that any of this happened," she sobbed into his shoulder. "He really hurt me."

"I know he did. I just wish I would have come sooner. Maybe I could have stopped it from happening."

"I think it would have happened anyway. He said so many things. He knew that you had been there. I think he was.... he was.... following me. He was watching me."

"I should have killed him, Terra. I shouldn't have stopped beating him. I hate him for touching you like that. I hate for any man to touch you." Suddenly Paul's arm grew tense around her as he started to control his breathing. She felt him counting. She understood those deep breaths.

"You can't just kill him..."

"I wish I could..." he answered between slow long breaths. "He deserves to be punished."

"That would make you no better than him... You have

to let karma...."

"I understand that.... but I really wish I didn't. I really wish I could have been there to protect you," he answered abruptly. "I don't know, maybe we shouldn't talk about it."

"I'm the one who went through it... not you," she whispered as she gently touched his hand.

"Yeah, you were and I'm sorry for that. I should have been there to protect you."

"You keep saying that... but it was just something that was going ..... to happen. I don't think either of us could have stopped it. I really wish that wasn't true, but I have no other explanation."

"You know what, I want to let you hear something. Will you be okay for a minute?" Paul whispered quietly, wrapping the blanket tightly around her.

Without waiting for a response, he rushed inside and found his guitar. It was a long shot, but maybe something that always helped him would speak to her somehow. Taking a seat on the ground beside her, he began to play. Starting with a few simple notes he felt himself begin to play to her. With each note the stars seemed to shine a little brighter and her face began to relax. Closing her eyes, Terra leaned her head against the bench and allowed herself to listen. It was beautiful to watch him as he lightly picked at each string with his hand moving up and down the neck of the acoustic guitar. This was the first time she had watched him play, but somehow it felt familiar. She felt her thoughts begin to slow as she focused on each sound as his music echoed against the trees. In her mind, she saw the stars glow brighter with each note and on the rare occurrence that he would miss one, the stars almost seemed to twinkle. Looking down at him from her blanket cocoon she saw his eyes close as he gently rocked in time with the music he was creating. And the trees seemed to drop their leaves like confetti around him as they, too, danced in time with his rhythm. Warmth echoed through her body like his touch as she watched and listened, but like anything, it had to eventually end. Looking into her eyes he rested his instrument against his body.

"What do you think?" he asked clearing his throat.

"That was beautiful. I guess I didn't realize you played like that," she answered with a small smile. "I hope you play for me a little more often."

"I would like that. I would keep going but it's getting colder and its late. We need to get you inside."

Gently taking her hand, he led her slowly up the stairs to his bedroom. Laying her down in the soft pillows, he lifted the covers to her chin and kissed her gently on the forehead. "Listen, I know I'm not perfect. I don't really try to be. I get angry. I assume too much. I want too much. I.... I.... protect too much. But I would never hurt you. I might hurt that son of a bitch that hurt you! But I will never hurt you," he answered cuddling up next to her. "I can't even touch you now, not without hurting you."

Closing her eyes, she let herself nestle up against him. She felt the tears melt away as the scent of his rich musky cologne took over her senses. Every ache, every pain in her body shook her mind as she rested her hand on his. It had been a long time since she had slept in a bed, especially next to someone. If only the day hadn't gone the way it had, she could have made love to him. She longed to kiss him, but every inch of her body was screaming with pain. Now more than anything, Terra wished she could forget, but there was no way she could pretend that Greg hadn't touched her. She had trusted him; he was supposed to be a friend, a confidant. Terra had always thought of him like a brother. He had been there when Autumn was born. He had always been there to support them and encourage them even in the rough times when Darren was never around. Had it all been an act? But deep inside, she knew that this was something she would never understand. She could only hope, as she lay in the arms of her defender, that she wouldn't experience yet another cruel twist of fate. For the past few months, her life had been nothing short of a nightmare.

Quietly, Paul laid beside her, watching her. Terra was stronger than any woman he had ever met. She was hurt, but she wasn't angry. With everything that she had been through, he couldn't help but admire her. Silently, she nestled against him. Her breath was slow as tiny snores escaped her lips. These little noises made him smile. He couldn't help but worry. What if she got pregnant? He didn't even know if she had been on birth control. What would she do if something like that happened? It could belong to either one of them. He had tried to be cautious, but accidents could still happen. Of course, it had seemed impossible for his ex to get pregnant, so maybe it was a problem with him. He had never been checked. The thought of a pregnancy right now could be devastating to Terra.

Right now, he knew that he had to stop thinking about Patricia. The bruises on the back of Terra's neck proved that. It seemed to grow darker by the moment. She had been brave going out tonight, and he had to appreciate that about her. But what would tomorrow bring? He knew that he had already fallen for her, and even though sometimes he thought of Patricia, he knew there was no comparison. He had wanted to be loved so much by her, but this woman beside him, this fragile creature so full of strength and passion had done more for him than his ex-wife ever had.

Watching her breathe, he couldn't help but imagine what life would be like with Terra by his side. She brought out the best in him. He was less violent, more patient, and made him want to be a better man. He wanted to be a man that could take care of her. He wanted to help her through this pain, but he knew that he had to wait for her. Paul knew that at any moment she could fall apart again, just because. She needed time. She needed to know that he would be there if she really wanted him. Slowly, he pulled his arms out from under her. There was something he needed to know.

Grabbing his phone, he headed into the hallway beside the bedroom and reached for the little slip of paper that he had hidden in his pocket. There it was, her name. Could it really be that Darren had been with Patricia? Did they know each other, somehow? And even if they did, did Terra need to know? Reaching for his phone, he slowly started to dial her number, not sure of what to say or what to ask.

"Patricia?" He spoke quietly into the phone. "I need to ask you something, and please don't ask why."

"What could you possibly want, Paul? Yes, I'm sure he's not your son. Yes, I had a DNA test done. No, I don't want you around. I never really did. You were a violent, abusive, well, you were an asshole. Now.... what's your question?" she spoke sarcastically into the phone. "Oh wait, I forgot... oh, never mind."

"Well, I'm not the same man that I used to be, but my question is...."

"People don't change.... I know that all too well."

"You know what, I wasn't that bad to you, Patty. I tried to take care of you, but any man would be angry at the way you treated me. But that has nothing to do with what I was going to ask... I just wanted to know if Chris's father was..." he mumbled into the phone.

"You don't need to know anything about his father! You knew him, you practically destroyed him, and now.... well, now... he's gone and my son has nothing of his. It's like he's a ghost," she screamed loudly into the phone. He heard the baby crying in the background, heard her clanging pans in their old kitchen, and then silence.

A ghost? Hadn't Terra said those same words? Paul found himself even more confused as he turned his phone down to silent. Her rudeness didn't surprise him, but her words did. They were cryptic and incriminating in so many ways. Still, it didn't answer his question. It just made him even more suspicious that yes, these two women might have something terrible in common. A man, but not just any man, Terra's husband. Could his fall into sickness really have started with being thrown out of their home that day? Patricia's words didn't exactly confirm it, but obviously the boy's father wasn't in the picture anymore. There was just too much to contemplate.

Looking back through the doorway, Paul watched Terra try to rollover on her back. He heard her gasp as she moved, her head tilted back as she tried to move around in his bed. He saw the pain on her face. She was restless. Her arms grabbed at the blanket around her and pulled it tighter against her. Watching her, he could feel her pain.

Maybe tonight he could just hold her. Maybe she could sleep. Hopefully, she would feel better in the morning. "Paul...." Terra whimpered as she rolled over in his bed. "Where are you?"

Sitting up in bed, she tried to let her eyes adjust to the light flowing in the windows. The soft covers surrounded her as she checked the pillow beside her. She saw a small indent where his head had been, but there was no other sign of him. Everything was quiet. She was really beginning to hate quiet. Pushing the covers back, she slowly slid her legs off the bed and tried to stand. She felt the pain shooting through her body as she put pressure on her legs. She felt her muscles ache where he had hit her. Her neck was stiff, and it felt like a thousand knives in her skin as she tried to sit even on the pillow soft mattress. Slowly, she pushed herself to stand. She needed to find him. Making small steps, she headed down stairs towards the fresh scent of coffee and bacon.

Standing at the doorway to the kitchen, she watched him silently. He had a few things already prepared and sitting on the large black marble island. There were beautiful strawberries, biscuits, and a couple of cups of coffee. He looked at home cooking for her. He had a sweet smile as he swiftly lifted the bacon into a bowl and whipped together a few eggs.

"Have you poured the coffee yet?" Terra asked meekly.

"Oh my!" Paul gasped as he turned quickly to face her. His eyes wide like a child that had been caught stealing candy. "When did you wake up? Yes, let me pour you a cup. I must warn you, though, I don't have any creamers or anything like that. I normally just drink it straight black. There's just something about the strong bitterness, the purity of it that I love."

"That's ok, I prefer it black, actually," she stated as she leaned up against the counter. "Thank you for breakfast."

"You're welcome. I figured it was the least I could do."

Climbing onto the stool, she watched him finish up and hand her a white plate. Everything smelled delicious and fresh. Grabbing her phone, she sat it beside her and tried to eat the meal he had prepared for her.

"I don't think I can stay at my apartment anymore. I'm not even sure I want to visit," she whispered more to herself than to him.

"I don't really blame you..."

"I can't expect you to take care of me all of the time either. I don't really know what to do."

"You can stay here as long as you need to, Terra," Paul answered touching her gently on the hand.

"I really can't do that to you. I have a little girl to think about. I don't even know how it went when you met. I might have to go stay with my mom for a little while," she sighed. "I hate doing that, but I'm afraid Greg or someone worse will come back. I have Autumn to think of. And while I know you're here to help, I can't just depend on you. I don't want to need you like that. It could ruin everything."

"Why do you think it would ruin everything? I enjoy being here for you."

"I know, but I was talking to my therapist about co-dependency... and I really don't want that for us. I don't think it ever turns out good. It's just not healthy."

"I don't think that's where this is going..... but, considering everything the two of us have gone through... I have to respect your opinion on that," he answered as he gently squeezed her hand. "What do you want me to do?"

"Well, I want us to be careful. But otherwise, I have so much that I need to do. I don't know where to start. I don't have much money at all, not really. I don't have much to offer or sell. So, I'm probably going to have to sell a bunch of stuff and leave the apartment behind. I really need to be able to take care of us, on my own. I haven't had a job in a long time. I never had to worry about it, but I'm going to have to, now. School just started so that will help a little I guess," Terra debated.

Looking down, she felt her phone start to vibrate. Quickly, she picked it up and slid away from the counter to take the call from her mom.

"Mom?" She answered taking a deep breath.

"Hey, has Greg tried to call you? He called me and was asking if I had heard from you. He said you weren't at your apartment this morning," Sheila questioned. "Where are you?"

"I'm somewhere safe, away from him," Terra snapped. "I don't want to ever speak to him again."

"Why? He was Darren's best friend. I figured he would be the first one you turned to."

"Well, not exactly. He's not a good person," she stuttered into the phone. "I actually want to ask you something. Can me and Autumn stay with you for a little while, just until I can get back on my feet? I just don't really want to be alone in that apartment. There are just too many memories," she answered, racing through her words.

"I don't understand. Why would you need to leave your apartment?"

"I just think that's what is best for us right now.

Maybe.... maybe I should try to start over."

"Well you know I will never turn you away if that's what you really want."

"Okay.... it's settled then. I just have to get a few things from the apartment, and I will have to stay there tonight if that's ok. I know it's short notice, but I can't spend another night there."

"Um, I had plans tonight."

"Keep your plans. I'm not going to interfere with your love life. I know what I'm getting myself into. I promise you won't even know I'm there."

"If you're sure, I guess we can make it work for a little while. But you need to get everything together. I don't want you guys staying forever. I don't have time for all of that! Wait, what are you going to do with all of your stuff?"

"I'm going to sell it, almost all of it. I will keep a few things, but I'm just going to open the apartment and put everything we don't need immediately.... up for sale. I think that's the best answer to all of this. I'm tired of being haunted by the past."

Hanging up the phone, she headed back to Paul. Grabbing her coffee, he quickly refilled it and silently held the door open to the outdoor patio. Watching her abrupt movements, he knew that she was trying to be strong. She was trying to find a way to escape her issues so she could heal. Starting over could be a good thing, and as much as he wanted to swoop in and save the day, it wasn't what she needed from him. Maybe the river would help to bring her peace as it often did him. Sitting together, they watched the river boats slowly pass by. It was a quiet morning. Neither one of them really said a word for a while. They just held each other's hand. He felt her pulse begin to slow down to normal, as she sipped her coffee. Above them, the clouds seemed to caress the sky like gentle wisps against the blue.

"Terra......" Paul softly whispered. "I think I'm in love with you."

Turning towards him, she raised her hand to his face and brought her lips to his. Gently she kissed him, her body sliding closer to him, she wrapped her arms around his shoulders as his lips pressed deeper into hers.

"I adore you.... I'm.... I'm just not ready to say that," she answered as her eyes locked with his. "I can't. I'm afraid. Please don't be mad at me."

"Why would I be mad? I guess I get mad easily, but not about something like this. I understand if you need more time. Just know that I really do love you. I always have. Watching you go through this..... I have never seen anyone as strong as you.... " he answered quietly as though he were measuring every word.

Cuddling into his embrace, Terra felt her eyes begin to water. He smelled so nice. His arm was so strong around her. Paul had been so sweet to let her stay the night at his place. How could she ever repay him? Of course, he didn't seem to want anything from her, not really. How was she supposed to react.? What was she supposed to do? The warm air had a crisp feel to it that morning. It was like a peek into the coming months. Around her she saw the trees starting to change. There were just a few hints of yellow and orange hidden in the foliage around them. But in the distance, warm golds and reds were taking center stage. Fall was an amazing time where old things, old habits, and old ways of life began to die. All of it preparing for something new, fresh, and beautiful. It was strange to think that the seasons were mirroring her own life. It had only been a few short months since Darren's death in the beginning of the summer, but summer was almost gone. She felt her heart breaking in different ways every day. There was so much pain, so much mystery surrounding him now that she didn't know what to think or how to feel. At least she was finding herself. Terra hated the idea of relying on someone else to take care of her and Autumn anymore. Now they were desperate for a new place to live. She wasn't even sure what she wanted to do with her life.

"Paul......" she questioned, looking up into his fern green eyes. "I don't know what to do, not anymore."

"What do you mean, sweetie..." he asked, pushing her hair away from her face.

"I think I should go back to school, get a career.... but I also want our own place, and to not be stuck at my mother's house. And all our things... I said that I would open up the apartment and sell most of it, but I don't even know where to start," she muttered. Sitting up, she placed her hands on either side of her legs and pushed herself to her feet. Walking a few feet away, she closed her eyes and took a deep breath. "I don't even know what I would want to do. I never really thought about it. The only thing I ever wanted was to be a wife and mother."

"I don't know what to tell you, other than just take it one day at a time. I can help you get everything sold, but as far as the rest of it goes, you need to find that for yourself. Maybe you could start with a couple classes or just go down to the little career college and see what they have. Maybe try something flexible. You can't figure it all out in one day. These things take time," he answered as he placed his hand on her arm. "You can do this. Just tell me what you want to do first."

"Well, first things first. I have to get away from that apartment. Apparently, Greg went back there today looking for me. He called my mom, too," she stated pacing between the two large oak trees. "I can't be alone with him again. I don't want to see him. I can't. I just can't." She sobbed into her hands.

"Ok, you shouldn't have to. I'm surprised he came back! I wasn't exactly being gentle!"

"I KNOW! And I hate to be this way, but I want this done, NOW! I can't be alone in that place. Can you go with me, help me grab what I need, and then I don't know," she demanded as she walked away from him again. "I just need to get something done. I feel like I've waited around for too long."

"Okay, let's go! I have a truck; we can make this happen!"

11

Darkness
swallows you
like a blanket
of rebirth.
It holds you firmly
in its grip.
It waits for you to awaken
and acknowledge that
it lives within you.

Surrounded by silence, Terra opened her eyes to the Gray. The darkness of the little stone house enveloped her in its embrace. There she found herself, hidden beneath the black glass bed that an older Autumn called home, but she was nowhere to be seen. Had she imagined it? Had she imagined this older version of her daughter guiding her from the black oil waters? Remembering the guards, she curved her body against the black stone walls that had hid her from the world of the Gray. What had happened to the little girl? It seemed impossible, but another look into the girl's eyes told her a story she couldn't deny. She knew those eyes anywhere. But how could her baby be here, in this place? Wasn't this just a dream, a nightmare that mirrored her own journey or was it something more?

The silence was deafening. The darkness made her eyes ache as she looked for a trace of light and then she saw it. Not far away, she saw traces of orange and red dancing in the reflection of the rock. Slowly, she slid along the side of the rock towards it. As the light grew closer, she began to feel the warmth of the fire.

"It's ok, you can come out. They're gone," Autumn stated dryly as she placed a large flat stone on the fire. "I dug us up some food. There's not a lot here." She gestured to her little pile of leaves and water."

"What is it?" Terra asked trying to see.

"A few leaves and nuts. I grow them from a small patch I found a long time ago. I keep my plants hidden in the rocks. They make a decent meal sometimes."

Placing a mix of items on the flat stone, Autumn began pressing them together almost into a paste as they melted on the fire. Taking a flattened stick, she spread it on a few leaves and rolled it like flour. Placing it back on the rock, she sat and quietly waited.

"How long have you been here, Terra?" she asked, staring up at her with wide eyes. "It can't be long. You don't even know to hide when the guards are around."

"I don't know, it doesn't seem like I'm here all at once. I thought it was just a dream."

"Well, I hope this isn't your idea of a good dream. This place sucks. There is literally nothing."

"I saw a few things, I guess they are landmarks for me to remember. But I still don't understand why I'm here," Terra answered.

"I definitely don't have the answer to that or else I wouldn't be here," Autumn laughed.

"Sometimes, when I go to sleep I imagine myself in a nice house, with a big bed, eating eggs and bacon for breakfast that my grandmother made. I love the smell of bacon."

"How long has it been since you had food like that?"

"If I've been here for five years, I'm pretty sure it's been at least that long," she stated, rolling her eyes. "What do you expect me to say?"

"What have you learned while you have been here, are we supposed to be learning something because this place just seems like a punishment. I don't understand it at all. It's like this place is trying to tell me something."

"Maybe it's trying to tell you something. But for me it just seems like I'm waiting, always waiting. In the beginning, I just wandered around. I tried to pull those people away from the waters. I tried to find shelter from the storms. I tried to run as far as I could, but after a while, I just ended up back here. I thought I would starve, but here, in this place, you don't need food. It's nice to have though. Maybe one day I will find a way out. I don't want to forget how to eat. It feels normal to have something. I'm glad that someone can hear me. All of these people are like zombies, or maybe robots."

"So, you're saying this place is like a loop? What all is out there?" Terra questioned.

"Basically, nothing. I mean there's the factory, my house here, the water and the door. The rest of it is like a desert. So, I just have had to occupy myself. I thought about going into the waters once, like you did. But nobody ever comes out of there. I can't give up. YOU CAN NEVER GIVE UP, Terra!"

"What makes you think I was giving up?"

"You were in the middle of the waters! What else would you be doing, going for a swim? I'm sure that's not what you were doing. If I've learned anything from being here, it's that you can never give up. There's always a reason to push forward. For instance, it's been lonely here, but now, I have you."

Handing her a plate the little girl sat down against the rocks and quickly ate the little jelly roll snack. It slid down her throat like honey as she swallowed it. Nervously, Terra copied her. Sitting beside her, Autumn noticed the scars on her ankles, the cuts on her legs, and the many callouses on her hands and feet. This had to be a rough life. She couldn't believe her daughter was here, had been here for so long, completely lost and alone. Why? Was the only thing she was able to think, the only thing she asked herself. Were they trapped? Was Autumn feeling like this in the real world too?

"I want to go back to the door. I want to see if I can see anything on the other side. I've never really looked," Terra stated, standing back up to her feet.

"If you want to do that, we better hurry before the guards come back. You understand that don't you?"

"No, not really. Have they ever captured you?"

"No, but they are always looking for something, always searching. It just doesn't seem like a good idea to get caught. They don't seem to have good intentions. Come on, follow me."

WITHIN THE GRAY

Silently they retraced their steps through the Gray. The rocks seemed harder this time, the heat more stifling as they approached the black oily waters of the deep. Crouching behind the rocks, the two of them watched another band of people heading for the waters. It almost seemed routine now, like a clock. Autumn seemed to time them as they slowly disappeared. Each of them was unique. Different faces, different bodies, but still all with the same purpose, to disappear. As the last one vanished, the little girl crept forward a little farther and waited.

"As long as nothing is disrupted, the guards don't come. Just give it a minute," she whispered. "I don't understand how you haven't been caught just wondering around out here in the open."

"I guess I just got lucky."

"Luck doesn't exist here."

After a few moments, the girls headed towards the door. The window seemed a little wider than it had before, and Terra saw clearly through it. On the other side, she watched pink cherry blossoms sway in the breeze that she couldn't feel. The sunlight was a warm gold as it kissed the rich green grass. She saw soft rain drops dripping from the leaves of trees and wild lilies whispering to one another. A long path seemed to follow the tree line into the distance. Placing her hand on the window, she felt the kiss of sunlight against her skin. It was real. She knew she had to find a way to break them free from their prison. Behind her, she could see a quick flash of red as Autumn began to tug at her arm. Looking up she watched the smoke grow thicker as the waters began to crash against the shore. It was happening. A new kind of storm was brewing, one that she could have never imagined. The waters were rising quickly, the broken sands were shifting under their feet as they began to run back towards their shelter. Terra could feel the smoke pushing against her as red lightning crashed against the rocks ahead of them. Darting back and forth between them, they ran as the lightning struck again and again. The broken sands were stirring up into the air as they arrived at the rock house. Rising and falling, she watched the sands break and shift while smaller rocks broke into pieces around them. Grabbing her hand, Autumn pulled her inside beneath the black rock bed. Covering their eyes, the girls waited for the storm to pass.

***

Gasping, Terra shot up from her position on Sheila's couch. She could feel her breaths coming in short bursts. Wiping her hand across her forehead, she could feel the beads of sweat that had risen to the surface. Another dream? She couldn't help but wonder if they would ever stop! How many had there been? Terra couldn't even remember anymore. All of those people, lost within the Gray. That place was one crazy nightmare that she kept visiting. It was unbelievable that she was seeing Autumn so much older, and it was her little girl. There was so much determination, the kind that only came from being like her mother. She acted the same way she had at ten years old. She had tried to think about it and understand that place before, but now it seemed urgent. The storm had been terrifying. It had been like nothing she had ever seen or heard of. She still felt the heat, the wind the swirling glass sands had felt like a thousand knives against her skin. She was still trying to catch her breath, and yet it had been her daughter trying to protect her, leading her to safety. The red lightening had seemed more like fingers of fire that were aiming straight for her than any kind of natural element that she had ever experienced. It all seemed so unnatural.

Looking around at the oak table beside her, she reached for a bottle of water, but it had disappeared. It was just like her mother to never leave anything alone. Running into the kitchen, she grabbed another bottle and headed back to her bed for the night. She hated sleeping on the couch, but they still had to wait on a new air mattress. She hadn't given Sheila any time to prepare, after all. The last thing she wanted was to keep Autumn awake because of her insomnia. Terra had been having so many nightmares that a restful night had quickly become a thing of the past. Glancing around the room, she remembered what she had stuffed in the bottom of her suitcase. It was Darren's journal. Until that moment, she had forgotten. Reaching for the dark brown leather book, she took a deep breath and opened it.

January 1st

Dear Journal, I don't know why I bought this thing, but I wanted to make a New Year's resolution that might help me with this. I feel bad all the time now. My chest hurts a lot sometimes, but I keep pushing through. I'm supposed to be okay. I guess I work too much, but when I see Terra, I wish I could give her the world. But then when she talks to me about her day and Autumn starting school... I get so mad. Sometimes I love her so much that I hate her. I hate that she is free to do whatever she wants. I hate that I can't give her everything. It doesn't seem to matter how hard I work; I never seem to have enough. It's not her fault. She doesn't know. I never tell her anything. She doesn't know about the women at work, constantly teasing me. We have this customer that keeps coming in to have her oil changed. I swear she just had it changed, but she keeps coming back. She always asks for me. Patricia, that's her name. She just saunters in like she owns the place. She can't keep her hands to herself and here I am acting stupid, not wanting to touch her back. I don't want to smile, but I do. It's such a thrill when she comes in. I swear it's about once a week and then I feel so guilty when I see Terra. She always wants me to be with her, make love to her. I think she wants another baby, but I can't afford it. I don't even want another child, not when I barely see the one I have. My beautiful wife. I love her so much, but when I get home, I just want to sleep. It's just not the same anymore. I only see her for a couple of hours at night. In the mornings, I'm wondering if I'm going to see that woman again. I'm a faithful man, but she is tempting. Patricia is very tempting. Heaven help me. I don't know what to do. Between that woman, and the guys bringing in their special brownies and energy drinks to get us through, I don't feel like I'm the same person anymore.

I better go, she's coming.... no doubt she needs attention. The kind of attention that I'm too tired to give her. It just makes me hate myself when I can't even make love to my wife. I guess I'm supposed to sign here; it is a bit of a letter to this journal, to myself, I don't really know. I just hope this helps me clear my head. I'm so confused.

-Darren

Slamming the book down beside her, Terra grabbed the cigarettes and headed outside. It was such a nasty habit, but she needed something to calm her down. Who was Patricia? She sounded like a bit of a home wrecker. What did it even mean? It sounded like he hadn't wanted anything to do with her anymore. She could feel her heart breaking. He had said that he hated her? She had never mentioned wanting another baby. The thought had never crossed her mind. But now it did. What would he have done if she had gotten pregnant on one of the rare occasions that they were together? It hadn't exactly sounded like he would have been supportive. Lighting a second cigarette, she began to pace the length of the driveway. Her hands shook as she brought it to her mouth. At that moment, she hated herself. She hated the way her mouth tasted, hated that she had tried so hard with Darren and hated that she missed him so much, especially considering he had never been around. Maybe Patricia was the reason for that. Who knows what the rest of the journal would reveal. That was just the first entry.

Heading back to the door of her mother's house, Terra took another deep breath and headed inside. There was no way she was going to be able to sleep. Grabbing the remote, she started flipping through the channels. As always, there was nothing on. Finally, she settled on a documentary and sat back with her bottled water and tried to forget what she had read, but it was impossible. She couldn't get the woman out of her mind. She couldn't stop imagining her talking to her husband. She could remember the smile he would get when she had first started dating him. It had been warm, charming, and breathtaking for her. Had this woman felt the same way? Is that why she had kept coming back? Stretching her legs out on the couch, Terra tried to lay down again and think about anything but him. It was too much to process. It didn't take long for Terra to grab the journal again. It was like a train wreck; she couldn't stop looking. She had so many questions that needed to be answered.

January 15th

Patricia came back today. This time she brought me a cup of coffee. She was here waiting on me when I got here. At least I wasn't covered in grease this time. We sat down outside on the bench and talked for a little while. It felt so nice when she put her hand on my leg. She just rested it there. I barely noticed that it was there. She kept talking about how her husband is gone all the time. He was always working is what she said. I don't know, but it seemed friendly to me, like she just needed someone to talk to. I know how that feels. I don't have anyone to talk to. How am I supposed to tell the guys that I never touch my wife anymore? How could I tell them that I'm not interested in sex? Isn't that what makes a man, a man? It was nice that she brought me coffee first thing in the morning. I wish I knew what she wanted from me. Greg keeps asking me about Terra. I don't know what to think. He's been like a brother to me for so long, maybe he could fill in for me. He keeps talking about stopping to check on her. He says that I need to look after my wife. Isn't that what I'm doing? I'm making sure she has a place to live, food on the table, and nice clothes. What else would she possibly want? What does he want? I don't even know why I'm asking that. I don't even know what I want, anymore.

-Darren

January 21st

Me and Greg got into it hard today. He made me so mad asking about Terra! Why does he keep asking about HER! I told him about last night. I was so tired, I had slept most of the day, but here comes Terra in some slinky little night gown thing. She looked sexy as hell, but I didn't really care. I thought it was funny. I told her no and fell asleep. She keeps trying. When will she figure out that I'm just not able to have sex anymore? It's not that I don't want her. It's that I just can't. I can't do it when I'm exhausted, full of so much caffeine that it's making me sick. Greg got mad when I told him about it! I told him that if he wanted her, he could have her because I can't do it anymore! I can't handle seeing her tears when she says she misses me! I adore her, but she's driving me crazy. It's so much stress, when all I want to do is quit working and sleep for a week. Maybe then I could make love to her. The way I see it, if Greg wants her, then maybe he should have her. That would be a lot less for me to worry about. He's lonely, and she's lonely. It makes me mad. I can't stand the thought of them being together, but maybe if they didn't tell me it would be okay. Then I would be free to spend extra time with Patricia. I haven't seen her in a few days.

She should be back around soon.

-Darren

January 22nd

I was right! She came back today, this time she was wearing cut off shorts and a little tank top. Her legs were so sexy and long I couldn't help but imagine them wrapped around me. For the first time in a long time, I felt excited. Patricia just kept talking about her husband never being around. It made me feel guilty for never being around Terra, so during my lunch break I went home just long enough to make love to her. It was so good, but every time I tried to focus on her, I thought of Patricia's long legs wrapped around me, pulling me into her. I love how she takes the extra time to really listen to me. It's nice. I hope she starts coming more often and without me having to change her oil again. I could use a cup of coffee every morning. I could get used to that kind of service!

-Darren

Throwing the book to the side, Terra began to sob. There was so much more to read. How could she possibly finish it, but at least now she was starting to learn the truth. She could remember the day he came home in the middle of the day. He had been attentive, passionate and even more tinder than he had been in years. She could still remember his gentle touch, the way he had kissed her neck, and the sweet way he had made love to her. It had been just like their first time. She had cherished that memory; it had been one of the last times they had been together. It could have even been THE last time they had made love. It was so long ago that she couldn't be sure. That was around the time Greg had started to come around more too, had he really meant for him to "TAKE CARE OF HER" like she was some sort of animal that needed to be fed? Terra couldn't believe what she had read, so she read it again and again, until finally, she fell asleep with the leather book in her hand.

***

Sitting back against his sofa, Paul grabbed his laptop and logged into social media. Maybe if he searched through Patricia's list of friends, he would see a familiar face. He thought he knew most of her friends, but there might be something there. He needed to know why her name was on that little slip of paper in Terra's bedroom. Thumbing through it, he saw so many names that he hadn't seen before. There were a lot of new guys on there. Switching to her newsfeed, he started scanning through her posts. Unfortunately, he had never been much for social media, so he had a lot to catch up on. There were so many pictures of her and her baby that it brought tears to his eyes. He had wanted a baby so badly. But it wasn't the thought of her with a baby, any baby pictures seemed to do that to him.

He wanted to have a part of himself out there in the world, something that he had helped create. Paul had always adored children and babies. He had always imagined having at least one of his own. For years, he had imagined what it would be like. He wanted sleepless nights, school projects, and all the challenges that came with parenting. A child would have been a blessing, but he was glad that he hadn't had one with her. At least now he had the chance to find someone who loved him in return. He had always wanted to have a family full of love, support, and encouragement. He had never experienced that for himself and had often found himself getting jealous of those who still had parents.

After scrolling for what seemed like hours, he saw something different. Right there in black and white was a post about losing a friend to a heart attack. She stated that she hadn't known him long but that they had grown close. She didn't know anything about his family, but they were in her prayers. Closing the laptop, Paul closed his eyes. He knew that it wasn't definite, but it was quite a coincidence. Living in a small town was strange. It made it harder to know for sure if his suspicions were true. He needed to know for sure if he had hurt the man that Terra loved. It hurt to imagine that in some way he could have caused her so much pain. He had always had a problem with anger. He had always been protective. But had he hurt the woman of his dreams by throwing that man out of his house that day? Patricia never had known how to mind her own business. She was always befriending guys wherever she went. She had been convinced that if you wanted good service, good food, or a discount, you had to get to know people. Unfortunately for him, that generally had meant a lot of flirting and her leaving her wedding ring in the car. He had grown to accept it and had never known what she was capable of until it was too late.

It was hard not to obsess over the situation. It was hard to not be angry with himself. After all, Paul really didn't know anything. He knew he was making assumptions. It wasn't for him to know. This was becoming dangerous for him. He had checked Darren's obituary, had visited where he had worked, searched public records, and had even tried to pay attention to the pictures that they packed away during Terra's move to her mother's. He had even considered going through her storage unit for more clues. He knew he was in dangerous territory. Why destroy the memory of the man that Terra mourned? There was only one more thing that he could do before he let it rest. He had to visit Patricia and see what she knew about him. Maybe she would say something that would tell him. He wasn't the best at telling if she was lying, but it was the only thing he had left.

Walking to the refrigerator, Paul grabbed something to drink and sat down again. He couldn't take his eyes off the screen and her post about Darren. She had never mentioned anything to him about losing a friend. Patricia would have used that to get attention. She had always seemed to want to make everything about her and loved to be the center of attention. He had always found it to be ridiculous because no matter what he did for her, it never seemed to be enough. He hated himself for trying to figure out if she had been Darren's mistress. It could have happened easily. She knew how to be friendly and had a knack for knowing when the right moment was to conquer her prey. Most men couldn't resist her charms.

Frustrated, he closed the laptop and folded his hands in front of him. He needed a plan. He needed to focus on what he really wanted and that wasn't a trip through the past. No, what he wanted was a family, even if it was one that was already made. Putting his head down, he took a deep breath. He knew what he needed to do. Terra needed space, but that didn't mean that he had to go away completely. Any good relationship is a journey, sometimes a long one. He knew it would be worth the time to get to know her better. The possibility of being a part of her life was exhilarating. She was a strong woman, and he knew that together they could really experience life. He wanted to go out and have fun even more than she did. Paul had forgotten how to be spontaneous, but he wanted to learn again. It was time to stop focusing on the past and start living the life he needed to live. As much as he was obsessing, he knew it wasn't healthy. He just had to find a way to stop and focus on the things that made him happy.

12

Grabbing the keys from the mantle, Paul headed for his truck. Going for a quick drive might do him some good. He loved to drive around town. It was always interesting to see how many lights were still on in the middle of the night. Sometimes he would sit at the park and watch to see if anyone was walking at night. It was never the same people, but it was clear that a lot of people in their little town were insomniacs. Tonight, however, the park was empty. The little park was covered in leaves now and was full and vibrant with color glowing in the moonlight. It would be a great night to go for a walk with Terra. He imagined her eyes sparkling in the light. Driving towards her house, he silently hoped that she would be outside, but hated what that meant. It was her first night there, and he had a feeling she wasn't sleeping well.

They had spent the day gathering her clothes and the things that they needed and taking them to her mother's or the storage unit. The rest she was planning to sell at an indoor yard sale. She had moved quickly. It had surprised him how fast she grabbed things and got out of that apartment. There was probably more being left behind than there needed to be. But she obviously wanted to get away from all of it. After all, who was he to argue? He had done something similar when he had sold his old house back to Patricia for next to nothing. He had started over, and it had been one of the best things he had ever done. After that, he hadn't felt tied down to her anymore. It had given the memories a chance to fade into the corners of his mind. Before that, they had taken center stage. The only thing that he had been able to think about was when he caught her with another man. While it had left a permanent scar on his heart, it didn't control his thoughts anymore. He thought a lot about the future now. It was a relief to be able to go for a midnight drive, go for a walk, and anything else he felt like doing without an explanation. Freedom was a beautiful thing.

Paul loved doing volunteer work. That was something he hadn't known about himself before leaving Patricia. He had learned so much about himself. He no longer surrounded himself with colors he didn't like. He no longer did things that he didn't enjoy and finally he was able to cook the foods he loved without her asking him to pick up fast food on the way home from work. He had planned on taking a weekend away soon, but he hadn't decided where to go. The idea of taking a drive, heading east and just going until he found a place to stop seemed like fun. After all, wouldn't it be interesting to just explore without the pressure of a deadline or a destination?

Turning down the street towards where Terra was staying, he couldn't decide if he wanted her to be asleep or awake. But then he saw her, sitting alone on the little wrought-iron bench. Her hair was pulled back in a ponytail, and she was sitting with her head in her hands. The lamp post behind cast a warm glow as she slowly rocked back and forth. The bushes behind her framed her like a portrait of beautiful pain. Pulling up in front of the house, he waited for her to look up. Standing up, she crossed her arms in front of her chest and began walking towards the door of the soft yellow house. She hadn't looked up. Swiftly, he parked the truck and headed for her.

"Hey, Terra... are you having trouble sleeping?" he asked quietly as he approached her.

"What are you doing here?" she asked, turning quickly.

"I couldn't sleep, so I went for a drive and saw you outside. I was wondering if you might want to join me?"

"I guess I could, but I'm not dressed," she stated, gesturing to her green satin gown. "How did you end up clear out here? It's a little out of the way. I think you might be spying on me," she giggled.

"I had a feeling that your night might have been going about the same as mine," Paul answered. Taking her hand, he kissed it gently. "Would you care to join me for a stroll in the moonlight? Just as you are, nobody is out tonight."

"I normally don't do that, but I might be able to make an exception. Let me go grab my purse." Walking inside, she grabbed Darren's journal and hid it under the cushion of the couch. Taking a quick glance around the room, she quietly turned off the television and headed back out to Paul.

The park was beautiful. The soft moonlight cast shadows on the ground like an abstract painting among the fallen leaves. The crisp air caressed her skin in the darkness. The birds were silent in the shadows, waiting for the first light of the morning. The usually bustling park was empty as the trees danced through the night breeze. The fountain had always been her favorite landmark with its marbled floor and concrete pillars. At night it was lit from within and glowed against the sky. The water hadn't run in it for years, but like her, it was a little broken.

Walking up behind her, Paul gently moved her hair to the side. She felt her body shiver as his hand gently caressed the back of her neck. Brushing her hair away from her neck, he leaned towards her and caressed her neck with his lips. Reaching down, Terra grabbed his arms and wrapped them around her waist. Nestled against him, she closed her eyes as his kisses continued down the soft curve of her neck. Taking her hands, she ran them up his arms, caressing his hands with her thumbs as they travelled up the front of her body while he kissed her from behind. Terra's body tingled with every touch as his lips pressed against her. Her blood rushed to her heart as she was engulfed with flames from his lips. Her breath caught in her throat while she leaned back, her body falling against him. Wrapping his arms tighter around her, he braced her against his body, squeezing her as a gasp escaped her parted lips. She wanted him closer, so much closer.

"Turn around, so I can kiss you," he whispered, nibbling on her ear.

Turning to face him, she wrapped her arms around his neck and pulled him into her embrace. Grabbing his lips with hers, she leaned against him. Her fingers grasped at his hair as she pulled his face towards her. Holding him tightly, she allowed her hands to explore his face as he moaned against her lips. His arms quickly grasped her messy hair and pulling her neck back, he began to trace the soft curve of her throat. His kisses were like a gentle embrace against her skin as her head fell into his hand. Still, he continued up her neck to her cheek and forehead as she struggled to catch her breath, wanting his lips against hers. Finally, he covered her mouth with his until she arched against him, pulling his face to hers while Terra's fingers brushed the side of his cheek.

"We're in public, Paul. We need to slow down... " she moaned between kisses.

"Well, then, let's get out of here."

"I want to so badly, so badly... but where would we go"

"There's always my place. It's only a couple blocks from here."

"Do you think it's a good idea?" she asked, brushing the hair from his eyes.

"I don't know, but at least we would be alone. I don't want to stop kissing you," he answered as his lips continued from her throat to her ear. "I just want your kisses, to feel you against me."

"Let's go...I just want to be with you," she whispered. "I'm just afraid..."

"That's all I want from you too. There's nothing to be afraid of, sweetie. I'm not going to let anything else bad ever happen to you. If you hurt, I hurt, remember that. I could never hurt you. I want to show you what it's like to be loved, without question. I want you to know that."

Swiftly, he lifted Terra into his arms and carried her back to the truck as his lips continued to caress hers. As they made their way inside his home, he held her tightly against him, cradling her in his arms with his lips occasionally caressing her forehead. Her green satin gown blended with the softness of her skin as she wrapped her arms his neck. His touch warm, his hands gentle as he held her safely against him. Closing her eyes, Terra tried to let go, allowing herself to feel his breath against her skin as he gently took her upstairs, laying her in bed. Opening her eyes, her body stiffened as he crawled in beside her and placed his arm around her. The last man that had touched her in bed hadn't been so gentle. *Paul said he just wants to be with me, will that change, will he expect me to...* Terra panicked as he got closer to her.

"I'm not going to hurt you, Terra," Paul answered her silent question. "Don't forget who you are with. I'm not him. You can trust me."

"I know, I'm sorry. I don't want you to think I don't trust you. I do! I just can't stop myself from reacting this way," she sobbed, trying to keep the tears from flowing.

"Shhh... Shhh... It's okay. Let me show you," he whispered in her ear with a gentle kiss.

Moving his body closer to Terra, Paul lay quietly on his side and propped himself up with his elbow. Watching her reactions closely, he allowed his fingers to barely move her hair from her cheek. As she closed her eyes, she felt his fingers travel across her forehead in a gentle massage. She barely felt his touch as he caressed her. Slowly, it got firmer as he explored her face and wiped away the tears that had escaped. In time, her breathing slowed again and she opened her eyes to see his smile.

"I told you, you can trust me."

"I know, Paul, I'm sorry," she stuttered as another tear escaped her eyes.

"It's okay to cry, I just hope this isn't a sad tear. I want to make you happy," he answered kissing it away.

"You do make me happy, it's just hard sometimes."

"It will get easier. I will make it easier. It just takes time."

As they lay together on his bed, he rolled even closer, letting his arm wrap around Terra, pulling her close. Reaching up, he cupped her face in his hands and felt her body push up against him. She felt so beautiful against him, warm, inviting. Slowly, he closed his eyes and let his lips touch hers, softly, like a whisper. As their lips met again, he felt the tingle of her lips against his, so soft, full, and tender. Tears filled his eyes as he kissed hers, returning the tenderness. As he pulled away, he touched his nose to hers and with a smile he caressed her face with his. She felt his breath against hers, as his cheeks caressed hers and their foreheads met. Looking longingly into her eyes, he held her tightly, lovingly as he grabbed her hand and caressed each of her fingers.

"There are many ways to make love, Terra. Sometimes, just the touch of your hand can be just as intimate, just as important, if you allow yourself to feel it."

"Is that why I feel like this? I can barely catch my breath."

"Yes, I'm trying to make love to you, but I don't want to hurt you. Your body isn't ready, but your hands, your lips, and your heart... they are ready. Words can be cheap, but this, it's not," Paul whispered, his fingers caressing her cheek. "It's been a really long time since I felt anything so tender, so sincere. Terra, you are absolutely breathtaking. I could kiss you all day."

Cuddled up against him, she felt herself drift away, allowing herself to surrender to his touch. Each caress of his fingers across her lips felt warm with a tenderness she had never experienced. His breath was heavy as he held her closely, pulling her to him. Butterflies filled her stomach as she gasped with every touch, each caress filled with electricity. Looking into his eyes, she felt intensely overwhelmed with passion. It was a fire that started deep within her and travelled up her body, taking her breath. Her eyelids collapsed as warmth overtook her and her heart quickened, ready to explode.

Resting her head against his chest, she rolled to her side and allowed his arms to wrap around her. His hands ran down her back to the bottom of her satin gown. Pushing it to the side his hands climbed beneath her gown as he explored her back his hands embracing her bare skin. Little moans escaped her lips as Paul covered her face with kisses until her body melted further into his. She felt like putty in his hands. She knew he could have done anything to her in that moment. Terra wanted to surrender to Paul, to submit in every way. She wanted to pull him into her body, closer with every moan his touch caused.

Yet, he didn't climb on top of her. Instead, his kisses continued, his touch firmly grasped her, pulling her closely, intimately without entering her. As passion overwhelmed him, he resisted the urge to make her his, instead he only explored her. His heart ready to explode, he collapsed on the bed, feeling his body respond to her touch, her skin, and the taste of her lips. Tears began to swell in his eyes as he experienced her intensity. This wasn't the first time he had tried to make love to a woman with just a kiss, but it was the first time one had responded so lovingly. Paul thought his theory was an impossibility to experience, but this moment was an intense reality he had only dreamed of. He wanted nothing more than to be inside her. But for him, it was too important to rest in that moment, to protect her, nurture her.

Trying to catch her breath, Terra laid her head against his chest, gently caressing the small patch of hair nestled there. As her mind raced, she tried to relax, to hope. Maybe she could finally rest peacefully. She relaxed against him. Eventually, her breath slowed, and she fell asleep in Paul's arms. Holding her close, he gently kissed her forehead. He still felt her heart racing against his chest. Her red hair fanned out wildly against the pillow. Taking a deep breath, he kissed her again and tucked the blanket around her.

For a while, they just laid there quietly, wrapped up in each other's arms, his hands gently rubbing her back helping her rest. Slowly, the sun began to peek through the curtains, and her eyes began to open, and together they silently watched the first peak of sunlight break through the horizon. He heard her sniffles, as the birds begin to sing outside through the small crack that he always left for fresh air. His breath warm against her neck, she knew it was a new day. *Things can be different.*

"I better get you home, Terra."

"I'm a grown woman, it will be ok," she giggled, rolling to face him.

"Maybe so, but they might think you were kidnapped or something."

"Who on earth would kidnap me?"

"Me, definitely without a doubt, me. As a matter of fact, I might not let you go at all."

"Hmmm... you think so, huh?"

Leaning towards her, he snatched her lips with his and pressed his body against her. Instantly, her hands wrapped around him and pushed him closer, her lips reaching for his as his kisses trailed down her body.

"Yes, I definitely think so. I probably wouldn't kidnap you if I didn't love the way you reach for me when I kiss you," Paul teased.

"Well, that's not fair."

"What's not fair about it, exactly?"

"You make me want to just lay here in bed with you all day, and wait for you to take me," she joked, pulling him in for another kiss.

"Believe me, I want to be inside of you very, very badly... but you're not ready."

"Don't I get to decide when I'm ready?"

"Not this time, you don't. You are too important to me to risk hurting you."

"Do you have a piece of paper? I feel a little bit inspired. I have to write this down!"

"Um, okay, that's a little random and weird," he laughed. "I know how that is, though. I do the same thing with music sometimes," he answered grabbing a notebook from the desk.

The Kiss

As coarseness captures silk
a moanful bliss escapes
the pout of crimson flesh.

Pulse flooded palms
reach within tender eloquence.

As your breath ignites
vein trails within.

A lavender clutched spine, dissolves-
in surrender to the passion
Without.

For a little while longer they cuddled and joked in bed. It felt nice for them to laugh again, to feel safe, even if for only a few moments. But they knew eventually she should return to her mother's house, so after a few breakfast sandwiches, they sat in front of Sheila's house. Silently, they stared at her mother's red door... waiting.

"Paul... that was beautiful. I didn't know it could be like that. You were so gentle and loving without expecting us to... have sex," Terra whispered as she refused to move from the truck.

"Holding you felt amazing, I'm glad I could show you what it's supposed to be like. You shouldn't be hurt the way you have been. It's important to me for you to know how it feels to be... cared for. I care... a lot."

"I know you care. I never knew something so simple could feel so beautiful," she smiled, caressing the back of his hand. "It's almost confusing. It was so much deeper than if we had..." she mumbled, afraid to look into his eyes. "Would you like to come inside... I think you have met Autumn and Sheila before, though, haven't you?"

"Yes and no, it was brief. And everything that was going on that day, I don't really remember anything."

"Well, come in. I'm sure they are already up, trying to figure out where I've been. I will get you a cup of coffee," she answered climbing out of the truck. "I wouldn't stay too long, though. I'm sure they are going to have plenty of questions. Maybe in a couple days I could make you dinner?"

"I would LOVE that. Of course, I would probably enjoy it more if we did it together," he smiled as they headed inside.

"That's right, I keep forgetting that you enjoy cooking." As she turned on the coffee pot, Terra grabbed two cups and gestured for him to take a seat at the little table in the corner. "Autumn should be up soon. I think I might have to take over her bed for a little while this afternoon," she sighed. "I have so much to get done today, though. I might have to stay up to make sure I sleep tonight. There's just so much to think about."

"I know what you mean. There's nothing like coffee in the morning to break up the magic of the night."

"Reality is harsh."

Taking a seat beside him, Terra watched Paul sip his coffee. His eyes were red and swollen but his hands were firm and steady as he gripped his cup. She couldn't help but smile into her cup as she watched him. She remembered the first time Sheila had seen him at the crisis center. She had said he was handsome and had suggested in her own way that she should seduce him. Of course, at that point they had already been talking. It was ironic that now the same man was sitting at her breakfast table, waiting to meet her. After all, could she dare to hope that this man would be in her future? The idea of growing old with someone seemed impossible since Darren had died. She wasn't sure about anything anymore. Reading his journal had only made it harder to believe in the concept. But THIS man was different. She found a strange beauty in a man who accepted her and her pain.

Shuffling her feet around the corner, Autumn took a seat beside Terra and leaned up against her. Looking up from her slippers, her eyes met Paul's as he took another sip of coffee.

"Hey, I remember you! You were there when Greg visited me last week at the apartment. Who are you anyways?" Autumn interrogated.

"I'm Paul. I'm a friend of your mother's, we met at the center."

"Why are you here so early?"

"Hmmm.... well, your mom and I went for an early morning walk together down at the park," he answered smiling.

"That's weird! Mommy never goes for walks, especially not this early! She hates mornings!" she answered swiftly.

"She seemed to enjoy it this time. Maybe it's something new, little lady."

"You can ask him all the questions you want after you

eat your breakfast, sweet pea," Terra answered as she got up to grab a bowl from the cabinet. "Will it be cinnamon squares or sugar flakes?"

"Sugar flakes, definitely!" she answered, forgetting about her game of fifty questions.

Once again, the table grew silent as they watched her eat her cereal. She ate quickly as she stared at Paul. Her eyes squinting, she gulped her milk down and took her dishes to the sink. As she took her seat, she rested her chin in her hands and glared up at him with purpose.

"So, what are your intentions with her?" she asked blankly. "You know, she just ran another man off, and then Daddy's friend, Greg, left, too. So, what makes you think you can stick around?"

"WOW! Autumn that's a bit much, don't you think?" Terra asked, almost choking on her coffee. "That's not quite what happened, little girl. Those are some harsh questions for a man you just met!"

"No... they're not. They are real questions that I want to know the answers to. I want to know why he is hanging around you."

"Well, I understand that you want to know, but you still need to be polite, young lady," she scolded her softly. "Maybe those aren't the questions you need answers to just yet. He said that he was a friend, and he is. I think you need to understand what really happened to Daddy and Uncle Greg before you start an interrogation on Paul."

"It's ok, sweetie. I don't mind answering her questions," Paul spoke up. "If you must know, I really like your mom and I'm not going anywhere. I'm a different kind of guy and she's special to me. I just want to be a friend and make her happy. Isn't that a good thing?"

"Well, yes, I guess so. That's all I wanted to know. It's not a big deal," Autumn answered as she stared into her hands.

"No, it's not a big deal, but you need to watch how you speak to people," Terra replied. "I wonder when Mom is going to join us. I think we are on a roll, already." She laughed nervously.

Once again, they heard shuffling footsteps coming from down the hall. These steps were slower as Sheila stumbled towards the breakfast table. Walking past the trio, she silently grabbed a cup and poured herself a cup of coffee and began piling on sugar and cream as everyone watched. Sitting the cup down, she adjusted her gown and plopped down beside Autumn at the table.

"Who the hell are you visiting my girls so early?" Sheila scoffed as she met his gaze.

"I'm Paul, we just went for a walk. I was dropping her back off."

"Well, if you just went for a walk, why did you have to drop her off? That seems kind of weird."

"Not really, I drove her down to the park."

"IF you say so..." she cooed into her coffee. "It doesn't really matter anyway. It's just odd that she's bringing you home so soon."

"I had probably better go and check in at the office. It's been a while. Thanks for the coffee, Terra. I'm going to leave you ladies to enjoy your morning. It was nice to meet you both again," Paul answered, as he stood to leave. "I hope to see you soon," He whispered gently as he placed a kiss on her forehead.

"Come back this afternoon... please..." Terra asked, as she caught his hand before walking away. "I'm sure Mom will be much nicer in a little bit."

"I will check on you in just a little bit if that's what you want."

Raising her eyebrows, Sheila sipped her coffee quietly as her eyes followed him out the door. Shaking her head, she glared at her daughter who sat quietly avoiding her gaze. She saw the frustration in her face as she sat there, staring. Unlike Autumn, Sheila had the ability to interrogate someone without ever asking a single question. Letting out a small sigh, Sheila placed her hand against the table and started tapping her nails against the wood on the table. Tap, tap, tap, tap.... the sound of her nails echoed across the room as she stared at her daughter. Looking away, Terra attempted to focus on her daughter as Sheila continued to tap her nails against the table. Tap, tap, tap, tap.... she continued. Without blinking, her mother raised her eyebrows again and glared harder into her eyes. She wasn't giving up that easily. Eventually, Sheila knew that she would meet her gaze. Tap, tap, tap, tap, tap, tap, her nails grew louder.

"UGH!!!" Terra exclaimed. "Why do you have to do THAT?"

"Do what, my dear? I didn't do anything," she answered with an evil smile.

"Oh, you know WHAT!"

"Well, since you're talking, who exactly was this FRIEND of yours?"

"Like he said, he's just a friend, anything beyond that is none of your business."

"I think it's my business when there's a strange man sitting at my breakfast table," she quipped as she got up for another cup of coffee. "And why are you not talking to

Greg? Like I said, he should have been your first choice."

"MOM! He's not my first choice. I never want to see him again. He's not a good man, MOTHER! You have to stop thinking you know what is best for me!"

"How is he not a good man? He was there for you when Darren died. He was always around when he was at work. You guys have always been close!"

"What? My Daddy died? Grandma! You said he ran away, you lied to me," Autumn interrupted with a scream. "Why would you lie to me? Mommy was right! I know what it means to die. Remember my goldfish died? You don't need to tell me stories. I'm a big girl," she continued as she hit the table with her little fists. "Well, are you going to answer me?"

"I'm, I'm, I'm sorry, Autumn. I just thought it would be easier if you thought your Daddy had run away," Sheila gasped nervously. "I wasn't trying to lie to you. I just wanted to protect you."

"And what about Uncle Greg, what really happened there? Why did he run away, Mom?"

"Well, he did something bad to me. He hurt me. My new friend, Paul, caught him hurting Mommy and asked him to leave," Terra answered. "I'm sorry that your Daddy is gone, baby girl. You have every right to be angry. I tried to tell you what happened." Kneeling beside her little girl, she wrapped her arms around the sobbing child and pulled her close. "It's going to be okay. I promise."

"I miss my Daddy...." she sobbed.

"I know you do, baby. I miss him too."

Picking Autumn up in her arms, Terra carried her into the living room and cradled her into her arms. Holding her tightly against her, she felt her own tears beginning to burn in her eyes as she rocked her little girl back and forth. She felt her chest rise and fall as she struggled to breathe through the tears. She had been so brave. This was the first time she had seen Autumn ask any real questions about Darren. It had to be difficult to lose your father before you even started school. He had really looked forward to her first day of Kindergarten and it was coming up soon. *If Sheila thought it would be easier for Autumn to think her father had disappeared, what really happened to mine?*

Brushing her hair out of her face Terra tried to wipe the tears away as Autumn continued to sob. Her whole body shook from the tears. Her breaths slowly started to deepen as she cried in her mother's arms. She was finally letting it out. Watching from the corner of the room, Terra saw Sheila's face grow pale. The older woman's eyes began to glisten as she watched her granddaughter moan in despair. The sound escaped Autumn's lips in gasps and whimpers as Terra cuddled up with her. Grabbing the tissues from the bathroom, Sheila handed them to Terra and sat beside them and placed a hand on Autumn's leg. Gently, she rubbed back and forth to console the child. It wasn't enough. Soon Autumn's tears grew louder, her breaths became sharper. There didn't seem to be anything they could do.

"Do you want me to get your teddy for you?" Sheila asked quietly. "He always makes you feel better."

"No, Grandma. I want my Daddy, and I don't want you to lie to me anymore," Autumn barked.

"You made me think it was all my mommy's fault and it's not," she stated as she kicked at Sheila. "How could you lie to me, Grandma. I thought Daddy was going to come see me soon," she screamed as she pulled Terra's arms tighter around her. "I'm never going to see him again. He won't be there when I sing at school. He won't see my drawing that I did in class. He won't get to meet my friends. He won't see my pictures of my first day of school. He won't see any of it. All my friends' daddies just live in a different house, but mine.... I guess he doesn't exist anymore. I don't have a daddy."

"Oh, Autumn, honey..." Terra sobbed. "He sees baby, he sees you from heaven. He will always be watching out for you. He will be there even when I'm not. Daddy is in heaven and he's smiling down at you. I know he's proud of you. And I know that if you close your eyes really, really tight you can still see him and talk to him in your dreams," she stuttered, trying to find the right words to console her.

"How do you know that, Mommy?" she asked looking up into her eyes.

"Well, that's because I can see him in my dreams."

Slowly the tears began to stop as she contemplated Terra's words. Taking a deep breath, Autumn closed her eyes really tightly and whispered to herself so low that nobody else heard. Relaxing her arms a little, she carried her little girl back to her bedroom and covered her with a blanket. Keeping her eyes closed, she felt around for her teddy bear and held it tightly against her chest. Her little lips mumbling something as she tried to control her sobs. Within a few moments, she fell asleep again, and Terra joined Sheila again in the kitchen for another cup of coffee. By now, she was covered in tears. Her top was wet with bitterness, as she glared down at her cup. She couldn't even look up at her mother. The only thing she could do was shake her head in disgust at what her daughter was going through. This was not the way that she needed to hear the truth about her father.

She felt her own tears building. She felt her body tense as the anger rose inside of her. She hadn't lied just a little bit, but extensively, enough for Autumn to have no idea what was really going on. Taking deep breaths, Terra tried to gain control before she lost herself in anger. She wanted to let it out. She needed to scream, cry, and sob the same way her daughter had. After all, she was right. He would never see any of her important moments. Darren would never walk her down the aisle. He wouldn't be the one to teach her how to drive. He was going to miss everything. When all the other children would be able to wave to their fathers at graduation, he wouldn't be there. But instead of reinforcing what Terra had told Autumn, Sheila had told her lies. She had told her that her daddy wasn't dead. Did she really think that she would never learn the truth? Terra had taken a lot of trouble to make sure Autumn had known what had happened, and Sheila had taken all of that away. No matter how mad she was at Darren, it didn't change that he was Autumn's dad.

"I'm, I'm... sorry," Sheila stated looking up from her cup. "I didn't mean to..."

"I don't want to hear it," Terra interrupted.

Slamming her cup down on the table, Terra grabbed her clothes and headed for the bathroom. In this moment, it didn't matter what Sheila had to say. There was no way she could fix what she had done. No amount of lies could change the truth. Ripping the hairbrush through her hair, she quickly got dressed and headed back to the living room. She wanted nothing more than to escape her mother's house for a few moments. Maybe a breath of fresh air would help her calm down before her anxiety sat in. It was going to be hard to leave Autumn alone for long. She needed to find a way to settle this between the two of them. It was going to be hard for all of them.

Sitting on the bench outside, Terra tried to calm herself. The sun was higher in the sky now, and she felt its warmth try to relax her. In the morning light, their loss was too real. She had made so much progress in the past few months, but now it all seemed to vanish with the morning dew. Grabbing a cigarette, she tried to clear her mind and think of other things. If she distracted herself for just a few moments, she knew that she would be able to figure this out. Right now, it all seemed impossible. She just wanted it to all go away. Looking across the lawn, she saw the mums that had begun to bloom into soft purple flowers. She had always loved them, and her Mother's were the biggest ones that she had ever seen. Taking another deep breath, Terra searched the sky for a cloud that would remind her of Darren. She was looking for a sign that it would be okay, but found nothing. She was on her own. Finally, she headed back inside, ready to confront Sheila. Sitting across from her at the table she could tell that Sheila had shed a few tears, but nothing compared to what her and Autumn had experienced.

"How could you lie to her so convincingly?" Terra growled.

"I didn't mean to. I just wanted it to be easier on her," Sheila sobbed.

"Well, you knew that I had spent quite a bit of time breaking the news to her. I told her the truth. Sometimes the truth is hard, but it's the truth. How were you going to try to hide the truth? How long did you think that would last?"

"I don't know, it just seemed easier for her."

"Easier for her or easier for you?"

"Both, I guess."

"Well, here's the thing. We should have been through the worst of it. This isn't going to go away. IF I EVER catch you lying to her about this again...I promise you that I will take us both out of here and I will never speak to you again. Do you understand me?"

"But I'm your mother, you can't-"

"If it's to protect the health of my child, I absolutely can. Don't try me."

"I love you two; I never meant to hurt either of you," Sheila stated as she tried to refill her cup for the third time. "Maybe if you just knew my story, if I sat down and told you what happened to me, to your father, what I went through... you would understand-"

"You need to start thinking before you speak. You need to think about the things you are saying. You don't know everything. I can't believe anything you tell me anyway, so don't bother! I love you, too, but you have to understand that what we are going through is NOTHING like what you went through," she stated. "Oh, and another thing, do not talk to Greg. I don't want him around me or Autumn, not ever."

"I don't understand, why don't you want to talk to him. He's your friend," her Mother questioned.

"He raped me, Mom, right there in our bed. That day that you came to pick up Autumn and Paul was there... he walked in on it, and he helped me. I'm so thankful that Autumn was upstairs. Greg hurt me so badly and all you want to do is question my motives," she cried through the anger. "I thank you for letting us stay here and helping me with the car and watching Autumn when you can, but please don't make any of this harder than it already is. Please, you have got to give me a break."

"Terra, I had no idea. I wish you would have told me!" she answered pulling her chair next to her daughter's. "I would have never imagined. Did he hurt you? I mean did he physically hurt you?"

"Yes, oh Lord, yes!" she sobbed pulling her hair back away from her neck. "There's this one, and there's a lot more. Come with me in the bathroom and I will show you."

Pulling her into the bathroom, Terra showed her everything. The bruise on her buttocks was starting to fade but was still a thick mustard color on both of her cheeks. Her back was still covered in dark spots, some were still painful to the touch and her thighs had begun to fade into a light yellow. They hadn't been as bad as some of the others.

"This looks really bad," Sheila gasped "Why didn't you call the police?"

"It would have just made it worse on Autumn. I'm hoping that she just forgets about him over time. They were never that close," she whispered. "Besides, Paul walked in and it didn't go very well for Greg. I really like Paul, Mom. I can't let something like that go back on him. Besides, you know how this town likes to gossip. What are they going to say if they know how quickly I started seeing someone?" Terra sobbed into her Mother's arms.

"I wouldn't care about what they think about that. You need to do what makes you happy. I know I talk a lot of crap, but it's the truth. Nobody can tell you when you are ready. Only you know that. Darren wouldn't have wanted you to be miserable and alone. He would have wanted you to feel love again," she declared. "And if I hear anything from Greg, I am going to give him a piece of my mind. He had better never show back up around here. I absolutely despise men like that. SOOOO many of THEM are such complete ASSES. I could tell you so many stories. And for one to rape and hit MY baby girl! There will be hell to pay if he ever crosses my path! I know a lot about men and I have tried to spare you, but that little bastard managed to slip past me, and that's not okay!"

"Thank you, Mom... I was just afraid to say anything because I know you care about everything and you are such a romantic..."

"Yeah, I am a romantic because of the crap I went through. It was terrible until I became the predator instead of the prey," Sheila scoffed. "I never wanted you to live that life. I should have protected you."

"I don't think there's anything you could have done," Terra answered reaching for her mom's hand. "Say... can Paul come back today, since you know a little more now... maybe you could give him a chance?"

"I will give him a chance. I'm sorry I was being so short with him. I didn't know... but maybe... it should just be you and Autumn. I might need to run out for a bit this afternoon," she winked, knowing where her plans would take her.

13

The air was cool and crisp as Paul followed the trail. It had been a while since he had travelled this path. The crimson and gold leaves covered the ground like a blanket as he strolled through them. Each step he took seemed to kick up leaves as he strolled carelessly among them. He loved the contrast of the warm colors and the cool air of late fall. The trees were like wooden sculptures stretching to the sky around him. Only a few leaves were holding on to the twisted limbs above him. Like an afterthought in his mind of the past few months, they clung needlessly to the past, waiting to let go, to be reborn.

He still checked in with everyone at the center occasionally, but his priorities had changed. Paul's journey of healing had been a struggle. Entering a new relationship had brought a lot of challenges that he thought he had conquered. He kept finding himself falling into old habits. The last thing he wanted was another unhealthy relationship. Regardless, he had fallen in love with Terra and had been through plenty of counseling to ensure that he wasn't repeating old habits.

Looking back, he was thankful that even though he had been struggling, the nightmares had stopped. He remembered them clearly. It was as though he had been trapped in a silent world completely lacking color. He remembered the water the most. He had watched people disappear into oily black waters as though they went willingly to their death. They would always come when he had least expected them. Time and again, he remembered waking up in a cold sweat. Everything around him would be scattered on the floor as if he had been fighting with himself throughout the night. Sometimes it would even happen during the day. The dreams did not discriminate but taunted him. He had been trapped in a world he could never escape. Then suddenly, just as they had begun, they had stopped.

Remembering that place only made him appreciate the beauty of the leaves even more. Taking in the colors of fall, he imagined what the coming months would be like. After all, Christmas was coming. It had been years since he had someone to share it with. This year while he wanted to help as much as he could with all the charitable causes that always seemed to need help, he kept thinking of only one thing. The idea of a family couldn't escape his mind. The town had been talking about covering the park with Christmas lights. It was a new display, and he wanted nothing more than to share it with Terra and Autumn. There were rumors of horse drawn carriages, singing, and a live nativity. It sounded like it would be like something from another world. It was a lot of excitement for a small town.

As he soaked in the rich array of his surroundings, he thought about the night ahead. Paul was finally going to be able to spend time with Autumn. He had always loved kids and had wanted a child of his own. Getting to know Terra's little girl was like getting to know an extension of her. He was hoping that they could have fun together. He had always dreamed of teaching children how to play basketball, how to swim, and so many other things. Their minds hadn't been tainted by disappointment. They were all looking for light in a dark world. They saw the world in a way that no adult could. It was that innocence and need for discovery that made him adore children. It helped him to remember what was important and what wasn't.

Heading back to his truck he couldn't help but smile. He couldn't wait to have dinner with Terra and Autumn. It was a big step for all of them. Soon, they would be together and hopefully he could find out how she was feeling. It had been quite a while since he had confessed his love for her and still, she hadn't done the same. Recently, it seemed like their relationship had changed. Terra had begun sharing things with him that she had never mentioned before. They had grown closer. She had a way of bringing out the best in him. She made him want to be a better person. There was a passion in her that he could not explain, not just for him, but for life. Her determination to survive ignited a fire within him that he had forgotten. It felt like they had been together for years, not months. They had gone from short visits at the crisis center to long discussions about life. They confided in one another in a way that he had never thought possible. Everything about their relationship seemed irrational, but in a beautiful way. His mind swam with thoughts of the future that he hoped he for. A future where all of them were together.

Tonight, would give him a glimpse of that or at least that's what he hoped. Climbing in the truck, he cranked up the radio and let the music relax him. Music had always spoke to him. Now instead of feeling hopelessness, he felt peace. That's what she had done for him. For the first time, he felt confident that he was ready. Paul had found his passion, his desire, and his lust for life. Together, they had learned to celebrate their gratitude for being alive. Pulling into the driveway, he quickly shut off the truck and almost ran for the door in excitement. He had been looking forward to this night for a long time.

"Paul! You're early! I wasn't quite ready for you," Terra laughed, running into his arms.

"Well, I finished my day early. I didn't think you would mind too terribly," he smiled.

"Are these for me?" she asked reaching for the bouquet that he held behind his back.

Taking the small bouquet of lilies, she ushered him inside. The scent of garlic filled the air as he headed for the small breakfast table in the corner. The kitchen was filled with all the necessary tools of a good cook. He adored a messy kitchen, at least while the creativity was happening. He couldn't help but smile as he watched Autumn trying to clean up after her mom. He had never seen a little girl so eager to help. Grabbing a bottle of wine, Terra poured a couple of glasses. Sitting across from him, she invited him to take a sip.

"It's from the local winery. Have you tried it?" Terra questioned.

"No, I don't believe I have. Thank you," he answered, grabbing the glass. He tilted it gently to her with a nod and took a small sip. "Mmm... this is nice. I had no idea you were a wine lover?"

"I'm not, not really. I don't like most of it, but this, it's different I guess," she smiled.

"Are you drinking mommy juice again?" Autumn asked, rushing up to them. "I thought only you could have mommy juice."

"Sometimes, I can share if I want to, you know, with another adult," Terra laughed as she reached down to tickle the little girl on the side. "Do you want Autumn juice?" she asked handing her a small cup of apple juice.

"Yes! Of course, I do," she answered quickly, grabbing the cup from her hand. "Hey, I want to go outside. All of this cooking has made me soooo tired."

"Go ahead, just stay where I can see you."

"NO! You BOTH must come with me. I want to show Paul my new swing set!" she pouted as she walked to the sliding glass doors. "Come on, he HAS to see it."

Without a word, Paul stood up and headed towards the door. Terra could see a smile on his face as she took his hand and led him away. It wasn't much of a swing set. It was closer to a giant wooden pirate ship. It was equipped with slides, swings, and plenty of places to explore. It was something Sheila had seen a model of at one of the local parks. She had always loved things that were hand built, so she had insisted. After all, she had felt guilty about lying to Autumn about her father. It was an obvious distraction, but a nice gesture nonetheless. Staying by the door, Terra watched Paul take in the sight of Autumn's new obsession. His eyes grew big as she took him on the grand tour. The solid oak structure was much bigger than he had anticipated. Carefully, he allowed himself to be drug all the way around the back yard. Grabbing his hand, she jumped up and down with excitement as she tried to explain the different parts of the ship. Obediently, he went down the slide, climbed inside, and then headed for the swings.

She had not heard Autumn laugh that much in a long time. Both were filled with smiles as he looked through the scope. She saw him talking to her in funny voices and gesturing to her like a pirate. They even looked for mermaids in the crimson and orange leaves around them. Climbing out of the ship, he grabbed a rake from beside the house and began piling the leaves together as she grabbed handfuls and threw them in front of the swings. Then he gently pushed her on the swing as she squealed for him to push her higher. Silently, Terra watched her little girl jump into the pile of leaves that he had made for her. Her little head disappeared into them before popping up and demanding to be on the swing yet again.

Watching it all unfold, she smiled as a feeling of warmth crept into her body. Her heart began to ache as all of Autumn's tears melted away. The little girl was once again full of life. She had gone from being sad and quiet, to laughing and exploring. Looking out at the two of them, Terra longed to walk up to him, grab his face and kiss him. For the first time in a long time, she saw the future. It was a future filled with warm summer days in the pool, hayrides, and cooking s'mores together on an open fire. Taking a deep breath, she filled her lungs with the crisp late-November air and began to let herself feel again. Yes, this was something special. In just a few short moments, she discovered something new. She was falling for him, too.

Standing in the doorway, she watched them rush back and forth across the yard. Autumn ran at full speed to the swings each time she jumped into the leaves. Again and again, he continued to chase her. As Paul pushed little strands of hair out of his face, she saw him start to sweat. Playfully, she watched him fall into the leaves. As he loosened the top couple of buttons on his shirt, Terra saw his labored breathing. But Autumn was merciless as she jumped on top of him and began burying him in the leaves. Quickly, he overcame her as his hands reached up and tickled her sides as she fell over, giggling in the leaves.

There was no doubt that what Terra felt was love. But it was not a new love, freshly sprouted in a moment. It was an appreciation for the man in front of her. Terra saw his faults, his clumsiness, and sometimes even his bad tempter. However, in that she also saw his determination, generosity, and patience. No, this was not new at all/ she had just been afraid to see how her own heart had grown towards him. There was no way to deny it.

After filling their bellies with lasagna and garlic bread, Terra and Paul tucked Autumn in bed for the night. She fell asleep quickly. Quietly, they watched her for a few moments. She laid there like an angel wrapped in her pink fuzzy blanket holding snow white teddy bear. Slowly, stars danced around the room from a carousel, lighting her face with their brilliance. The pair crept away to the living room where they could be alone. Sheila was gone for the night, and now, maybe Terra could find the courage to confess her new discovery to Paul. Her heart had been aching to hold him and tell him her secret for hours.

"Do you want to go outside, maybe get some fresh air?" she asked, opening the door for him.

"I guess so, but I had plenty of fresh air tonight," he laughed.

Looking up at the stars, Terra lifted his arms and wrapped them around her. Leaning towards her, he gently kissed her forehead and pulled her closer to him. The couple shone a little brighter than night in the late autumn air. Sitting on the wrought-iron bench, she gently pulled him down beside her and looked longingly into his eyes.

"I loved watching you with Autumn, tonight."

"She's a lot of fun," he smiled. "I hope you didn't mind that I jumped right in there with her?"

"No of course, not... it actually made me realize something."

"Oh, really, what's that? I'm a little childish and would be a pain to have around all the time?" he laughed gently.

"No," she giggled. "I'm trying to be serious for a second." Leaning closer to him, she slowly caressed her lips with his and slowly made her way to his ear with gentle kisses. "I love you, Paul."

Pulling away, she looked into his eyes again as a single tear trailed down her cheek. Her heart was pounding as she waited for him to say something, anything. In that moment it had seemed like forever since he had confessed his love for her. She had never repeated it. Her body began to shake as every second felt like an eternity. But instead of saying anything, he pulled her closer to him, his lips pressing firmly against hers.

"I love you, too. I love you so much that it hurts," he whispered between kisses. "Do you know what I want?"

"No... what?" she asked, surprised by his question.

"I wish I could explore you and kiss every inch of you," he winked. "I want to show you pleasure, deep, intense... pleasure."

"I think I might need another cigarette," Terra

stuttered, fumbling for her cigarettes.

"Why, are you nervous? Afraid?"

"Yes, no... It's been a really, really long time. Darren couldn't... do... that."

"Can I?"

"Umm... yes, I guess," she blushed under his gaze.

As Terra threw down her cigarette, she reached for his hand. Her heart quickened as she entered her mother's home and headed for the other spare bedroom. Terra had never slept there because she had been more comfortable on the couch, closer to her daughter, but now she wanted to be as far from her as possible.

"Is it safe here?" he asked surveying the room.

Taking a deep breath, Terra sat on the edge of the queen size bed and reached her hand out to him. "Yes, Paul. It's ok."

"I want to make this special for you."

"You don't need to do anything to make it special. It already is," she whimpered, clinging to him.

Walking to her place on the side of the bed, Paul leaned over and cupped her face in his hand. As he leaned down to her, he gently brushed his lips against her forehead. Like a whisper, he kissed down her nose until he found her lips. With the tip of his tongue, Paul teased her. Pulling forward, she tried to kiss him, but he quickly pulled away with a knowing laugh.

"Patience..." he whispered.

Tracing her lips with his tongue, he gently laid her on the bed, holding her head in his hand. As she finally rested against the pillows, he pushed his lips against hers, engulfing her with kisses. Positioning himself on top of her, he began to tease the soft curve of her neck, tasting every ounce of her skin. Slowly, he worked his way down her body, unbuttoning her top as his mouth followed his hands down her body. Gently, he pulled her bra to the side and as she gasped, he sucked her nipple into his mouth, wrapping his hand around her breast he pulled her flesh deeper into his mouth. With a moan escaping her lips, Terra ran her fingers through his hair arching her chest up to meet him. Exposing the other breast, he gently caressed her other nipple until his lips found it. His eyes closed, he heard her heart echo in her chest, pounding like a drum.

Traveling down her body, his tongue discovered her belly button as her hands began to push him even lower. Arching her back, she slowly spread her legs inviting him downward. As she teased him with her hips, she felt his tongue dart quickly inside her belly button while his fingers laced themselves through the sides of her panties. Each kiss that he gave went lower on her abdomen as he slowly slid them down, exposing her soft flesh to him. With a gentle slide he followed her panties down her thighs to the tips of her toes until they finally fell on the floor and every inch of her body had been exposed to his tongue, except for her most sensitive places. Looking down at her, he watched her chest rise and fall as she anticipated his next move. As he leaned over her, he gently kissed her belly button and travelled farther down her body. Lifting her legs around his shoulders he lowered his face down to her awaiting flesh. Gently, he traced her lower lips with his tongue, teasing her with tiny licks and kisses. Slowly, he teased her with kisses against her thigh, waiting for the right moment. His hands drifted, caressing her legs as they spread open before him. He could smell her anticipation, and it made him hunger for her more.

Terra felt her heart quicken as he finally buried his face between her legs. His kisses were slow at first as he explored her, tasted her. His tongue strengthened as she arched her back to push him closer and he dove his tongue into her as he kissed and sucked on each part of her. She felt her body surge against him as he mercilessly teased her flesh, paying attention to each tiny part of her. Draping her legs around his shoulders, she grabbed his hair and pulled it gently as she moaned, squirming under his tongue. Warmth spread through her body as his tongue teased her, wrapping itself around her clitoris, sucking tenderly on her lips. Pressing his tongue hard against her, he pushed his mouth against her body. His breath felt like fire against her bare skin as he continued. Until finally, he latched his lips against the most sensitive part of her and began to flick it with his tongue. Within a few minutes of his teasing, her body began to squirm, tensing against his head. Pushing herself up from her pillow, Terra grabbed his hair and watched his face disappear between her legs. Finally, she collapsed, falling back against the bed, her body exploded with passion.

Instead of stopping, his tongue slowed as she relaxed her legs against him and he began to caress her with his fingertips. Working his way to her hips, he cupped her cheeks in his hands kissing her gently, waiting, patiently. When her body relaxed completely, Paul once again buried his face between her legs, repeating his path, flicking his tongue against her, smothering himself in the evidence of her passion. Once again, her heart quickened, and she arched her body against him, only stronger this time as she exploded. As she gasped for air, she struggled to muffle her screams of pleasure. Grabbing the nearest pillow, she clung to it, covering her mouth in an attempt to muffle her screams. But with her hands occupied, Paul was left to do as he pleased and took the opportunity to pull back the flesh that hid her clitoris, exposing it to his hot breath and the passion of his tongue. Holding onto the pillow, Terra tried to free herself from his grasp before she screamed out in pleasure yet again. He had made her so sensitive that every touch sent a shock wave of electricity through her body. Wave after wave of pleasure crashed through her as he explored her.

"Stop! Please stop, she begged. It's just too much."

"Are you sure you want me to stop?" Paul chuckled. "I could do this all night."

"I'm sure, definitely sure," she gasped, pulling his arms up so he could lay beside her.

Laying her head against his chest, Terra slowly began to unbutton his shirt as she tried to catch her breath. Moments later, she watched his eyes close while her hands uncovered his chest. Consumed with passion, she tried to be gentle but seeing him lying there was overwhelming. Sitting up, she quickly pulled his shirt from his body and with one hand she grabbed his belt, releasing his pants from their grasp. Pulling at the button of his jeans, she quickly ripped his pants from his waist as his manhood fell into the open air.

Finally, able to see his hidden treasure, she forced herself to slow down. Taking it in her hands, she began to trace her fingers along his shaft in a gentle caress. Feeling it throb in her hand only increased the fire that raged within. Glancing up at him, she watched his hands reach for her and gently caress her back as she lowered her mouth onto him. At first, she began with a tiny lick on the head of his penis, a simple tease against his body. For a while, she covered him with gentle kisses, until finally she released her passion and took him completely in her mouth. Playfully, she nibbled on him. Not wanting to do anything more than to love him, she teased his body with her tongue, with tiny kisses that occasionally traveled down the length of his shaft. Her hands massaged his legs as he softly moaned. Her tongue danced around every part of his manhood, slowly, gently, until she could no longer resist him and latched on to the head of his penis and forcefully sucked it into her mouth. Wrapping her hand around him she stroked him, extending the pleasure of her mouth as he entered it, sucking hard against his tip. Taking him fully, she enveloped his penis, massaging it with her tongue as she stroked him. Gently, he ran his hands through her hair, his hips arching to meet her lips, not pushing her, not controlling her.

"I can't do this anymore," she gasped, pulling away to kneel beside him. "I need you inside me."

"Are you sure, sweetie?" he asked as his lips met hers again.

"I want you," she answered, staring lovingly into his eyes. Glancing around at the rest of the room, she remembered the last time a man had been inside of her and felt a cold chill settle into her stomach. "I want to try, but... as much as I want to, I'm afraid. What if it hurts, Paul? What if my body still needs to heal? What if we have to stop?" she asked with a sudden panic in her eyes. "I don't want to disappoint you. I want to please you so badly, but what if I can't. You have set me on fire, but what if..."

"You could never disappoint me, not ever. I want you,

but I know how to stop. I would never hurt you. You can trust me." he soothed. "From what I can tell, you responded very well. I think you will be ok. Do you want me?"

"Of course, I do," she whimpered.

"Have you ever been made love to? I don't mean sex; I mean, been made love to."

"I don't know what you mean?"

Reaching for the pillows, Paul lifted her head with his hand and placed them underneath her. His eyes gazed into hers as he lowered his face to hers, kissing her cheek. "I love you, Terra."

"I love you too, Paul." she answered as she ran her fingers along his jawline. "I want you inside of me. Show me..."

As he leaned above her, he reached down and kissed her forehead as her legs opened for him. She watched his face come closer to hers as his body came into full view, her hands gently caressing his shoulders as she looked up into his eyes. She waited, wanting to feel the weight of his body against hers, but loving the way he looked above her. His lips were parted as he made shallow breaths while he lowered himself onto her. She had never known that a moment could be beautiful until she saw him like that. He looked into her eyes with more passion and love than she had ever imagined possible. The lamp light behind him made his hair glow and his eyes sparkle as he gently wrapped his arm around her head, his fingers caressing her hair. He hadn't begun to make love to her, but she was ready to surrender her body to him.

Forgetting her fears, she searched his eyes and memorized the way his body looked as he prepared to make love to her. She never wanted to forget the way he looked in that moment. She knew she would have been happy to stay there forever as he held her, his lips caressing her forehead. With her lips, she reached for his kisses, wanting to feel them against hers. Terra wrapped her arms around his shoulders and began to run her legs against his, waiting, wanting.

As her hands ran down his back, she felt his hips arch and slowly; gently, he entered her. The strength of his erection glided within her, parting her flesh. His warmth rushed through her body as he became a part of her, opening her tenderness with his strength. Clinging to his body, she felt him gasp against her neck as his body slid in and out of her. Each thrust, a little deeper, a little harder but still gentler than anything she had ever experienced. Her heart ached, wanting to stay in that moment, wanting to breathe in his essence as his body danced with hers in the darkened room. Her legs wrapped tightly against his legs, and her arms clung to his as they collided in the ultimate embrace. Soon, her moans echoed his as she forgot to care about breaking the silence of the house. Growing louder as his thrusts quickened, she clung to him, showering his arms with kisses as he knelt above her. Lifting himself from her body, he took her legs in his and spread her thighs open against him, caressing them with his hands. His neck arched back and his eyes closed as he continued to express his passion with every thrust.

Wanting to feel the weight of his body against hers, she pulled at his arms and lifted her body to his. Wrapping her hands around his neck, she pulled him down to her, straining to meet him with another kiss without interrupting him. With her teeth, she gently nibbled at his lower lip and sucked it into her mouth. Moaning, he wrapped his arms around her and began to kiss her delicately as his breath quickened and his body began to tense against her. As her body began to quiver, she watched the veins on his neck tighten as he began to quicken his pace. Arching her hips to his, she pulled him deeper into her. Pulling her legs away, she surrendered to him allowing him to take over her body, loving him. Until finally, his body shook against hers and he held himself tightly inside of her.

Slowly he lowered himself on top of her and pulled her into his arms. She felt his heart pounding as he lay there, looking longingly into her eyes. Their foreheads resting against each other's, he kissed her, wrapping his hands in her hair. Reaching her hand up, Terra placed it over his heart and listened to the healthy rhythm that pounded deep beneath the surface. Instead of sickness, it was an echo of passionate release. Instead of pain, she marveled in the sweetness of his afterglow knowing he loved her, feeling his loyalty.

As she leaned into his bare chest, she wiped a tear away that had fallen from her eyes. Trying to hide her tears, she buried her face in him. She didn't want him to misunderstand her tears as she cried in relief. He had been gentler than she had ever imagined.

"Are you ok?" he whispered, trying not to disturb the moment.

"I'm okay," she sobbed. "That was beautiful. Thank you for being so gentle, so sweet."

"I told you, I would never dream of hurting you. Thank you for giving me a chance to show you that," he answered, pulling her chin up to look into her eyes.

Without a second thought, he kissed the trail where her tears had been. "Wait, what was that?" he asked, looking around.

"What? I didn't hear anything," she replied pulling away.

"I heard a thud; I think it was coming from Autumn's room."

Jumping up from the bed, he headed down the hall and opened her door with Terra only steps behind him. There they found the little carousel of stars laying in the floor. Autumn's hands were flying wildly as she tossed in her bed. Flipping on the light, they both ran to the side of her bed.

"Wake up, baby girl. What's wrong?" Terra pleaded, shaking the little girl gently.

Slowly, her little eyes opened, and she wrapped her arms around her mother's neck.

"Mommy!" she sobbed, "I dreamed of this terrible place. People were walking into a black bunch of water. They were disappearing and I could not hear anything. It was hot. I could not breathe. It was so scary, Mommy. I could not find you. I was stuck there." She stumbled, trying to hold onto her Mom.

"What do you mean?"

"I don't know, it was scary. My feet and legs were hurting. I was bleeding from all the glass. There was nowhere to go. I felt like something was pulling into the black water."

"I know, I know, sweetie it was just a dream. It is all over now. It's going to be okay, baby."

Pulling her out of bed, Paul carried Autumn to the little table beside the kitchen while Terra grabbed a glass of water from the faucet. Pulling the chair closer to her, she wrapped her arms around the sobbing little girl and began wiping her tears away. Rubbing her back she tried desperately to soothe the little girl as the tears continued to fall. Her little face had grown red. Her body shook in terror.

"What was that place? Mommy, I'm scared," Autumn pleaded.

"I don't know, but you know what," Terra answered softly. "I've had dreams like that."

"Really?" she asked, looking up into her eyes.

"Yes, I think it's just a place we go when we are sad, hurt, or confused."

"But, I'm not sad. I had a great day playing outside."

"I know, but sometimes maybe it just reminds us that we are going through something. Have you been thinking a lot about Daddy?"

"Yes, but you said Daddy is in heaven looking down on me."

"He is, baby, he is," she whispered, pulling her onto her lap. "I just think it's a scary place that finds us somehow. But there is nothing to worry about. It's all over now."

With her arms around her, Terra took Autumn back to her bed while Paul fixed her starlight carousel. As they tucked her in, they both placed a small kiss on her cheek and waited for her to go to sleep. Thankfully, it didn't take long her for her to drift away again and the two of them headed back to the living room.

"You've had dreams like that?" Paul asked seriously.

"Yes, several times. It is a reoccurring nightmare. It is always the same place, just a little different. It is hard to explain. Why do you ask?"

"I've had dreams like that, too. It's not something you forget."

"Really? How is that possible? Are you sure it's the same place?"

"Yes, it has to be. I remember standing on a shoreline made of broken glass, watching people walk into this black water. But it was not really water, it was like oil. They just walked to their death, one by one." he answered taking her hand. "Is that what you dreamed?"

"Yes, and so much worse. Maybe it's just our minds playing tricks on us," she answered shaking her head. "Maybe there's some sort of thing on television that triggered it, somehow."

"Are those things that Autumn would have seen?" he questioned, trying to help her find the answer.

"No, of course not, but I'm not always around."

"There has to be some sort of explanation."

14

Looking over at Paul, Terra hesitated for a moment before getting out of the truck. It was a spontaneous stop during their date, but still a serious one. A stop that he had encouraged her to take. It was one of those turning points, a push in the right direction. A degree in business. It is something she had thought about for a long time but had never done because she had been busy taking care of everyone else. She had so many ideas about helping with customer experiences, helping others succeed. She had always been good with people and had always been a natural leader. It was a versatile degree even if she just managed to get an associates while Autumn was in school.

Looking across the parking lot at the store-front sign of the little community college, she imagined the challenges that lay ahead. Thoughts of homework, school projects, and exams seemed intimidating, but she knew it would be worth it. She knew she needed to focus on the future so that she could heal from the past. Even if it were a little bit at a time, every step would be worth it in the end. Terra wanted Autumn to see her mother succeed.

More than anything, she wanted to be a good example for her to follow. Stepping out of the truck, she headed inside the small building to gather information and start the process of enrolling. Spontaneous life decisions had never really happened to her before, but she knew if she started the process, she would go through with it. After all, how bad could it be?

***

Watching her disappear into the building, Paul rolled down the windows, threw his head back and closed his eyes. He remembered how intimidating it had been to go back to school as an adult, but it had been worth it. It had been terrifying to be around all the younger kids that were just out of high school. There could be so much gossip and distractions, but he had remained focused. He had made it a priority, and he knew that Terra would, too. Thinking back, he remembered every step he had been through since Patricia. He had felt so empty and alone that he thought death was the only answer. He had no purpose and nobody that had really wanted him around. That is why he had tried to kill himself. The emptiness was too much to bear even with his career. His family had abandoned him years before. There had been no one to talk to, except the pill bottle on the nightstand. He did not want that for Terra. He had fallen for her. She was all he thought about it, and he could not help but worry that he just needed someone to take care of. One of his greatest fears was that it was not really love, but just another one of his obsessions. But, maybe with a little help, he would find a way to make sure it was healthy. The first thing to do was to give her room to grow and heal. It was her turn to become who she needed to be, with or without him.

Today, he just wanted to be near her. She had called him because she wanted to get away from the house. It was not going to be anything fancy. He just enjoyed spending time with her. He had not mentioned his feelings to her in a while. Paul did not want to make her feel uncomfortable. He had been allowing her to take the lead. She had needed time with her daughter. Now, he just waited.

A couple of hours later, she emerged from the small building full of smiles. "Well, that took longer than I expected," he smiled as she climbed into the truck. "What happened?"

"I'm so excited!" she squealed. "I signed up for classes, financial aid, and even took a couple of placement tests! I did well! I start in a couple weeks. Let's celebrate!"

"ABSOLUTELY!! WOW, how did you accomplish so much?"

"Good timing, I guess, and maybe a little persistence," she laughed with a sparkle in her eyes.

"Persistence is important! Where would you like to go? I am at your service my lady," he asked, playfully.

"To an early dinner, sir. Something with ice cream would be preferred."

"Ice cream it is, and then, maybe pop-corn and a movie. That would be my suggestion for the evening. That is if it agrees with your mood, of course."

"But, of course! Now fire up the chariot, kind sir," she giggled as she copied his playful tone.

"And would you prefer the indoor or outdoor ice cream experience?" he asked as he pulled back onto the road.

"Outdoor would be preferred if you can find a way to accomplish such a feat."

"Your wish is my command."

After hitting the drive-thru, the two of them spotted a couple of picnic tables close to the movie theatre and sat enjoying their hot dogs and ice cream. Terra adored hot dogs, especially the foot-long kind with sauce and cheese. It was refreshing that Paul seemed to echo the simplicity of her dinner choices. There was nothing quite like hot dogs, burgers, and milk shakes. She was a firm believer that dates did not need to be expensive. It was the time and the experiences that really mattered to her.

Looking into his eyes, she saw warmth and tenderness. He was not fake when he smiled at her. Terra had always preferred to look a man in the eyes so that she could really see them. She had never really been interested in them for their looks, their money, or what they could do for her. It was all about their heart. Because of that, she had never really had a specific type. Of course, she was good at being wrong about people too.

As she looked into his eyes, she knew he was not complicated. The way his eyes seemed to close a little when he smiled was charming and sincere. When he was thinking, he tended to bite his lip just a little in the left corner and when he was excited, Paul always seemed to purse his lips together as if he were holding something back. There was a kindness to him that she rarely had seen. When he was being playful, he was a joy to be around. This was a man she imagined teaching Autumn how to play basketball. After all, he seemed to be able to appreciate the little things in life. Sometimes, the little things made the biggest difference. The thought of forever terrified her, but she took comfort in knowing that Darren would not have wanted her to be alone.

That night, Terra wrapped herself in the moment. At the movies, she simply rested in his arms. She had spent so much time watching his expressions and caressing his hand that she missed the movie entirely. Seeing him in the darkness with only the dim flicker of the screen, she had been captivated. She could not take her eyes away from him.

"Paul," she muttered as they headed back to the truck. "I really enjoyed today."

"Me, too," he answered hopefully. "We should do this more often. What do you think?"

"I would love to, of course. But... I do want to talk to you about some things, though. It's not about us," she stated reassuringly. "I just need to talk about, you know, other stuff."

"I don't mind if you need to get some things off of your chest," he replied squeezing her hand. "Are you sure? We have had so much fun tonight. I don't want to ruin it."

"Absolutely. Let's just go somewhere a little quieter. Is my place okay?"

Shrugging her shoulders, Terra let him drive her home. His outdoor patio was beautiful after all and maybe the warmth of the fire would be comforting. There was so much she needed to get off her chest. She hoped it would be good for her to open a little, even though she hated bringing him into all the crazy things she had been reading.

Once they arrived, he lit the fire and they sat side by side on his wicker sofa looking out at the river. It was beautiful, like something from a post card. The trees surrounded them with passionate fall colors as the mixed tones of the fire and moon enticed their senses.

"Paul..." she stated facing him. "I know this doesn't really matter anymore, especially not to you, but I think Darren was cheating on me. It had started out as just a rumor I had heard. Then I found his journal and he keeps mentioning this girl, Patricia."

"Patricia?" he questioned. "That's my ex's name." He answered glancing down at the ground before meeting her gaze again. "What does he say in the journal."

"It doesn't say anything bad, mostly that he cannot stop thinking about her and that she kept dropping by the car lot. She brought him coffee, stuff like that. I stopped reading it," she stuttered. "It was getting hard to see his words. I'm afraid of what I will find."

"That actually sounds a little bit like something she would do."

"Didn't you say that she cheated on you? That she was pregnant? You don't think?"

"I don't know, I honestly just don't know. I wish I remembered what he looked like, but I was so angry that day that I barely remember anything," he replied squeezing her hand. "We might not ever know. Not unless you read more of the journals."

"I don't know, I might skip ahead. I do not want to put myself through reading all of them. There's a lot, honestly."

"Skipping ahead isn't a bad idea. I would tell you to get rid of the journal, but I think that you would regret it. You will eventually need to know to give yourself some peace. You need closure on that."

"I know. It is like he died AND we got a divorce because

I'm finding out that the man I loved didn't seem to love me as much as I thought he did. I feel so betrayed. I thought that everything was okay. I thought that he was working all the extra hours for us, but maybe he wasn't working that much extra after all. Maybe I was just too naïve to see it."

"There's nothing wrong with wanting answers," he replied softly. "You need to read ahead and find out what happened. Or if anything happened at all. You don't need me to tell you that, Terra."

"I know, it's just nice to say it out loud."

Leaning towards her, he gently caressed her cheek with the back of his hand as a tear began to fall slowly from her bright blue eyes. Swiftly, he pulled her hair away from her face and brought his lips to hers. Her lips tasted like flower petals as he caressed them with his own. Pulling her tightly against him, his hands began to wander down her body. As he lifted her shirt, he began to caress her belly. Slowly he inched his way upwards towards her breasts as his kisses began to deepen. He felt her breathing change as she nestled in closer to him, surrendering to his touch.

Reaching for him, she leaned back on the outdoor sofa and looked up at the stars as they lit the night sky. She saw the moon peaking behind the clouds as though it was trying to hide them in the darkness of the evening. But nothing shone brighter than his eyes as he searched her own for approval.

Pulling his shirt above his head, Terra placed her hand on his chest. She loved running her fingers through the dark hair that covered his body. She loved feeling the warmth of his skin against hers. She had never had a man touch her so gently. Releasing her neck, she closed her eyes and took in the smell of the outdoors and the crispness of the air.

But then, like a flash, she saw Greg. She felt his powerful hands on her body, forcing her down on the mattress. She felt the pain as he had hit her and ripped into her body. Quickly, she sat up against Paul and pushed him away.

"I'm sorry, I don't know what happened," she gasped. "I was enjoying you, wanting you, needing you and then all I saw, heard or felt was Greg." She sobbed trying to catch her breath. "I don't understand. You're nothing like him," she cried reaching for him again.

"It's okay, Terra. It is going to be okay," he sighed. "It's probably just a flashback. I know you can't help it."

Pulling his shirt back over his head, Paul reached for her again. This time he held her quietly as she cried. But inside, all he felt was rage as he tried to comfort her. His thoughts kept returning to the man that had scarred her so deeply. Fantasies of what his face felt like against his fist invaded his mind as he watched the woman he loved tremble at even a gentle touch. Quietly, he watched her cry in his arms. In a moment, she had forgotten about how beautiful the day had been and how much they had accomplished. She had gone from being a bold passionate rose, to a trembling and dying leaf that had fallen from the trees in a matter of seconds.

Closing his eyes, he fought against the rage that was boiling inside of him. Taking deep breaths, he attempted to count, he attempted to breathe, and he tried desperately to forget what he had seen. Desperately, he fought for his own peace while he attempted to help her come back from the memory of her violation.

15

As he poured a cup of coffee, Paul headed outside to the brick patio. It was chilly, but the view was worth it. Looking out over the river, he watched a barge slowly pass as he took a sip. The leaves were gone from the trees now, and the ground glistened with frost like a coating of sugar in the cold morning air. The transition through the seasons always caught him off guard. The hot cup steamed in his hands as his breath left a cloud of mist in the air.

As he tightened his robe around him, Paul reached for his phone. It had always been his morning routine to check social media just to see what was going on in the community. There was no better way to keep an eye on the community than checking his timeline. Everyone seemed to share all the local news on social media before any other source seemed to pick it up. Then he saw her name again, Patricia. He had almost forgotten about the mystery behind her and Darren. He had almost forgotten about discovering who the father of her child was. Paul's mind began to race. He remembered when he had found the slip of paper with her name on it, hidden in Darren's drawer. He remembered her post on social media and all the entries in Darren's journal. Living in a small town was difficult. Everyone seemed to know everyone and all their business. Gallipolis was a quiet and peaceful town, but nobody ever escaped the gossip. Regardless, it was torturing him, not for himself, but for Terra. She deserved to know the truth. Suddenly, the phone began to vibrate in his hand.

"Hello..." he answered, scratching his head.

"Hey, it's me, I need to ask you a favor," Patricia stuttered. "I hate to ask you, but I could use a little help."

"What KIND of favor? What exactly do you need from me, Patty? The last time we talked you didn't exactly want to be friendly?"

"I know... I am sorry about that. I know that you have done a lot for me already, but.... I really need diapers. Is there any way you can pick me up some? I can't get anyone to help me."

"What about his father?" Paul asked, hoping for a little more information.

"He doesn't exactly come around. I told you, he's like a ghost," she sobbed quietly on the other line. "There's no way he can help."

"Well, I don't really mind helping, just don't get any ideas, ok?"

"I won't, I promise. How soon can you bring them?"

"I will be there soon. Just give me a few minutes. I will drop them off on the way to work," he sighed begrudgingly. She was not exactly giving him the information he needed to know. "I wish you could have asked me sooner, how long you have been out?"

"I'm not out, I just used the last one. I have been trying

to get someone else to help. Believe me, you're the last person I wanted to call."

"Ok, well, it's funny that you ask me for help now, when you refused to speak to me a few weeks ago. Don't worry, I'm not going to let your son suffer."

Quickly, Paul hung up his phone and headed into town. Maybe he would learn something from all of this. He hated helping her because you could never really tell if she had other motives. But she sounded desperate and a few dollars for a pack of diapers might give him the opportunity to find out what he needed to know to give himself and Terra a little peace.

When he pulled into his old driveway, she immediately ran outside. Her short blonde hair bobbed up and down as she clutched her short bright pink robe around her waist. True to her style, she was barely dressed. Yet, she had obviously taken the time to apply her makeup and find her best robe. She looked alive and a bit mischievous. Her smile was wide, and her face was flushed as she waited for him on the porch of their old home.

Climbing out of the car, he grabbed the bag and headed towards her slowly. After all, he knew her better than anyone. He knew how she tried to seduce and manipulate when she wanted something. Paul had been her victim many times before. Her smile was contagious, after all.

"Paul! I'm so happy to see you," Patricia cooed as he approached. "Thank you so much for coming to the rescue."

"I'm not here to rescue you, just to help out your son," he answered coldly, handing her the bag. "Oh, but you must come in, you know you can spare a few minutes for me."

Staring at him widely she ran her fingers through her hair and let her robe fall slightly to reveal her lack of clothing underneath. Her tan skin glistened in the cold air as she clutched her arms together shivering. Approaching her, he held out the bag to her and when she did not take it, he placed it beside the door on the porch and turned to walk away. But she was not done with him just yet. Grabbing his arm, she pulled him back towards her and kissed him forcefully on the cheek.

"Why don't you come inside, Paul. I've really missed you," she begged.

"You probably have, Patty, but I haven't missed you. I told you, don't try anything."

"But I'm not trying anything, honest," she giggled with a wink in her eye.

"I brought you the diapers, now I have to get to work."

"Of course, always working, never playing. Maybe if you would take some time off you would still be with me. Don't you regret leaving me, over some silly misunderstanding?"

"No," he laughed. "I don't miss you at all."

Pulling away from her grip, he headed back down the sidewalk to his truck. He felt her sulking eyes glaring into his back as walked away, but he didn't dare to turn back to her. He was done talking to her. The past was gone, and she had betrayed him many, many times. She was a trickster. What he wanted was something real, and Patricia had never been real.

As he reached for the handle of his truck, he froze in shock as another man pulled into the driveway. He knew that face. They had met not once, but twice. Each time the man had met him in Paul's anger. This time, he saw the outline of bruises along his jawline from their last encounter. He could see the coy smile as he looked at Patricia and he knew. It was Greg.

Taking a deep breath, Paul tried to calm himself. There was no need to be angry. He had already taken care of business, twice. This was the man that had raped Terra and had been seduced by his ex-wife. He was the father of her child. He almost felt sorry for him. That is, until he quickly jumped out of his car and headed towards Patricia. Greg didn't seem to notice him standing there.

"What do you think you're doing calling him?" he screamed up at her.

"I needed diapers, I told you that. You said you were not going to come. I had no one else to call," she begged backing away from him.

"I told you to never speak to him again! I bet you kissed him, didn't you?"

"No, of course not, I wouldn't. You're the man that I love," she begged.

Paul quietly climbed into the truck and picked up his phone, ready to call the police. He had a bad feeling about what he was witnessing. Watching them carefully, he could not hear their words anymore as their voices grew quieter, but he understood body language.

After a few more moments, Greg pulled his arm back and slapped Patricia across the face. Holding her hand against her cheek, he saw her cry as Paul dialed the phone. "Yes, I need to report a domestic violence dispute in progress at 156 water street. Please hurry," he told the police dispatch. "It's brutal."

Setting his phone up in the windshield he started recording the incident as he jumped back out of the truck.

Greg had knocked her to the ground as she cried. Paul watched him spit on her as she laid there trembling and he kicked her repeatedly in the head and the stomach. He was out of control and was not slowing down.

Paul wanted this time to be different. He deserved to go to jail for what he had done to Terra and now Patricia. They might not have been able to get him for rape, but they could get him for assault.

Locking Greg's arms behind him, Paul pulled him away from his ex-wife and took him to the ground to stop him. Taking deep breaths, he resisted the urge to hit him. He wanted so badly to cause him more pain, but he knew he had to control his anger. He knew he had to do the right thing to bring this man to justice. Quietly, he sat and waited. Each time the man moved, he imagined grabbing his head and slamming it into the concrete. He wanted to see this man bleed. He wanted to see him unconscious, fighting for his life for what he had done. Paul remembered everything as he held Greg down. He remembered Patricia clinging to him in their bathroom, his laughter, and everything that he had done to Terra. Every muscle in his body shook as he held him down, praying that the police would hurry. He hoped he had enough on his phone camera to help them make a conviction. He wanted to be smart this time. He knew he needed to stop taking matters into his own hands. After all, they could do a lot more damage than he could.

He heard the baby crying in the back of the house. It was screaming at the top of its lungs, but Paul could not move. It had been quiet, a few moments before, now it seemed to be crying out in terror.

"Patty, you have to get up if you can. You must get to

him. I know you're hurting, but you have to get up," he pleaded. "I'm not going to let this creep go."

"I can't move, I can't," she sobbed looking up at him with blood in her eyes.

"Yes, you can. You are ok. Help is on the way," he pleaded as he struggled against Greg as he thrashed beneath him. "You can do this."

Just then a police car pulled in and two officers jumped out of the vehicle running up to them. Grabbing Greg, they quickly pulled Paul away and started asking questions. As Paul explained the situation, they loosened their grip on him. As he told them about the phone, they quickly reviewed the video, cuffed Greg, and headed towards Patricia. Running inside, Paul grabbed the baby and tried to console him as he watched them take the other man away.

Pulling up a stretcher, they carefully lifted Patricia into the ambulance. He saw the flash of the camera going off as they documented the damage Greg had done from inside their vehicle. Then they closed the doors, and she, too ,was gone, leaving Paul standing, holding her baby in his arms.

For hours, Paul waited to hear back from Patricia and finally relief arrived. He had held the baby for hours. He had bathed him, fed him, and put him back to sleep in his crib by the time that his mother arrived. Walking out of the house, he had mixed emotions. He had enjoyed spending a few hours with the little boy, but his thoughts were on Terra. How would she react when he told her about what had happened that morning? It was too much to believe. So many things had happened. He could not help but be relieved that finally Greg was in custody, where he belonged and now, he knew that Darren hadn't fathered another child. Had he cheated on Terra? He was not sure, but maybe there would be more clues in his journal. Leaving his old home behind, he headed to her, hoping that she had experienced a better morning than he had. As he arrived, he knocked quietly on the door and waited, not knowing about the night that Terra had been through.

***

Around her the dust was beginning to settle as she looked over at Autumn. The storm was finally over, but the heat had grown more intense as they had waited. Around them, their shelter had fallen only leaving fresh glass covering the ground around them. In the distance she saw the red lightning strikes pulsing across the sky as they clung to each other. She had never seen a storm like it before.

"How have you survived here for so long?" Terra asked nervously.

"I don't know, I just do. But I have never seen anything like that before. It was like it was chasing us away from the door."

"Why would it do that?"

"I don't know, but it's clear that we don't need to be going back there. Every time you get close to that door, something crazy happens."

"Maybe that means we are getting close to discovering something?"

"I don't think a little discovery is really worth the risk," Autumn laughed.

Looking down at her shredded dress, Terra sobbed. Her breaths came in gasps as she looked around at how much her daughter had grown. She could not imagine all that she had to endure within the Gray. What had she done to survive? She had only been a little girl when would have first arrived. How many nights did she cry and suffer alone? Had she looked for her mother? How could a child so innocent and small survive in a place so full of darkness?

The black mirror shards taunted her with their reflection as the lights pulsed and the smoke raged in the distance. She was tired of not being able to breathe. She was tired of the heat and the pain from walking in that desolate land. Looking at all the mirrors that surrounded her, she saw her daughter's tears. She saw her slowly growing from a little girl to a young lady. Her face had gone from the look of innocence to confusion and finally into a calculating expression that only a woman well beyond her years could have. She watched her child's memories play out in front of her. Day after day, month after month, and year after year, she had searched. She had looked for meaning, a reason, and a way to survive until finally, she had found Terra. She felt the tears and heard the screams. Terra felt her heart breaking as she looked into Autumn's eyes.

"We have to do something, there has to be a way out," Terra demanded.

"I have never found it, and believe me I don't want to give up. I just don't know what to do anymore," Autumn scoffed. "It's not like a key is just going to magically show up, now is it?"

"I've never been one to believe in magic, but I don't

want to give up. This place is driving me crazy and I'm pretty crazy to begin with."

"Then let us do it; let's find a way out. Maybe this storm stirred something up! If there are two of us, we stand a better chance of figuring this place out."

Grabbing Autumn's hand, Terra ran back towards the black oily waters and the door. Swiftly, she stopped at every large rock and began to roll them over, looking for anything hidden. There had to be something, somewhere. With each stone that she lifted, she grimaced in pain as the sharp edges cut into her hand. She was bleeding, not just from her feet, but from her legs, her arms, and her hands. This time pain was not going to get the best of her.

In the distance, she felt the ground shake as people appeared again marching for the waters. From this angle, she saw their faces more clearly. This time they seemed the same. Hundreds of copies of her and Autumn headed for the waves that crashed hard against the glassy shore, each of them at different ages and different stages. Some of them were crying, some of them smiled peacefully, and some of them were screaming in anguish trying to resist the pull to the waters. They had always been calm before, but this time it was different. It was like the Gray knew that they were looking for something, anything. There had to be a clue, something to discover to help them escape.

Quickly they searched, turning over every stone until they reached the water's edge. Gasping for air, they collapsed on the broken shore. Silently, they stared at one another as together, they watched copies of themselves disappearing into the depths. None of them stopped, like a pounding in their heads, each step that they took echoed within their minds.

"We can't give up..." Autumn sobbed. "Don't give up on me now, Mom."

"You know who I am?" Sitting up, Terra grabbed Autumn and held her in her arms.

"Yes, of course, I've always known. How could I not know you? I've been waiting for you forever," the girl cried.

Terra watched as black tears streamed down the girl's face. Around them, the pounding had stopped. Everything had frozen in a moment. It was like time was standing still. Everything grew darker around them as they held each other close. Everything, except the door. Along the edges, the door began to glow with lights. At first it was just a sliver of gold. Steadily, it grew wider and warmer, beckoning towards to them. Around them, the darkness seemed to melt away as the light grew brighter and the warmth grew louder. Staring at it from over Autumn's shoulder, Terra watched the light continue to reach for them, like the warm embrace of sunlight it spread. That is when she saw it. Hidden against the tide was a post and, on that post, hung a key.

Grabbing her hand, she pulled her daughter up and stumbled for the door, afraid to look away. The light strobed around them as her hand grasped at the key. The metal burnt like fire against her skin, but still she refused to drop it as she fumbled around for the knob and the hole underneath. The light was blinding now as she pushed the key in and quickly turned it. Finally, after a few tries, the door creaked open and the girls stepped inside.

Blinking against the light, Terra grasped Autumn's hand as they felt the wet grass kiss their feet. They smelled the mixture of honeysuckle in the fresh breeze. Around them cherry blossoms floated in the air from the trees that surrounded them. The limbs gently swayed as though they were welcoming them within. With a slam, the door shut behind them and the Gray... disappeared. Ahead of them they saw a waterfall falling to a small lake that gently licked the edge of the grass. Like a whisper, it fell as the birds sang a song of welcome. Ahead of them, they saw the ghostly figure of a man walking towards them. At first it was just an outline. Each step was slowly measured in rhythm with the sway of the trees, but then it was gone. At that moment, a different kind of chill spread up Terra's spine as though someone had taken ice and poured it on her head. Around her the trees froze and the specks that had been floating in the sunlight vanished. Her paradise had been frozen like a painting in a museum and just as quickly Autumn vanished, swept away like pollen in a frozen breeze. She was alone. She felt the heat raging behind her as she stared ahead unable to move, frozen within the painting and in the distance, she smelled the familiar stench of sulfur and oil as it engulfed her. The place she thought she had left behind was following her into the most beautiful place she had ever imagined. Closing her eyes against the light, she held her breath and waited... as a sudden burst of heat came from behind her. Ash and smoke blew through her hair with a mighty gust as she fell to the ground. Around her she felt the atmosphere change as her hands fell into smoking embers where grass had once been. As tears filled her eyes, she opened them just long enough to see the weeping cherry trees fall into a raging fire. With a scream, she fell into the ashes as her body shook. She was never going to escape. Yet again, she awoke to face another day, knowing her journey wasn't complete.

"Mommy! You're not going to believe what happened!" Autumn squealed, jumping into Terra's bed. "I saw Daddy!"

"What do you mean, baby?" Terra tried to answer through the tears.

"Are you okay, Mommy?"

"Yes, I just woke up. Now... how did you see Daddy?"

"Well! I went back to that place, and you were there, and we went through this door, but I was older and it was weird. But he came out of the trees, he was invisible at first and then, he wasn't, but I ran to him and he hugged me and told me he loved me he said I was brave and strong and that I need to make sure to take care of you... It was time for me to go back home, but he said it wasn't your time yet. You weren't ready to come home, but you're here so I don't understand that. Anyways... it was sad to leave you! But I got to see Daddy and he said I wouldn't have any more nightmares!" she rambled between gasps as she bounced on the bed around Terra's head. "Oh, Mommy! I'm so glad it's over, I love you so much! I hope your nightmares stop soon!"

"Me too, baby girl, me too..." she answered, trying to hold back the tears. "I'm so glad it's over for you. I was soooo worried!" she answered as she snatched Autumn and consumed her with kisses. "I'm sure mine will be over soon. But... I just woke up; can you give me a few minutes?"

"Yes, Mommy. I'm going to have my cereal; you go back to sleep."

"Okay, I'll try that... get something small and when I get up, we will make pancakes to celebrate. Does that sound good?"

"WHOO HOO!!! PAN!!! CAKES!!!!" she screamed down the hall.

Lying awake, Terra stared up at the ceiling and counted the tiles. Soon enough, her pillow was wet from tears as she wondered how long she would have nightmares... how long would she be trapped within the Gray. It felt like nearly a year had passed since her first dreams had appeared. She remembered the pain, the smell, and the utter darkness. It was a world she felt she would never escape from. Being awake hadn't even stopped the dreams. Every time that she was afraid, the Gray would appear like a fog that enveloped her. It didn't matter where she was or what she was doing, for a moment she would be lost to it. But while it felt like she was there for hours, only seconds would have passed. She was exhausted. She never knew when it would appear or where she would be, but it would happen, like a bad record on repeat. They had grown less frequent and at least she knew that it was possible to escape. Terra just didn't know how. But now, regardless of what happened in her mind she had to move forward.

"Good morning beautiful, how's your morning?" he asked as Terra answered the door that morning.

"We were just sitting down for pancakes. I know it's a little late, but I needed a little time. Those dreams just keep getting harder," she sighed, opening the door for him. "Would you like some?"

"I'm honestly not sure I can eat. How bad was the dream?"

"Pretty bad... Autumn was there and she just... vanished. I don't think they are ever going to stop."

"They will, eventually. They can't keep coming forever."

Sitting down beside them at their breakfast table, he took the coffee that she gave him and watched them eat for a few moments. Autumn's hair was messy and still in braids from the day before. Her pink nightgown wrinkled from the night.

"Any more bad dreams?" he asked quietly.

"Nope. Thankfully, I am bad dream free! I had an amazing dream and I even saw Daddy. He had A LOT to say," the little girl giggled. "But I've been thinking a lot about our next pirate adventure. I'm going to make you walk the plank."

"Oh, I don't think so, young lady."

"You know you will let me win," she laughed as she ate another bite of her pancakes. "Never."

Sitting back, he watched his two favorite ladies finish their breakfast. It was so peaceful when he was around them. Their lighthearted banter always seemed to make a rough day go a little easier. Finishing his coffee, he nodded for Terra to meet him in the living room. Sitting quietly on the sofa, he waited for Terra to start a video for Autumn in the other room before she joined him.

"Something's wrong," she stated from behind him. "What happened?"

"I ran some diapers out to Patricia this morning...." he slowly began. "It was fine, I dropped them off, and as I was leaving Greg showed up. It turns out that he must have been the father of her baby."

"Greg has another child?" she questioned. Sitting down beside him, she noticed the scratches on his arms. "What did you do?"

"Nothing really, at least I didn't do what I wanted to do," Paul replied, grabbing her hand. "I saw him slap her, and then he threw her on the ground and started beating her. Long story short, he got arrested, and she's in the hospital."

"Oh my God, Paul! That's awful," she proclaimed, holding onto him. "I'm proud of you, though. You must have really held it together to have not put him in the hospital, too."

"Don't get me wrong, I really wanted to," he shrugged, forcing a laugh. "But I took a video and held him until the police arrived. They can do more than I can, but I wasn't about to let him hurt anyone else. At least he will get a little of what he deserves now."

Snuggling up against him, Terra rubbed his arm gently. His eyes were tired as he looked down at her. Taking his hand in hers, she gently squeezed it. As she sat up, Terra opened up her lap and let him lay down against her. Gently, she ran her fingers through his hair as he rested up against her.

"Well, I guess it's good news that she didn't have Darren's baby. That would have been weird," she stated softly. "I mean I know this isn't about me at all, but it's a relief. I could just imagine what Christmas would be like with your ex-wife."

"Yeah, that's not something I want to imagine," he laughed. "I wish I knew what happened between her and Darren, though. Have you looked any farther in the journals?"

"No, I haven't been able to bring myself to. I'm not sure I want to know."

"I think you need to know. I think it will help you in

the long run. You don't need that question stirring around in your mind."

"There's just too much to read. It hurts, and right now, I can't do it. Maybe one of these days, but not now. I have more important things to worry about," she stated blankly. Reaching under the sofa, she pulled the journal out and handed it to Paul. "I trust that you can find out for me? Just let me know? I can't handle all of the details, not now...."

"You keep saying, not now...." he questioned, taking the journal from her hands. "I can do this for you, that's fine, but what's up?"

Sitting up, Paul wrapped his arm around her and looked down into her eyes. He saw something new in her expression, something different. Nervously, she slowly smiled as she nestled into his arms.

"I went to the doctor, yesterday.... "

"Are you okay? I didn't know you had an appointment? Why didn't you tell me?" he asked nervously.

"It was just a routine exam, nothing major, but...."

"But what?"

"Well, if you would let me finish, I would tell you," she laughed.

"I'm sorry, it's just the way our luck has been going.... I'm just a little nervous, that's all," he answered, wiping the sweat from his forehead.

"Well, they found something. Well they found a couple of things actually." Reaching down into her purse, she pulled out a strip of paper and handed it to him. "I'm pregnant."

Opening the paper, he looked down at the sonogram picture. There was barely anything to be seen, just a couple of little circles with a tiny dot in the middle of each. His heart dropped as he thought about what Greg had done to her, but in his mind he silently hoped. As he looked up into Terra's eyes, he saw the most beautiful smile he had ever seen. Her face was glowing as she showed him the little dots.

"This looks different, could it be his?"

"Well, they can't be his, no," she smiled. "I haven't even missed my period yet. They were going to do an x-ray, but my test came back positive. I'm only a few weeks along. So, no, it's not possible. That was a couple of months ago."

"Are you sure?" he asked, looking down at the paper. "Wait, you keep saying they."

"Yes, I'm sure, Paul. They are yours. We are going to have twins," she blushed. "Remember, a few weeks ago, right after I told you that I loved you for the very first time."

"Really? I thought there was something wrong with me," he beamed. "Can it really be true? I didn't think they could tell anything that early!"

"It's true, here let me show you."

Taking the sonogram picture from him, she explained how little the two babies were. Each of them in their own little sack. She was so newly pregnant that they appeared like tiny dots in the picture. Two beautiful little dots. His eyes filled with tears as he looked at the pictures. Finally, he was going to be a father. Together they held each other and cried tears of joy as they contemplated the idea of not one but two babies. They were going to be a family. After so much turmoil and heartache, something was finally going in his favor.

Taking her into his arms, he kissed her gently. He could tell that she was a little more tired than usual already. After all, carrying twins would take a toll on her almost immediately, especially with all the sleepless nights with Autumn. Quietly, they sat, both dreaming of having two beautiful babies to love until Terra drifted off into a restful sleep. Taking care not to disturb her, Paul slipped his arm away and took the journal to the kitchen table. He had to know, neither one of them needed anything else hanging over their heads.

16

February 10th

Patricia came back today. We sat beside each other for a while. As always, she brought me coffee, which is always nice, but this time she kept running her hand up my thigh. It was exciting to feel her touching me. Her fingernails felt so sexy as she got higher and higher on my leg. She will probably be back tomorrow. I hope I get the chance to kiss her soon. I really want to taste her lips.

-Darren

February 14th

Patricia's husband was stuck in meetings all day today, so I had flowers, chocolates, and a stuffed dragon delivered to her house today. I was richly rewarded when she showed up this afternoon in a slinky red dress, and fishnet stockings. It was a great way to celebrate Valentine's Day. I took her into one of the cars we were working on, an old Cadillac. She kissed me so deeply and so intensely that I was thinking about it all night. Unfortunately, another customer came in and she had to leave before we had any real fun. But when I brought home dinner to my wife, I made sure to take out my frustrations on her. She was happy that I gave her any attention at all. I almost felt guilty, but I wasn't really thinking about her anyways. I was thinking of those stockings and the way that woman kissed me in the back of the car.

-Darren

Paul couldn't believe what he was reading. He remembered that day, that dress, and the flowers that she swore her mother had sent. There hadn't been a card. Yes, this was the same woman. Still he needed to know a little more. As he read, he questioned what he had discovered about her baby that day. Flipping forward in the journal, he continued as a knot began to build in the pit of his stomach.

April 21st

I felt terrible when Patricia stopped by today. We kissed again, and then, she handed me the key to her house. She told me to stop by in the morning and she would give me a breakfast to remember. As I stared at the key, I knew I wanted her. But I knew she wasn't worth it. She's not worth destroying my marriage. Terra and I just need a little excitement. After all, don't all married couples go through this? Maybe I should just let Greg have her. They seem to have a lot in common. One thing is for sure, I can't do this to my wife anymore. She doesn't deserve this. I can't speak to this woman ever again. I can't kiss her. She's too distracting. What will this woman even get me? When it comes down to it, she's not my wife, who has seen me through everything. I cannot trade all of that for a moment of lust. I'm giving Greg her address. He can have her. I've already gone too far as it is. I'm not going any further. I'm not going to give up on my wife.

-Darren

As he heard the doorknob rattle Paul tried to hide the journal but there was nowhere to hide it from Sheila so he tucked it under his arm and headed for the coffee pot.

"I see Terra is finally getting some rest," Sheila stated dryly, plopping down on of the kitchen chairs. "Probably a good thing. That girl never sleeps."

"Yeah, she fell asleep, and I just covered her up and left her there."

"I'm surprised you didn't leave."

"Why would I do that? I don't want her to think I bailed on her."

"Most guys don't have a problem with that," Sheila laughed.

"Well, I do. She was telling me some pretty important things," He sighed sitting down across from her.

"Well, I promised her I would give you a chance, so... thank you for helping Terra with Greg. I had no idea. He was Darren's best friend. It just doesn't make any sense... after everything she did for him. Of course, I'm hearing a lot about him cheating on her, too. It just reminds me what I went through when me and her father split up."

"What do you mean?"

"You don't want to hear any of this, Paul."

"Of course, I do..."

"Well, I had a lot of guys cheat on me, lie to me, and just basically try to use me. That's when I knew I could only rely on myself. Of course, I have Michael now, and he's completely different. I don't know what I would do without him, but before that... I had to develop my own set of survival skills."

"Is that why you come across so mean sometimes?"

"I come across as mean? Damn... that sucks, but no... I just know what a woman must do to survive around here. It's not always pretty. If you are as good of a guy as she says you are... then she's lucky to have you."

"Hopefully, I can live up to your expectations."

"Well, you haven't run off yet, so that's definitely in your favor. Time will tell, though," she answered with a knowing glare. "You hurt her... you die... it's as simple as that. So, you said she was talking to you about something important?"

"Yeah... she... was," he answered looking down at the journal, knowing it was better to talk about its contents than the pregnancy. Sheila had already brought up Darren so it was the perfect excuse. "Well, funny you should mention those rumors about her late husband."

"I am SOOO pissed that he cheated! If I could dig him

up and kill him again, I would."

"Well, she found his journal."

"OH??" her voice raised as she sat up in her chair. "Is that what you're holding onto?"

"Yeah, it is actually... Terra just couldn't read anymore. That's why she hasn't been sleeping. She..."

"Give me that!" she demanded, grabbing it out of his hands. "She might not be able to, but I can."

"That was my idea, too," he laughed, letting her take it from his grip. This was the better option, after all. She knew he would be dead for sure if he told Sheila that Terra was pregnant... with twins. The idea of it gave him a chilling excitement.

Flipping through the pages, Sheila found the first letter and slowly read it. Her eyes narrowed as she read and forcefully flipped the page. Clearing her throat, her eyes reddened and her breaths shortened as she continued. "Get me a cup of coffee..." she demanded as she continued reading. "Man... this is pissing me off."

Dutifully Paul headed to the machine and poured her a cup of coffee and took it, with her sugar and creamer, to the table. By then, her eyes had narrowed into tiny slivers and she was making weird noises. It could only be described as the death call of Sheila. As he looked over to Terra's sleeping face, he felt regret. It was unimaginable that her late husband had been caught up in one of Patricia's traps, but at least he had survived. But now they were together which just increased the irony.

"I wonder who this Patricia person is..." Sheila asked as she felt around for her coffee cup.

"Actually, it's my ex-wife."

With a snort, she spat her coffee halfway across the

table and stared up at him. "So you know where I can kill her...? I mean, find her? Good thing you got away from THAT!"

"That won't be necessary. She's had her reward, unfortunately."

"OH... I must hear more about that. Sounds juicy. Give me a minute to finish this up."

"Uh-huh..."

"Shit... that was really something. At least he didn't cheat on her. I could still dig him up and kill him again, though... for even considering it, kissing that woman, being stupid... dying," she grunted through sips of coffee. "But... wait... you said that this Patricia is your ex-wife?"

"Yeah, unfortunately... talk about a mess."

"So, you were married to her during this? Wait... how do you know it's your ex?"

"Because I remember the flowers... everything like he described in that book, I remember. She told me her mom bought them."

"Huh... imagine that. So how has she had her reward, exactly? Is that why you guys got a divorce?"

"No, she got pregnant with Greg's baby and that's why we got a divorce. She was cheating on me, trying to find a baby daddy, I guess. Then... I caught them, kicked him out of our house..."

"So, you knew him before the incident with Terra?"

"No, I never really saw his face. It wasn't until the other day..."

"Oh?! What happened!?" Sheila exclaimed.

"I went to help Patricia with diapers because she said she didn't have anyone to call..."

"Sounds like total crap to me... go on..."

"Well, Greg showed up at about the same time. I went to my car... and then... he hit her. A couple of times. I recorded it on my phone, called the police, and stopped him."

"Did you beat the crap out of him?"

"No, just held him down until the police got there. I thought jail was a rather good place for him. Do you want to see the video?" he asked, dangling his phone like a carrot in front of Sheila.

"Of course!" she exclaimed, grabbing the phone from his hand. "I am really starting to like you, Paul... you get me!" She laughed almost to herself. "You know, I still want to dig him up. Terra is way better that your ex, and he kissed her. He was stupid, I guess. But I'm telling you, most men are from my experience. You better not be stupid, got that? And I like you, so I might REALLY kill you if you hurt her."

"One of these days... I really want to hear YOUR story."

17

Stepping out of her car, Terra took in the sunshine around her. The air was bitter, but the day was bright. As she took her books in her arms, she headed inside to the small community college. It was her first day, and she hadn't been this excited about learning in a long time. The past few weeks had been so full of new developments that her mind was still spinning with the knowledge that Darren hadn't given up on her. It had been a relief to know that even though he had made some mistakes, in the end he had honored their marriage. As she made her way to the classroom, she thought about the two miracles growing inside of her. It was going to be hard, but Terra knew that going back to college was the right thing to do for all of them. This would give her the opportunity to be able to take care of all of them, no matter what happened. She had always loved business and marketing. Many years before, she had started taking classes, but she had met Darren and after they were married, she had given up. Allowing him to take care of her and Autumn had seemed like the right thing to do at the time. As she looked back on her decision, she knew that it would have been better for him if she had been able to share the load. She would have been able to do more when he got gotten sick. She loved staying home and raising her, but she needed the confidence to know that she made it on her own.

The room was bright and full of eager young students from all walks of life. As she sat down, she couldn't be sure where to look or who to talk to. They were all so different from her. From the girl wearing all black and pigtails, to the blonde with perfectly straight hair and glasses, everyone seemed to smile and were eager to learn, except for the girl in the seat ahead of her who was bent over her notebook and chewing on her fingernails. Her hair was frizzy and tied up in what was almost a ponytail. She directly reflected how Terra felt. Surrounded by people who appeared to be at least ten years younger than herself, she was nervous. It was hard to imagine how well she would do in college level classes when she had completely dedicated her life to Darren and Autumn. None of it was going to be exactly what she expected. Then again, nothing ever was. Life was unpredictable. Still, even at thirty years old, she wasn't confident about being one of the oldest ones in class. Clutching her coat around her, she waited for the instructor to appear. She had her notebook ready, pencils lined up, and her book opened. She was determined to make this work and hoped that nobody noticed her leg shaking underneath the table.

Smiling, she thought back to when she first told Paul about the twins. He had so much doubt, but it was a miracle that she had found out about them so quickly. It seemed unheard of, but after a little research she discovered that it wasn't all that unusual after all. Autumn was so excited to be a big sister and her dreams had vanished.

Thinking back to the last six months or so, Terra couldn't believe how far she had come. It seemed like only yesterday that she was struggling to leave her room at the crisis center. She had been afraid to speak to anyone, afraid to be seen, and afraid of embarrassing herself. She remembered when the nightmares had started. She was never sure whether the crisis center or the dreams were real. For weeks, she hadn't left that little room. It had felt as though she had been lost in a barren waste land with no hope of escape. By the time she had met Paul, she had completely isolated herself. It had been ages since she had taken a shower or bothered to brush her hair. He had changed that for her. He had pushed her just enough and showed her kindness. It was odd that with so many people in the center, nobody else had tried to comfort her or had even bothered to speak to her.

Still she pushed forward, trying to resolve her issues. At first, every little step had felt forced. It had been a struggle and a journey. After a while, she had become so focused on caring for Darren that she had lost a little of herself. It took time to find those things, and now here she was. Finally, she felt free of the guilt, the anger, and the self-pity. She had accepted his death. Now she could finally cherish the memories that he had given her and prepare for the rest of her life.

After class, she headed back to her car. She couldn't be sure she had learned anything more than what was expected out of a college student, but at least she had the syllabus. Terra had found herself drifting away as the professor discussed term papers, rules, and how to not plagiarize. Everything that he discussed was written on the handout, and she was a fast reader. What it took him an hour to discuss in class, she had read in five minutes.

Then, as she drifted away...

***

Slowly his form became clearer. His hand reached out for her as he approached and then with a thick southern accent, he spoke...

"I have been waiting for you." Darren's voice echoed against the trees. "I have a lot to tell you."

"What do you mean? You died? How can you be in this place? Are I?" Terra asked in shock.

"No, you are not dead, far from it actually," he stated walking beside her. "This place is more than just a dream. It's real. Many people come here, but few make it through the door. You two didn't give up. For others, it's a place that will haunt them forever. They will look at this door and never try to reach for it. Many will spend their lives struggling. They may live their whole lives in mourning, never really living." Turning, he gestured back towards the door where they had entered the peaceful garden. "You had a lot to learn, but you fought to get here. You need to know that it's okay to move on. It's okay to cherish the memories, but remember they are just memories. If you never allow yourself to move forward, you destroy yourself. That's how you become the lost. Those that enter the waters are the ones who blame others or never forgive themselves. They are the ones who never learn to love again. You need to live your life now that I'm gone. There's nothing holding you back. It is time. Don't look back to this time in sorrow. This has been a journey of discovery, not only for yourself, but for the world around you."

Gesturing towards the center of the path, she watched the sky open with a bright beam of light. Turning towards her, he pulled her into his arms and kissed her gently on the cheek.

"It's time for me to move on now. I know that you will find happiness. Don't let your memories hold you back. There is something better for you. Just remember that I love you, I believe in you, and none of this has been your fault. I have to go, but I will always live in your thoughts and in your heart."

Pulling away, Darren slowly turned towards the light and in an instant, he was gone. Letting her eyes follow the stream that ribboned through the grass, she slowly turned around to trace it to its destination. Watching the water reach the door, the cold strength of the window that had teased her dissolved into the sand. Quickly, the water reached the black shores and everything that it touched came alive again, and as it reached the oily ocean, she watched black turn to blue. And as glass turned to sand, she watched the future play out in front of her.

Against the shore that once was black was now sparkling turquoise as the sun cast its light upon it like a million diamonds. Just beneath a bending palm sat Terra and Paul. He was sitting with his legs crossed, leaning against the tree, as she laid down next to him, listening to him play the guitar that sat on his lap. She saw her own gentle smile looking up at him. The breeze caressed her skin like a kiss from the ocean, as a little boy and a little girl ran up to them with buckets of sand. She watched the sand transform into a castle within moments, the team of four quickly built their dream home in the sand. In the distance, she saw Autumn laughing in the waves as she twirled and jumped while the waves crashed against her. Closing her eyes, Terra felt the sun warm her skin as wave after wave crashed against the white sand with rhythmic splendor. The smell of coconuts and salt-water overwhelmed her senses as she watched their family play in the sand. But she knew she didn't have long to wait until the brief glimpse of the future was taken from her. Closing her eyes, she waited. Soon the summer sand became the chill of a classroom.

As she lifted tearful eyes, she rushed to gather her books and pretended that she had been alert for the class as she followed everyone to the parking lot. As the cold air hit her, Terra kept her head down and placed her books in the back of the car. Then she saw Paul watching her as he always seemed to, leaning against the hood of his truck, shivering in the cold.

"Hey, how was your first day?" he asked smiling.

"I don't know. It was all about following the rules, don't cheat, show up for class.... that kind of stuff," she laughed.

"Do you feel smarter yet?"

"Yes, I do, because I'm smarter than a lot of the people in the class. With age comes wisdom, after all," she joked.

"Well, hop in, I want to show you something." Opening the door to the truck, Paul held out his hand to help her climb in. Thankfully, the truck was warm and cozy as she scooted to the middle of the bench seat.

"Where are you taking me?" she asked, teasing. "Are you going to kidnap me?"

"No, of course not. Well, actually, I am a little bit."

Together they laughed as he drove them to a different park than they usually travelled. It was a small state park that was usually full of family reunions, church picnics, and field trips during the spring and summer. She hadn't been there in years. As he drove, she became more and more curious as he headed up the hill to a section she wasn't as familiar with.

Around them snow covered the many bushes and trees that framed the drive to the top of the hill. Shelter houses were barren now and covered with fresh snow. There were no footsteps anymore and hardly any tire prints in the parking lots. Finally, as they reached the top, she saw the newest structure, a snow-white gazebo surrounded by empty flower beds. It stood alone with just a small amount of parking places close by. In the distance, she saw the trees glistening like ice sculptures on the horizon. In the middle of the gazebo, she saw the concrete that was still white and new. It obviously hadn't been around for long. As the truck came to a stop, Paul nervously opened her door and wrapped his arm around her as they headed for the gazebo.

"It's beautiful, isn't it?" he asked, holding onto her hand. "I just heard about this place a couple of weeks ago. And then I was showing a house nearby and I knew you had to see it."

"The snow makes it looks so different. I haven't been up here in years. I wonder how long this place has been here," she asked strolling over to admire the ornate trim.

Looking above her, she was hypnotized by the beams that circled them and arched to meet one another in the center of the structure. From below them, she saw the gentle curves of the gazebo as they artfully met and swirled around each other. She saw the hooks hanging in each opening, waiting for flower baskets to be hung in the spring. As the wind blew, she watched fresh snowflakes begin to dust away their footprints on the walkway. Everything felt beautiful and new.

Glancing back over at Paul, she watched a smile creep across his face as he took her hand and went down on one knee in front of her. His eyes filled with tears as he reached into his pocket. He pulled out a little blue box...

"Terra, you have made me such a happy man. You gave me hope when I thought there was nothing left for me," he stuttered, wiping away the tears that ran down his cheek. "You are everything I have ever imagined that I thought didn't exist. I never thought a woman like you would walk into my life. When I first met you, I think... I knew. You were raw, natural and had a delicate strength that I hadn't seen before. In a moment, what was dark in me... vanished as though you were an angel bringing light into my life. I used to want to be alone, to avoid women and just live in peace, but now... I can't imagine my life without you. You are the bravest and the strongest woman I've ever met. Ever since the moment I told you that I loved you, I have wanted nothing more than to be with you. I don't want us to just live together. I want to be there for you when you cry. I want you to reach for your dreams and I will be there to make sure you achieve them. I want to cheer you on as you get your degree. I want to be the one standing by your side as the world around us discovers what I already know. You are the most beautiful, intelligent, and amazing woman I have ever known. And as we both move forward in our lives I would be honored if I could be your husband." Opening the box, he held out a beautiful ring glistening with diamonds. "Terra, will you marry me?"

***

Standing above his snow covered grave, Terra looked down to Darren's headstone and wiped the ice from his name. He had been gone over a year, and a week hadn't gone by that she didn't visit him. Each time she had a sense that he was standing next to her watching her cry. This time a rush of warmth filled her mind as she placed new yellow roses at the base of the stone. They had always been his favorite. Since her last vision, she knew that he wasn't there. He had moved on just as he needed to. This was just a stone that represented where his body laid. She knew that was the only thing left, an empty body. He wasn't there anymore, and for the first time, she truly felt his absence. Now, she felt him in her essence. He was a part of her, and she knew that he would always be there, but he had asked her to live life in a way that he never could. As much as it hurt, she knew his time was gone and her time was just beginning. Their life together had been a beautiful gift, but life was waiting. She couldn't freeze time any longer. She knew that the best way to honor him was to live. He loved her enough to want her to create beautiful moments in whatever time she had.

Looking down to her blossoming belly, she thought of the twins that would soon arrive and the new diamond on her finger. Taking a another look at his grave, she knew that it was time to let go. And, finally... Terra walked away.

ABOUT ATMOSPHERE PRESS

Atmosphere Press is an independent, full-service publisher for excellent books in all genres and for all audiences. Learn more about what we do at atmospherepress.com.

We encourage you to check out some of Atmosphere's latest releases, which are available at Amazon.com and via order from your local bookstore:

An Expectation of Plenty, a novel by Thomas Bazar
Sink or Swim, Brooklyn, a novel by Ron Kemper
Lost and Found, a novel by Kevin Gardner
Skinny Vanilla Crisis, a novel by Colleen Alles
The Mommy Clique, a novel by Barbara Altamirano
Eaten Alive, a novel by Tim Galati
The Sacrifice Zone, a novel by Roger S. Gottlicb
Olive, a novel by Barbara Braendlein
Itsuki, a novel by Zach MacDonald
A Surprising Measure of Subliminal Sadness,
    short stories by Sue Powers
Saint Lazarus Day, short stories by R. Conrad Speer
The Lower Canyons, a novel by John Manuel
Shiftless, a novel by Anthony C. Murphy
Connie Undone, a novel by Kristine Brown
A Cage Called Freedom, a novel by Paul P.S. Berg
The Escapist, a novel by Karahn Washington
Buildings Without Murders, a novel by Dan Gutstein

ABOUT THE AUTHOR

Jenna Ashlyn currently resides in Gallipolis, Ohio but plans to relocate in the coming years. She has studied writing and literature at both the University of Rio Grande and Marshall University, where she worked for the campus literary Magazine *Et Cetera*. Her work has appeared in several publications including *The Atwood Review*, *Night Roses*,  *Poet's Choice*, and many others. She was also a 2019 Maier Award nominee, and won the StarJewel talent showcase award for best writer in 2015. She is the mother of three teenagers, and while she works in business, her greatest passion has always been expressing herself through the arts, and she began writing at a young age.

CPSIA information can be obtained
at www.ICGtesting.com
Printed in the USA
LVHW021720160920
666192LV00007B/1226